This book purchased
in memory of
Irvin & Lucile Van Raden
2005

P9-CEV-908

PHI   Phillips, Carly.

             Summer lovin'

$16.95   /

DATE			
AG 23 05	JE 26 06		
SE 0 / 05	AG 0 9 06		
SE 28 05	FE 19 08		
OC 05 05	AP 07 08		
10.19	JE 05 10		
NO 16 05			
NO 29 05			
DE 13 05			
FE 13 06			
MR 11 06			
AP 04 06			
MY 16 06			

FORRESTON PUBLIC LIBRARY
P. O. BOX 605
FORRESTON, IL 61030

BAKER & TAYLOR

Summer Lovin'

CARLY PHILLIPS

Summer Lovin'

HQN™

ISBN 0-373-77019-7

SUMMER LOVIN'

Copyright © 2005 by Karen Drogin

All rights reserved. Except for use in any review, the reproduction or utilization of this work in whole or in part in any form by any electronic, mechanical or other means, now known or hereafter invented, including xerography, photocopying and recording, or in any information storage or retrieval system, is forbidden without the written permission of the publisher, Harlequin Enterprises Limited, 225 Duncan Mill Road, Don Mills, Ontario M3B 3K9, Canada.

All characters in this book have no existence outside the imagination of the author and have no relation whatsoever to anyone bearing the same name or names. They are not even distantly inspired by any individual known or unknown to the author, and all incidents are pure invention.

This edition published by arrangement with Harlequin Books S.A.

® and TM are trademarks of the publisher. Trademarks indicated with ® are registered in the United States Patent and Trademark Office, the Canadian Trade Marks Office and in other countries.

www.HQNBooks.com

Printed in U.S.A.

To Brenda Chin and everyone at Harlequin—you gave me my start and you worked hard to make sure I came back home. Brenda, who'd have thought when we started that one day we'd be doing hardcover together? Thank you! You're the best!

To the Plotmonkeys—Janelle Denison, Julie Leto and Leslie Kelly. Not only do we need a stinking plot but we need each other! Happy 40th to us all. XXX OOO.

And a special acknowledgment to the Greek friends in my life: my college roommate Ariane Economon Mastrototaro and Tony and Lori Karayianni. Thanks for answering a question or two, and please...don't hold any mistakes against me!

Also by Carly Phillips

HOT NUMBER
HOT STUFF
STROKE OF MIDNIGHT
UNDER THE BOARDWALK
SIMPLY SENSUAL
SIMPLY SCANDALOUS
SIMPLY SINFUL
THE HEARTBREAKER
THE PLAYBOY
THE BACHELOR

Watch for the next installment of The Hot Zone series
HOT ITEM
Coming summer 2006

Chapter One

THE COSTASES' BACKYARD was packed with people all circling the capuchin monkey, who was performing on a makeshift stage set up on the green grass. Though a party would always draw a crowd, these folks had been excited to see Spank, a monkey with a fondness for mooning anyone in sight. Zoe Costas stood with her twin sister, Ari, and watched the capuchin perform in honor of their foster sister Sam's fourteenth birthday.

Sam missed the monkey since Spank had been forced to move out of the Costas family home after they discovered that owning a pet monkey violated the law. Since Sam had lost too many people and things in her young life, they still tried to maintain her strong bond with the animal, whom she loved dearly. Zoe kept in touch with the trainer who'd taken the monkey, and she made sure Spank was present on special occasions like today.

Zoe glanced at her foster sister and smiled. They were celebrating Sam's first anniversary as part of the family and Zoe was glad the teenager would get to experience a spirited celebration surrounded by people who cared about her. The young girl had come to Zoe's parents through Quinn Donovan, Ari's husband. They'd taken the young girl in and now Zoe's parents were on the road to adoption.

But Sam had been in foster care for six years, unwanted for too long and so distrustful she acted out and tested the family in every way possible. Only lately had she begun to trust and settle into the crazy Costas clan.

Someone in the audience whistled and Spank dropped her pants, then the monkey smacked her bottom with both of her hands.

Ari groaned and covered her eyes.

Zoe chuckled. "You lived with Spank last year. I would have thought you were way past being mortified," she said, unable to hold back a grin.

Ari shrugged. "What can I say? Spank always takes me by surprise."

"That's because you still expect everyone around you to be sane and calm." Zoe waved a finger in front of her twin's face. "It's your shrink training," she said.

"You say that like expecting normalcy is a crime."

Zoe laughed. "Shame, shame, Ariana. You ought to know better than to expect the ordinary from anyone named Costas."

"Frankly, accepting the family's unique qualities has done wonders to help my own sanity."

After a period of estrangement, they could finally talk and joke about Ari's saner tendencies. Her twin had always been the straitlaced sister, the one who felt she didn't fit into their eccentric family. As a result she'd moved to Vermont, far from the Jersey Shore, and kept her distance from the Costas clan, Zoe included. But it was Zoe's recent so-called disappearance that had brought Ari home to stay. Zoe welcomed the chance to renew the closeness they'd shared as young children.

Suddenly Ari nudged her sister in the ribs and pointed toward Spank, who was spitting into the crowd.

Zoe cringed. "Like I said, ordinary and the name Costas do not go hand in hand."

"Would it do any good to remind you that Spank the monkey is *not* a relative?" Ari ran a hand through the long, black hair she'd grown back after trying a bob a few months back. Now the twins looked even more alike again, something Zoe loved, since she felt it helped strengthen their bond.

"Look, Ari, the family may no longer perform their Atlantic City Boardwalk Addams Family Act, but Dad is still as bald as Uncle Fester, Mom still wiggles her hips like Morticia, and Aunt Dee swears that Great-Aunt Deliria was engaged to a chimp, which means Spank could very well be a long-lost relative."

Ari sighed. "Spank's a capuchin not a chimp."

"And your last name once was Costas. Nothing is as it seems," Zoe said, laughing.

"She's got a point," their mother, Elena, said, joining her daughters just as Spank's first act ended.

"Hi, Mom," Ari said.

"Hi," Zoe echoed.

"My beautiful girls." Elena enveloped them in a hug, made more suffocating by the long, flowing sleeves of the kimonos she favored now that she'd packed away her Morticia Addams black dresses.

Zoe supposed the outfits had something to do with owning a spa and working as a licensed masseuse. But she wasn't certain what that connection was any more than she knew why her mother had decided to wear her geisha-girl outfit to Sam's birthday party. And darned if she'd ask. Nobody could stop Elena's wacky ways and, in truth, nobody tried. In their small hometown of Ocean Isle, New Jersey, everyone expected the Costas family to act, well, *odd*. Zoe had long since stopped trying to figure out their eccentric mother. She'd rather just love her instead.

"I've come up with the perfect name for your new business," Elena said to Zoe.

After years of working for the Secret Service, protecting government officials visiting New Jersey, she'd begun to chafe under the tight rules and regulations. No surprise there since she was a Costas and liked to do things her own way. Her new business would give her the opportunity to do just that. She and her partners would be protecting visiting stars and dignitaries on their trips to Atlantic City's casinos.

"I heard that." Quinn, Ari's ex-cop husband, came up beside his wife and pulled her against his side. "What wacky idea have you got this time?" he asked his mother-in-law.

Elena raised her arms, as though on stage. "Safe Sex—protection is our business," she said, punctuating each word with her hands. "So what do you think?" her mother asked, smiling proudly at her idea.

Quinn blinked. His hazel eyes focused on Elena as if she were insane, although he knew better. He'd married Ari knowing full well the family was merely eccentric.

Connor Brennan, who Zoe hadn't realized had joined them, choked on his cola. Connor was Quinn's best friend. They'd grown up in the same foster-care system and had worked together as detectives for the police department. As partners with Zoe in the new venture, both Connor and Quinn had a vested interest in the business Elena wanted to name.

Zoe knew better than to dignify her mother's idea with a response or she'd start expanding on it and before Zoe knew it, a Safe Sex sign would be hanging over their new office space and the cops would arrive to shut them down.

"Mom, don't you have more important things to do? Like corralling Sam's friends for cake?" She pointed to the group of teenage girls gathered in the yard.

"Good idea. I'll get the kids," Ari said, escaping while she had the chance.

Elena patted Zoe's cheek. "Okay, I can see you aren't ready to talk business. Later, then. But you should think about registering the name before somebody else takes it."

"Like who? A porn shop?" Zoe asked, raising an eyebrow.

Quinn shook his head and laughed. He'd always enjoyed his in-laws much more than any man should. "I think I'll go help Ari gather the troops."

"Not yet." Elena waved an arm in the air, her long sleeve blowing in the summer breeze. "I have one more game for the girls to play before we sing 'Happy Birthday' and open presents," Elena said.

Connor adjusted his sunglasses on the bridge of his nose. "What game is that?"

"You'll be sorry you asked," Quinn promised his friend.

Zoe nodded.

Undeterred, Elena pulled out a red cut-out heart from one of her kimono pockets. "Since they're too old for Pin the Tail on the Donkey, they're going to Pin the Heart on Orlando

Bloom," she said, pronouncing *heart on* so quickly the phrase sounded like *hard-on.*

This time Connor spit out his drink. "Pin the *what* on *whom?*"

Thankfully, his fiancée, Maria, came up behind him and pulled him away, rescuing the poor man from any more of Elena's antics.

"They're happy," Zoe said of the couple.

Quinn nodded. "Connor was a goner the first time he laid eyes on Maria working as a cocktail waitress at the casino. I was just amazed he so easily accepted that she had a kid."

Foster care and their rough upbringing had scarred both Connor and Quinn, Zoe thought sadly. But they had each come around in the end, accepting that the future could be much better, if only they gave it a chance.

"The things people do for love," she said lightly. More lightly than she actually felt.

After all, she really wouldn't know what love would do to a person. She'd never fallen hard for any man. After growing up witnessing the intensity of her parents' relationship, their love and their fights, most of the time she was glad Cupid had passed her by. Experience showed her that her mother often caved in to make her father happy, and Zoe couldn't imagine sacrificing her independence for any man. As for a family of her own, Zoe wasn't holding her breath, because without love, there would be no family, no babies. It wasn't something she gave much thought to, perhaps because her immediate family took up so much of her time and energy. She was never alone unless she wanted to be.

"You'll see for yourself one day," Quinn said, an amused

smirk on his face. "In the meantime, why don't we meet to-morrow morning at the new office and discuss business there?" he suggested.

"Sounds like a good plan." Better they talk when there were no prying eyes or ears and nobody to offer their well-meaning, off-the-wall suggestions on how to run the new venture.

Zoe had been out of work for almost a year, and it had been Costas meddling that had gotten her into trouble in her former job. To help her mother, Zoe had taken a gig as a showgirl for a casino owner to whom Elena owed money. Within a few hours, she'd realized her mother was up to one of her tricks, this time matchmaking between Zoe and the casino owner. Unfortunately, despite his good looks, the man oozed slime and Zoe's instincts had kicked in. In no time she'd discovered a money-laundering scheme. which had put her in danger and the cops already investigating the case—namely Quinn—in a foul mood. He'd forced her into protective custody until their investigation was over and they'd had to tell her family she was missing and presumed dead. *Not* Zoe's finest hour.

Meanwhile her superiors had been royally ticked that she hadn't come to them as soon as she'd uncovered the illegal operation and had suspended her. She'd quit instead. She hated the rules and restrictions that were part and parcel of government work, so as soon as the case had ended, she'd returned home and settled back into her life, surrounded by her chaotic family. All her time in the safe house had made her realize she didn't enjoy her job as much as she should. Not when the job was all she had. For a while she'd helped her parents in their new spa business venture but playing bookkeeper and receptionist didn't suit her. She missed the action and day-to-day surprises on the job.

The action had drawn her to the FBI to begin with. The training at Quantico and subsequent job had more than filled her need for excitement. Too bad rules and regulations had been part of the package. She hoped her new business would give her back the satisfaction of thrills on the job. And she looked forward to working for only herself and her partners, planning and implementing security detail.

Once the business was established, she could turn her attention to finding a place of her own. Residing with her parents had worked while she'd been on the road on assignment, living out of hotels more often than being home. But she'd turn thirty next week and it was past time for her to grow up and move out.

Her parents accused her of being afraid of committing to anything, any man or any place. She didn't like to think of herself as afraid of anything.

"We'll talk tomorrow. Right now I'm going to find Ari," Quinn said, interrupting her thoughts.

Zoe cleared her throat. "Good idea. Maybe *she* can talk Mom out of embarrassing Sam with this Pin the Hard-on game, or at least get it over with before the social worker gets here."

Despite the seriousness of the caseworker's visit, she and Quinn couldn't help but laugh. They both found the Costas clan uniquely amusing. They were one big family, including Sam, whom they were intent on protecting and making happy.

Zoe understood how important it was for Sam to feel loved and she had to admit, for all their oddball tendencies, love was what the Costas family did best.

ALMOST THERE. Ryan Baldwin glanced at the directions supplied by the private investigator and turned right. Two more blocks and his search for his runaway sister's child would finally be at an end. A bittersweet end after a long, nearly fruitless search.

Faith had left home when she was seventeen—hopelessly hooked on drugs—but Ryan hadn't been able to begin searching for her until five years later, when he'd turned eighteen. By then her trail had turned cold. He hadn't given up looking, but Faith had changed her name so many times that the P.I. had had one hell of a time finding out what had happened to her.

Only recently had his P.I. stumbled onto information from a convict who had some link to Faith, and more facts had come to light. Ryan was still reeling from the painful discovery that his sister had been shot and killed six years ago by a bullet meant for her drug-dealer boyfriend, a guy now serving a life sentence. Ryan was also floored by the news that Faith had had a child.

He glanced down and realized he'd clenched his fists too tightly around the steering wheel, and loosened his grip. Thinking of Faith was always difficult. More so now that he understood what had happened after she'd run away.

Growing up, Ryan had alternated between missing his older sister and envying her the freedom he felt sure she'd finally found. Their conservative upbringing in an elite suburb of Boston, Massachusetts had never matched his sister's wilder personality. As his older brother, J.T., had already moved out, her running away had left Ryan as the only child at home. His parents had disowned Faith because of her defiance, and Ryan had caught on quickly, always behaving as expected.

Since J.T. had followed tradition and gone into the family department-store business to help his father and uncle, Ryan had become an attorney with the family's blessing. He was a partner in a firm downtown, distancing himself in ways his sister couldn't while she'd lived at home.

That distance had given him the strength to continue the search for his sister and it had finally paid off. He was on his way to meet his niece, a fourteen-year-old girl named Samantha who had been in and out of foster care since her mother's death six years ago. He planned to rescue his niece from that hellish fate and bring her home where she belonged.

He pulled up to a well-kept house in a suburban Jersey neighborhood. The clapboard siding was painted a cheery yellow with white trim and on the front lawn was a sign that read Costas Day Spa. Evening Hours Available.

He shrugged at the absurdity of the sign and turned off the ignition. The investigator had given him background information on the current family Samantha resided with and they were an odd bunch. Just a year ago, they'd made their living performing a Jersey Shore comedy act based on the Addams family. Now they ran a spa. With clients coming in and out, Ryan didn't consider it the ideal place to raise a child.

Surely his niece would be thrilled to find out she had a

sane and stable uncle and family who wanted her. Well, *he* wanted her. The rest of the family, with the exception of his uncle Russ, wasn't so keen on bringing "his delinquent sister's child" back into the fold. He'd have to deal with his uptight parents later. In the meantime, he drew a deep breath, stepped from the car and straightened his tie before heading toward the house.

Music and laughter sounded from behind the home and when nobody answered the doorbell, he followed the path that led to the backyard. He looked around, taking in the sights. A disc jockey played loud music while a monkey—he blinked, certain he was seeing things, and looked again. Damn, it *was* a monkey, dancing onstage with a pretty blond teen.

He wondered if the girl was his niece and his heart twisted tight in his chest. A bunch of kids ran by him, laughing and giggling. He glanced up at the clear blue sky and for the first time he noticed, draped between two large trees, a banner that said Happy Birthday, Sam. Welcome to the Family.

A sick feeling of unease settled in his gut as he realized he wouldn't be waltzing in and *rescuing* his sister's child from an unfit, uncaring environment. Certain he needed to re-think and devise a new approach, he turned to leave when a light touch on his arm stopped him.

"You're here!" a female voice said.

He turned to see an attractive woman wearing a bright red kimono with long black hair flowing over her shoulders. Her outfit was unique and inexplicable. Where he came from, women dressed in designer dresses and suits. He didn't know what to make of the middle-aged geisha woman appraising him with frank, interested green eyes that made him squirm.

"I'm Elena Costas." She treated him to a welcoming smile. "You must be the new man from Social Services. I know our caseworker is on vacation but she promised she'd send someone in her place to wish Sam a happy birthday—which you can do in a minute. Please, first come and meet my husband."

A hint of Greek accented her speech and she spoke quickly without taking a breath, giving him no time to insert a word until she'd finished.

He wasn't the man from Social Services and it was best she knew it up front. "I think you're confusing me—"

Ignoring his protest, she grabbed his hand, pulling him farther into the crowd.

He groaned aloud but resigned himself to going along. Short of digging in his heels, nothing would stop this determined woman, but that didn't ease his sense of guilt. Trained by his parents, Ryan typically behaved above reproach. He preferred not to lie or cheat, but this woman had presented him with an opportunity. If Sam's foster family thought he was a social worker, they wouldn't turn him away.

Besides, he had no idea how Sam would react to him showing up in her life and he appreciated the chance to observe his niece and figure out a plan that would benefit them both. He assuaged his conscience by promising himself he'd correct the false assumption before any real damage was done.

Unfortunately they didn't get far before they were stopped again.

"Halt," demanded a beautiful woman, a younger version of the one holding his hand.

Ryan couldn't help but stare. Her silky black hair twisted

around shoulders bared by a lime-green halter top tucked into a pair of faded jeans. The shirt's bright color complemented her Mediterranean skin tone, which glowed beneath the afternoon sun. She completely entranced him.

The older woman he'd begun to think of as a tornado came to a stop and uttered a few words in Greek to her that he didn't understand before switching to perfect English.

"Zoe, this man is the replacement from Social Services, so make nice. I want him to meet your papa. Have you seen him?"

"He's inside getting the cake." She gestured toward the house. "Mama, why don't you go round up Sam and her friends and get ready to sing?"

She possessed a deep voice that reminded him of hot sex and he felt himself begin to sweat beneath the afternoon sun.

Her mother nodded. "I forgot to defrost the cake so I hope your father remembers to bring hot water to dip the knife. And your aunt Kassie better behave because you know how badly she wanted to bake the cake. But we had to please Sam on her special day." She glanced at Ryan and smiled broadly. "Carvel is Sam's favorite. Do you like ice-cream cake, Mr....?"

"Baldwin. Ryan Baldwin." His head was already spinning from his dealings with Elena Costas and he opted to use his real name for fear he'd confuse himself otherwise. With his sister's myriad name changes, he had no fear they'd connect him to Sara Morgan, Faith's last known name.

He forced a comfortable smile. "I love cake, especially Carvel."

"Then let's do it so we can get to the gifts. I can't wait for Sam to see what we bought for her," Elena said.

"Maybe we should wait until tonight when we're alone." Zoe shot a pointed glance at Ryan.

Her mother shook her head. "Nonsense. Mr. Baldwin seems like the kind of man who'd want a young girl to be happy. I'm right, yes?" she asked.

"Uh, of course." But he wondered what kind of gift Sam would be receiving that had Zoe uncomfortable.

"You see?" Elena took his hand once more, grabbed Zoe and headed deeper into the yard.

They came to a stop by a picnic table and while Elena busied herself gathering the girls, Zoe turned to Ryan, her eyes intense and serious. "You'll have to excuse my mother but she's so excited about this party. She just adores Sam and wants everything to be perfect. You'll like my family," she assured Ryan, her need for his acceptance blatant.

In her mind, he was the social worker whose opinion would help determine whether they were an appropriate home for his niece. They needed to impress him. He needed for them to fail any inspection.

But as he observed her expressive face and the obvious pleasure she took in this entire day, he realized this was no act for a social worker. Zoe's love for his niece was so real, he couldn't help but like her for it.

"I'm sure I'll like your family," he told her. Even if what he'd seen so far showed him a carnival atmosphere he couldn't possibly understand.

Zoe's shoulders eased and she seemed to relax. "How's Katherine's mother? We were all so sorry to hear she couldn't make it today because of her mother's fall."

Katherine must be the missing social worker, he realized, the moment of panic passing. "She'll be okay." He hoped he was telling the truth.

"Okay, cake time," a male voice boomed through the loudspeakers. "Everyone gather." He spoke slowly and with a more distinct accent than Zoe's mother had possessed.

"Where's Samantha?" Ryan asked, nerves jumbled together inside him.

"There," Zoe said, pointing.

Ryan followed her direction and once again felt sure he was hallucinating. The monkey he'd seen earlier stood on the back of a large dog, balancing with ease. The animals came to a halt when a bald man carrying a huge ice-cream cake stepped forward. By his side walked a beautiful blond teenager, her hand tight in the crook of his elbow.

"Faith," he said aloud.

"Sam. That's my soon-to-be sister, Samantha," Zoe said with pride. "Of course we already think of her as part of the family," she quickly assured him.

He nodded but couldn't speak any more than he could take his eyes off the girl who was the spitting image of his sister. At fourteen, Sam was three years younger than Faith had been at the time she'd run away. Sam possessed the same long, blond hair and similar features, with one marked difference. Where Faith had been morose, constrained by their conservative family's demands and expectations, Sam appeared vibrant, happy and full of life.

He swallowed over the lump in his throat. "She's a beautiful child."

"Yes, she is. I'm sure the picture in Social Services files doesn't do her justice," Zoe said.

He muttered a noncommittal reply.

Their conversation ended when the "Happy Birthday" song began. The monkey blew out the candles before Sam could get to them. Laughing, she gave the animal a high five and in turn the monkey blew her a raspberry and then shot her a huge grin followed by a kiss.

The routine seemed practiced. "It seems like she knows the monkey," he said, wondering if he sounded as stupid as he felt.

"She does," Zoe said, unfazed. "Spank lived here for a while."

"Spank?"

"The monkey." Zoe rolled her eyes. "Please don't ask, okay? She's gone. She lives with her trainer and we're not violating any laws or rules and we would never, ever put Sam or any other child in danger." Zoe's once self-confident voice took on a pleading tone as she obviously realized she'd slipped with her admission.

Once more, he sought to reassure her. "I can see that you wouldn't." Unable to stop himself, he reached out and touched her hand.

The spark of awareness was instant and energizing. His gaze immediately flew to hers and in those green eyes, he saw equal doses of surprise and pleasure.

He felt the same and knew he shouldn't because of who he was. But he let his fingertips linger. Her skin was soft, the texture as intriguing as the woman herself. He'd never felt such instant desire. How ironic it would be with a woman he couldn't allow himself to get close to.

She met his gaze and smiled, a full, honest, interested smile. Ryan didn't find trouble often, but he'd found it with Zoe Costas.

"Do you want to meet Sam? See for yourself how happy she is with my parents?" Her voice was a touch hoarser than before. The desire and awareness between them might be unspoken but it was now a tangible thing.

He nodded. "I'd like to meet her."

"Sam!" Zoe called and the girl came running.

Her eyes lit up as she reached Zoe. "Hey, sis. Having fun?"

Sis. He shuddered at the memory the word evoked and at the fact that his niece obviously already felt like part of the family.

"The best. I want you to meet someone." Zoe gestured toward Ryan.

He straightened his shoulders, suddenly feeling stiff and uncomfortable as Sam looked him over from head to toe, then frowned. "I hope he's not your boyfriend." She wrinkled her nose in the disgust only a teenager could demonstrate.

Clearly he'd come up lacking. He tried not to let it bother him since she didn't know him yet.

"Sam, that's not nice," Zoe chided. "And Mr. Baldwin happens to be Katherine's replacement. He's your social worker, not my boyfriend."

"Oh, man, I'm sorry." The young girl glanced down and began fingering old keys that dangled from a chain around her neck.

Scared? Chastised? He wasn't sure but finally she looked up again, meeting his gaze.

"Hey, mister, I bet I can tell you where you got them

shoes," Sam said, her joke an obvious attempt at bravado in the face of her mistake.

He shot Zoe a questioning look.

She grinned, clearly amused but not giving away any of Sam's secrets.

He shrugged. "Okay, I'll play. Where'd I get my shoes?"

"You got 'em on your feet," Sam said and burst into belly-aching laughter at her own joke.

He didn't catch on immediately and when he did, he realized Zoe was laughing along with Sam.

Zoe shook her head and tried to control herself. Sam's old, tired joke wasn't what had her laughing but poor Ryan Baldwin and his blank, lost stare. She wondered if it was painful to be that uptight and straitlaced. Oh, well. As Sam's new social worker, a couple of days with the Costas clan would cure him in no time.

She had to admit that his sandy-blond hair and brown eyes made for a darn cute package, despite that he was a social worker and by definition a stickler for rules. She reminded herself that he was a man who would no doubt make her feel strangled and constrained way more than even the safe house had done. Still, she found herself tempted to test the waters and wondered how he'd react if she reached out and pinched his—

"He's got a stick up his butt—" Sam said in a stage whisper.

Ryan's eyes opened in shock.

Zoe refrained from laughing and instead leveled Sam with a stern glare. Thankfully Sam got the message and gazed downward, appearing contrite for Ryan's sake. Zoe knew she was probably anything but.

"Sorry," she muttered.

"That's okay," Ryan said.

"I've got to go talk to my friend Stacey," Sam said.

Zoe nodded. "That's a good idea."

Before leaving, Sam glanced at Ryan. "Nice meeting you, Mr. Baldwin. You're gonna let me stay with Elena and Nicholas, right?"

Zoe's heart clenched, not just at Sam's plea but at her sudden polite tone. That wasn't who Sam was and Zoe hated the anxiety and insecurity Sam was forced to live with every single day.

"Go have fun. Nobody's making any decisions today." Zoe ruffled the girl's long hair, and after Sam had sped away, she turned to Ryan.

"If there's anything you can do to speed this process along, it'll be better for everyone, believe me. In the best interest of the child," she said, parroting Katherine and everyone else in the government bureaucracy. "I mean since that's what you're all about, and we are what Sam wants..." Zoe trailed off as Ryan's expression shut down.

Apparently she'd crossed the line. The Costas clan tended to do that too often. Pleasing the social worker and worrying about conforming to someone else's standards was the one thing that had the entire family on edge. They were an out-of-the-box sort of group and nothing, not even adopting a child, could change that.

Thankfully Social Services had agreed to the foster placement and the past few months had been uneventful. Now if she could just get her mother to stall Sam's birthday present until Ryan Baldwin left, she'd feel much better.

"I'm sorry. No more pushing. I promise. So, how about a tour of the house?" she asked with forced cheer, recalling that had been one of the first things the other social worker had requested.

He seemed to relax and even crack a smile. "Has anyone ever told you you're just like your mother?"

She cocked her head to one side. "If you mean because I'm pushy, tend to ramble, and usually get what I want, then yeah, people do think my mother and I are alike."

"I was thinking that you're both like a tornado of sorts." The corners of his eyes crinkled. "But I have to admit, you two can be somewhat refreshing."

"That's one way of putting it, and coming from someone more... How shall I put this delicately? Coming from someone more stuffy than I am, I think I'll even consider it a compliment."

He laughed at that, two dimples suddenly becoming evident. With his guard down and his smile genuine and unstrained, Zoe was struck again by how handsome he truly was. It was strange that she'd notice him at all, since a "suit" was the last kind of guy she'd normally be attracted to, but what the heck. The rush of adrenaline proved she wasn't dead, as her mother accused her of being.

"I'd like to take that tour now," he said, changing the subject back to business.

"Come." Zoe grabbed his hand and pulled him toward the house.

She kept things light as she pointed out the spa and how it was completely separate from the house. Entrances on opposite sides of the property meant nobody could get in or out of the house from the spa. She showed him all the safety precautions they'd taken and couldn't help but show her pride in the business her family had made a success in such a short time.

He asked questions and she answered. He even laughed a time or two at her jokes. And all the while, she couldn't shake the heat his touch generated or the sense that his big hand had imprinted itself on her smaller one. She hadn't liked the other social worker's unexpected visits but she could get used to this guy hanging around.

They ended their tour in the kitchen and Zoe hopped up to sit on the counter. "So what do you think?"

He nodded in what seemed reluctant approval. "It's a different setup but you've definitely made sure the family is separate and protected from spa guests. The cowbell was a unique touch."

She rolled her eyes. It figured. Zoe had pointed out their high-tech protection, the video cameras and the alarm system and he'd focused on Elena's personal method of insuring nobody entered the private part of the house unnoticed—a cowbell hanging over the door, virtually impossible to move or disable. She'd used the same technique on Zoe and Ari when they were younger to make sure neither sneaked out of the house or came in too late.

Zoe shrugged. "What can I say? Mom and Dad have got their own ways. But they did their job as parents and did it well."

He strode closer. So close she smelled his rich, musky scent and a warm, tingling feeling arose in her chest.

"Your family is certainly different," he said.

"I take it you're from a more conservative bunch?" She laughed and yanked on his tie playfully before remembering who he was. The social worker who would determine Sam's fate.

She started to pull back but he touched her hand, stilling her movement, and his eyes locked on hers. The air around them grew heavy, pulsing with anticipatory awareness. She couldn't remember the last time she'd been this drawn to a man on first meeting.

Zoe had a healthy sex life but not a *love* life. That description she reserved for soul mates, people like her parents, or Quinn and Ari. In fact, she reserved the description for many people, really, with the exception of herself. She didn't know how people made a lifetime commitment and kept it. She hadn't even been able to accomplish that with a job.

She understood these things about herself and though she accepted them, she was taking steps to lead a more adult life. Her sister's marriage had made her realize it was time to make changes. Zoe supposed it was a good thing that love had never happened for her. One less decision she'd had to make and stick with, she thought wryly.

And since she was approaching her thirtieth birthday in a matter of days, she had long since stopped expecting love at all. Besides, she enjoyed her freedom too much to give it all up for one man.

She glanced at the good-looking man before her and realized that her sex life had been status quo for so long even this overwhelming chemistry came as a surprise. As a woman who liked excitement, she welcomed the rush of adrenaline in her veins and she had no trouble acting on their mutual attraction.

As long as she didn't jeopardize Sam's future in the process. Thankfully, the ringing of the telephone interrupted their prolonged silence and she reached for the phone. "Hello."

"Elena?" a voice asked.

"No, this is Zoe."

She gave Ryan an apologetic look and held up one finger, asking him to wait a minute while she took the call.

"It's Katherine Farr, Samantha's social worker," the voice on the other end of the phone said. "I just wanted to apologize that neither myself nor my colleague could make it to Sam's party today."

Zoe narrowed her gaze. "But…"

"I know you're disappointed and so is Samantha, but it can't be helped. My mother needs me for another few weeks and my colleagues will be tied up with urgent cases. I hope you understand."

"Sort of." Zoe shot a covert glance at Ryan beneath her lashes.

"It's a compliment and a testament to your family's skills with Samantha. She's come such a long way. I know she's safe and in good hands, so I have no problem with the final evaluation being postponed for a few weeks until I'm back."

"Okay." She didn't want to give anything away to her companion who stood with his back to her, staring at the photographs on the refrigerator.

"My colleagues will need to focus on the more problematic cases in order to cover my absence," Katherine explained.

"I understand. And I hope things work out for your mother."

"Thank you, dear. You'll relay the message to your parents?"

"I certainly will." Zoe hung up the phone and focused on the stranger in her kitchen.

A man who'd stirred something inside her that had been dormant for too long. A man who obviously had an agenda.

She walked up behind him and tugged on his arm.

"Is this you and Sam?" He gestured to the picture of Zoe, Ari and Sam with orange spray-on tans on their faces and arms, smiling for the camera.

"We were recreating an old childhood memory," she said laughing, before she caught herself. "Never mind that."

He narrowed his gaze. "What is it? What's wrong?"

"*You're* wrong, Ryan Baldwin, if that's even your name. Since I just spoke to Sam's social worker on the phone and I know she couldn't get someone to replace her, I'd like to know just who the hell you are. And what the hell you're doing snooping around my family and my house."

Chapter Two

RYAN REALIZED THE MOMENT his cover had been blown and his stomach churned with a combination of relief that he could end his deception and anticipation that a confrontation was sure to follow. He'd been preparing himself the entire car ride from Boston and he was ready now.

He glanced at Zoe. Gone was the solicitous woman who'd sought to charm and accommodate him. Instead he looked into deep green eyes, which only minutes ago had flickered with warmth and interest, and that now held cold contempt.

"Who the hell are you?" Zoe asked again.

Ryan welcomed the intervention of fate. "I'm Sam's uncle."

"Sam has no family." She folded her arms across her chest defensively. "Care to cough up another lie?"

"It's the truth. My sister, Faith, was Sam's mother."

"Sam's mother's name was Sara."

He reached into his pocket for the papers he'd received from the P.I. and handed them over.

Zoe glanced through the sheets, which acknowledged her words and verified his, and paled. "I'm assuming these are copies?"

He nodded. "Feel free to keep them."

She rolled them tight, hanging on to the documents with

one hand. "Even if you're telling the truth, wouldn't you say you took your sweet time coming around?"

"Faith ran away from home when she was seventeen. I was only thirteen. She got involved with drugs and changed her name so many times, her trail grew cold. But make no mistake, Sam is my niece."

"And?" She spat out the word.

"And I want to bring her home."

"What if that isn't what Sam wants? After years of being shuffled from foster home to foster home, she finally has a family. Here. With us."

If Ryan had admired this woman before his revelation, her spunk fired his blood now. Even their differences didn't stop the desire racing through his veins.

"Do you really think you can show up, wave some documents that proclaim you're a blood relative and whisk her away? Think again. You're years too late to do Sam one bit of good."

He swallowed hard, because Zoe had voiced his biggest fear. But that didn't mean he'd back down. He leaned closer, getting into her personal space. "No court's going to hold it against me because I was too young to track Sam down sooner."

Court? Zoe grew dizzy, feeling the blood rush out of her head. Her family might pass inspection with a social worker. But if a judge was faced with choosing between this man, who had blood ties to Sam and who seemed impeccably normal, or her wacky family, the Costas clan didn't stand a chance.

She understood this just as she understood the ramifications of Ryan Baldwin's claim. A claim she intended to check out ASAP. In the meantime, while she got Quinn and Connor digging into the man's past and present, she needed to buy her and her family some time.

No way could he reveal the truth to Sam or Social Services just yet. "Please don't tell me you think you can snap your fingers and all will go your way," she said with sugared sweetness.

He shrugged, but there was a definite arrogance to him she hadn't noticed earlier. Hadn't wanted to notice, she was forced to admit. She'd been taken in by his good looks and suckered by his claim that he was a public servant.

Now that she allowed her training to kick in and looked more closely, she realized his European suit was more expensive than any social worker could afford and his voice held a trace of a fine New England accent. Which meant he not only had the intent to fight her family in court, should it come to that, but probably the financial means, as well.

The Costas family didn't.

She gathered her wits and her defenses and pulled on every shred of self-confidence she could muster to go toe-to-toe with him. Her family and Sam's emotional well-being were at stake. "Okay, let's agree on a few points, shall we?"

He raised an eyebrow. "Go on."

"Right now my family has custody and controls access to your niece. You need that access as well as a smooth introduction. Are we on the same page so far?"

"So far, yes." He studied her with those astute brown eyes.

"I'm also sure you don't think we're just going to hand Sam over to a complete stranger, blood relation or not. We're going to want to know what kind of home you plan to provide for her. Fair?"

He inclined his head, but didn't answer.

She studied his expression closely. A muscle ticked in his jaw, telling her that something she'd just said had put him on edge.

She intended to push him a little further. "Are you married?"

"No."

"Engaged?"

He shook his head.

"So you're a single guy then. Interesting," she said, referring to more than his ability to raise a teenage girl. "You mentioned that your sister ran away when you were young but you never mentioned other family. Are your parents still alive?"

"Yes." His expression grew more shuttered.

She narrowed her gaze. "That's it? Yes? Do they know you found your sister's child?"

"Yes." His jaw tightened, almost imperceptibly.

"Yet they aren't here with you."

He paused, then said, "We thought it best I come down and check out the situation first." The tick in his jaw became more pronounced.

She made a mental note to have Quinn look deeply into their family history. If he had been thirteen when his sister ran away, what had his parents done about finding Faith *before* the trail had grown cold? Ryan Baldwin's silence spoke louder than any words could and perhaps whatever was behind that reticence would provide her with the leverage she needed to stall his revelation to Sam.

She sidled up beside him, this time more aware of his expensive cologne, a scent that under other circumstances she could definitely get used to. "I'd like to propose a deal. A quid pro quo of sorts."

"Again, I'm listening."

"You just can't spring this on my family or Sam. She's fragile and needs to get to know you first."

He nodded in understanding, his expression softening. "That sounds fair. What are you proposing?"

"Katherine, the social worker, has put off the final evaluation a few weeks while she's away on a family emergency. They're so overburdened they can't spare anyone for this case. I suggest you hold off telling Social Services or Sam who you claim to be."

"Who I *am*."

She shook her head, refusing to accept him at his word just yet. "Whatever. What I'm suggesting is that you continue your charade. Pretend to be a social worker and come by as often as you like during these last few weeks of the evaluation period. You'll get to know Sam and see her in her element here."

He frowned. "That sounds awfully one-sided. What do I get out of this?"

"My cooperation in getting to know Sam. If you dump this news on her, I can promise you every defensive mechanism she has will surface and your chances of winning her over will be slim. She considers me her sister. She trusts my judgment. Like it or not, you need me, Mr. Baldwin. So do we have a deal?" She held out her hand.

He hesitated for a second, before grasping her hand. If Zoe

thought the first sparks between them were a fluke, she immediately discovered she'd been mistaken. The man might have lied from their first meeting, might be the biggest threat to the Costas family since her father's bout with cancer, but somehow the attraction was there, strong and undeniable.

She gathered her composure—which wasn't easy when she *liked* the feelings he evoked—and yanked her hand back. "One more thing."

"What's that?" he asked, flexing his fingers as if he needed to shake himself free of her touch.

She understood and had to force herself to focus on their predicament. "When Sam gets her birthday gift, you will grin and laugh and look the other way."

"What's the gift?" he asked warily.

"You'll see." Despite herself, she couldn't help but grin.

RYAN TRIED TO MAKE HIMSELF comfortable at the party. With the truth out in the open between himself and Zoe, he felt as if he'd just dodged a bullet and also knew for a fact that he'd bought himself some time at the Costas home. As tough as it was to admit, Zoe had raised many good points, the most important of which was that he needed her. Zoe's parents were Sam's guardians, which put them at a legal advantage. Emotionally, they also had the upper hand since they *knew* Sam and understood how she would react to his sudden appearance in her life. He'd foolishly thought he'd be rescuing her from hell and she'd greet him with open arms. Zoe made him realize Sam might well resent him for all the years she'd suffered in foster care, and now that he thought about it, such a reaction would be understandable.

No fourteen-year-old would be able to rationalize the situation enough to forgive and forget immediately, no matter how much he wished otherwise. Still, he tried to play devil's advocate, to think through all possibilities. Though there was a chance that Zoe was trying to discourage him with her warnings about Sam's defense mechanisms springing into place, he decided it was unlikely Zoe would lie about something so important.

As an attorney, he'd learned to read people and trust his instincts, and Zoe Costas, for all her family's eccentricity, seemed to be honest and upfront. Most important, it was obvious that she loved Sam—enough not to put her emotions at risk. He felt the same way and that's why he'd agreed not to rush into revealing who he was.

An hour after she'd uncovered his real identity, the last of the guests had left the party and only the family remained gathered in the family room. They were a large group, Elena and her husband Nicholas; Zoe's twin, Ari, and her husband, ex-cop Quinn Donovan; Quinn's best friend, Connor Brennan, and his fiancée, Maria; Nicholas's sister, Kassie, who owned a local diner called Paradeisos; a man named Gus; Elena's sister, Dee, and her husband, John…the list went on and on.

All except for the monkey, who thankfully had departed with her trainer, but not before dropping her pants and mooning the crowd one last time. Sam had slipped the monkey five dollars, tucking the folded bill into the white-lace panties beneath the primate's dress. Spank had changed clothing before leaving, much as a bride would prior to her departure with her groom.

Ryan had been speechless. He still couldn't believe this day, which had been filled with one shock after another. Had his family seen the spectacle of that monkey, his mother would have passed out on the spot while his father would have called for Hilton, the butler, to show the animal to the door. The only one in his family Ryan could picture enjoying the animal was Faith, and she was long gone. Only her daughter remained, her legacy and a testament to her free spirit.

With the huge family surrounding him, he sensed the surprises weren't over yet. There weren't enough chairs to hold all the relatives, but no one seemed to mind, and though he tried to give any one of the women his seat, they'd refused. He was the *guest,* they'd informed him. He knew they meant *the social worker* and all were on their best behavior.

Only Sam seemed oblivious to his presence as she bounced from person to person, begging for clues about her birthday gift. Nobody was speaking on the subject, leaving both Sam and Ryan in the dark.

Without warning, Ryan heard a drumroll and turned to see Nicholas playing a small set of drums, deliberately building anticipation.

"Come on, I want to see!" Sam said, her enthusiasm tangible and contagious.

Even his stomach churned with unfamiliar excitement. Growing up, the most exciting birthday gift his parents had ever given him was a savings bond. At least he'd had Uncle Russ, his father's brother, for the kind of fun gifts a kid needed like a bike or the latest gadget.

This large gathering and the love in the room was as alien to him as the young girl who was his niece. Not for the first time, he realized he had his work cut out for him when it came to winning her trust.

He glanced at Zoe, who sat on the arm of the sofa beside him. By the way she glared at him when she sensed no one else was looking, she obviously hadn't forgiven him for his lie. Despite the fact that they were adversaries, she hadn't thrown him out, at least not yet. Instead he sensed that for the time being, they were on the same side, though solely for Sam's benefit.

He owed her for that and as he met her gaze, an odd sense of gratitude filled him. Who was he kidding? When he looked at the raven-haired beauty, a hell of a lot more than gratitude washed over him.

"Introducing Sam's birthday gift and the newest member of the family!" Elena said, interrupting his thoughts as she walked into the room, holding a leash in one hand.

"Ooh, what is it?" Sam asked.

Ryan tried to see, but she darted in front of him, blocking his view. He heard a loud squeal that could have come from Sam, but his gut instinct told him the sound was from an animal.

Of the swine variety, if he wasn't mistaken.

"It can't be," he muttered.

"It is," Zoe retorted.

He hadn't realized he'd spoken aloud.

"And you will be nice about it." She treated him to a forced smile.

He rose and stepped around the couch to catch his first

glimpse of the…pig. A tiny, black-and-white pig. Snout and all. "It's gratifying to know my hearing's not going."

"Your mind's not playing tricks on you, either," Zoe said helpfully.

"Gee, thanks."

Elena leaned down beside Sam and patted the space beside her. "Come sit quietly."

Sam did as Elena instructed, both women sitting cross-legged on the floor. Everyone else had grown silent, too, respecting the fact that the tiny piglet was shaking like a leaf.

"Sam, meet Ima. Ima, meet Sam," Elena said, lifting the pig and placing her gently in Sam's lap.

"Ima?" Sam asked. She paused, her nose crinkling as she thought about the name. "Oh I get it!" she finally said and began giggling.

"I don't," Ryan muttered.

Every eye in the room turned his way.

"I'm a pig, doofus," Sam said, grinning. "Get it? Her name's Ima Pig." When Ryan didn't answer right away, Sam rolled her eyes. "See, Zoe, I told you he's got a—"

"Samantha!" Elena and Nicholas said at the same time.

Elena gently took Sam's chin in her hand and turned her face toward her own. "Be nice to Mr. Baldwin. He's a guest in our home and he's your elder. In this house we respect our elders."

Sam glanced down before looking his way, her features contrite. "Sorry, mister," she said, her hands gripping the old keys around her neck.

Ryan struggled for air. She was being reprimanded for being fresh to him while he sat here and lied to her face. It wasn't right or fair. The charade he'd begun had already started to weigh on him and he wondered how he'd manage to play social worker for any stretch of time.

"That's okay," he managed to tell her. "It's your birthday and you're excited. I understand." Though he sensed it wouldn't matter what day it was. Sam's tough exterior had been formed long ago.

Excusing himself, he made his way into the kitchen. Above the whispers of the family, he heard Elena's instructions about how to care for the animal, how not to scare it, how Ima would think anyone coming for her from above was a predator and so Sam should always approach the pig from the side. She'd obviously done her research on the care and feeding of pigs. If her actions with Sam were any indication, Elena Costas was a loving, caring parent and the thought scared him spitless.

But he was Sam's uncle. Her flesh and blood. Surely that counted for something…didn't it?

SITTING IN HER FAMILY HOME and watching Sam unwrap gifts reminded Zoe of past birthdays and holidays. All involving family fun and unbelievable presents. Zoe remembered the dog she'd been given for her tenth birthday. Ari had received a cat. And somehow, maybe because the Costases had said so, they'd all gotten along, she recalled. This feeling of family made her whole and she wanted the same for Sam.

That's why Zoe had let Ryan watch her family interact with the teenager for a while before she'd come up beside him, and why she gave him a few minutes alone in the kitchen to think things over before joining him in the other room. She wanted him to realize how well Sam fit in with them.

"Hey there, Mr. Social Worker, how's it going?" she asked.

"It's fine and I'm confused. She's really excited about the pig," he said, shaking his head.

"It's a legal pet to replace the monkey. Not replace it in her heart, but in the house—"

"I get it. I just couldn't believe your mother walked in with a freaking pig."

Zoe blinked, startled. Something told her Mr. Uptight, Conservative Bostonian didn't curse often. "A Vietnamese potbellied pig, in case you were wondering."

"I wasn't."

"Liar."

To her surprise, he burst out laughing. "Are you people for real?"

"Last time I checked." She nodded toward her family gathered in the other room. "We may be different, but we love each other so if you're thinking you can use our uniqueness against us—"

"Whoa." He held up a hand. "I didn't mean anything except you're all nothing like what I'm used to."

Zoe stopped, smiled slightly, then placed her hand on the back of his larger one and gently pushed it down, keeping her fingers lightly closed around his. "And what would that be? Proper decorum at all times," she teased softly.

A dimpled grin worked its way across his face, but his stare remained fixed on their hands. She suspected he also felt the heat passing between them.

No doubt he needed an explanation for her behavior when they were supposed to be on opposing sides. She wished she could understand it herself. How could she be so attracted to a man she knew was lying? A man who was, in essence, forcing *her* to lie to her family?

Yet she *was* attracted. Very attracted. Enough that she couldn't control the smiles he evoked or the warmth surging through her body right now.

He also deserved an explanation. "What can I say? You may be a lying creep, but you interest me." In fact, her insides tingled, making her aware of sensations that had been dormant for a while. She couldn't remember the last time simply touching a man had caused her breasts to grow heavy and her nipples to tighten against her shirt.

Oh yes, she liked how this man made her feel.

When she'd worked for the Secret Service, the agency had frowned on mixing work and pleasure. She'd resented the rule at the time and had bent it on occasion, but with Ryan's relationship to Sam between them, she'd be smart to follow a no-fraternization rule now.

On the other hand, he was hard to resist; his pull was magnetic. And he'd be around for a few weeks, underfoot, watching them and getting to know Sam. She couldn't deny the desire to get to know him equally well. Without a doubt she knew he'd give her all the heat she desperately needed without being any threat to her resolution to advance her career and her life. It was an ideal situation.

"You see? Not only are you one big, loving group, but you say what you think." He shook his head in disbelief.

She swung their clasped hands back and forth. "Better than keeping your feelings bottled up until you explode."

"Or run away," he muttered.

She paused. "Your sister?"

He nodded. "She chafed under rules and restrictions."

"And your parents had a lot of them?" she guessed without too much difficulty.

"You could say that. Ever hear the term *upper crust?*"

"Of course."

"Well imagine all that term implies. My brother and I conformed. She didn't."

Zoe raised an eyebrow, interested in his background for reasons that went beyond Sam. "How many brothers and sisters do you have?"

"There were three of us in total. There's the oldest, J.T., then came Faith, then me." His eyes glazed over at the mention of his sister's name.

"So Faith was the only girl."

He nodded. "My parents had high hopes for her. They expected her to have a traditional coming-out when she turned sixteen, but Faith was anything but traditional."

Being so close to her family, and knowing what Ari had gone through when Zoe'd had to fake her disappearance, she could empathize with his pain over his sister.

She squeezed his hand tight. "I really am sorry." And she was, despite that he might want to take Sam away. "So your folks must be thrilled that you've found Sam." Her voice caught in her throat, this time at *her* pain over the fear of losing someone.

"My family is adjusting to the news," he said vaguely. "So how do you care for a pig?"

A not-so-subtle change of subject and Zoe made a mental note to mention it to Quinn and Connor during their meeting tomorrow morning. Planning the discussion at the office seemed like an even better idea now, since she didn't want to run the risk of Sam or anyone else in the family over-hearing. And now that she'd found out some more in-formation on Ryan Baldwin, she decided to play along with his topic change.

"You can feed and train the pig like any other domestic animal. Don't you read the papers? George Clooney has one and he loves that animal more than any woman he's met yet. Want to go meet Ima?" she asked.

"Ima Pig," he said and shuddered. "No thanks. I'll avoid it for now."

"Chicken." Zoe grinned. "So where are you staying?"

"Trump Plaza."

"All the way in Atlantic City?" she asked. With their house right by the beach, there were a number of small, but nice hotels and motels closer to Ocean Isle.

"It's only twenty minutes according to AAA."

She rolled her eyes. "Let me guess. A motel close by never even crossed your highfalutin mind."

He opened his mouth to speak, then shook his head. "Never mind. You already seem to have my number."

"That I do, Mr. Baldwin. Just tell me that you're going to honor our deal." Because she had no choice but to trust him.

Trust that he wouldn't go to Social Services and announce his status as Sam's uncle. Trust that he wouldn't tell her par-ents and completely freak them out, sending them into a tailspin and likely triggering a reaction she didn't even want to imagine. And worse, she had to trust that he wouldn't tell Sam.

Zoe swallowed hard.

This time he squeezed her hand tight. She'd grown so comfortable, she'd forgotten they were still standing that way.

"I realize you don't know me well and that I just showed up out of nowhere and turned your life upside down. But if there's one thing I can promise you, it's that despite my social-worker lie, I'm a man of my word. If I make you a promise, you can believe in me." His voice grew low and husky.

"And?" she asked.

"And I promise to keep my end of the deal." Those deep brown eyes met hers, warm and compelling. Sexy and real.

She had to be a fool—because she believed him. "I have a meeting tomorrow morning so I'd appreciate it if you didn't show up here until after noon."

He nodded. "I can do that."

She had one more question before she walked him to the door. "What do you do that you can take time off so easily and hang around Ocean Isle until this gets resolved?"

"I'm a lawyer."

Swell, she thought, but she'd had to ask. "Family practice, I take it?"

He shook his head. "I might have conformed better than my sister, but there are still things I do my own way." In his gaze, she thought she saw a hint of mischief. A sexual warning of sorts.

But then she reminded herself that this was Mr. Conservative and she had to be mistaken. Still, she couldn't help but think of him doing things to her *his own way*.

"I'll keep that in mind," she heard herself say before pulling him back to the family for his goodbyes.

THE NEXT DAY, Zoe showed up early for the meeting with her partners so she could prep what to tell the two men. Both had a soft spot for very few people, but Sam was at the top of their list. Now Zoe paced the office space she, Quinn and Connor had recently rented, located about a block from the rec center where the men volunteered and where Sam hung out after school. On a clear day like today, the large office windows provided a nice view of the ocean. It was a decent amount of space for their rental money. All that was missing was a firm name, but what had been a priority yesterday seemed insignificant today in comparison to the problem Ryan Baldwin presented.

"Are you going to tell us what's wrong or are you just going to wear out the new carpet?" Quinn asked, his voice tight with frustration.

Zoe groaned and detailed all she'd learned from Ryan yesterday, including his true identity.

"He's Sam's *what?*" Quinn yelled, shaking the walls if not the foundation.

Zoe winced. If anyone had a stake in Sam's future, it was the man who'd secured her first one foster home, then another in an effort to find her a good, solid home. Being a product of the foster-care system, Quinn understood only too well how abandoned, traumatized and confused Sam would feel upon learning the truth.

If it was the truth. But after a few hours in Ryan's company, Zoe believed him.

She handed Quinn the papers Ryan had given her. "I'd handle digging into Baldwin's family and background myself except that I want to be around the house at all times.

I don't want him alone with Sam, or my parents, for that matter. I need what little control I can get over him and this situation."

Quinn ran a hand through his brown hair as he flipped through the papers. "His sister's birth certificate, even her death certificate... Holy hell," he muttered. "All this bastard has to do is demand a DNA test and he can prove he's family. From there, a judge would only be too happy to hand her over."

"Jeez, Quinn. Thanks for the vote of confidence. He says he's from Boston, has two siblings including Sam's mother, and from what I can gather, they're on the uptight side."

"That much was obvious from the way he jumped out of the way when Sam tried to put the pig in his arms," Connor said, chuckling.

"And you're one to talk. My family still gives you hives." Zoe laughed.

Connor had the grace to flush red in his cheeks. "Only because I'm not used to so many wacky people in the room at one time."

"He was probably afraid the pig would soil his designer duds," Quinn offered helpfully.

Zoe drew a deep breath before giving her opinion. "He seems nice enough. In fact I wish I'd met him under other circumstances. If I could just get him to loosen up a little, we could have some fun."

"Changing from tight-ass briefs to boxers would accomplish the same thing." Connor rolled a pen between his palms as he contemplated the thought. "Seriously, Zoe, you can't get involved with the guy. Talk about a conflict of interest!"

"Hell yes, she can," Quinn said.

Zoe and Connor's gaze flew to their partner's. "What?" they asked simultaneously.

"You already made the decision to stick close to home until we figure out how to handle the guy, right?" Quinn leaned forward, elbows on his desk, and pinned Zoe with a determined glare.

Too bad she'd long ago learned how to handle wannabe bad guys like Quinn. "Yes. But you don't scare me, so lose the Bad Cop look. I'm already on your team," she reminded him. "Of course I'm sticking by Sam's side. What's your point?"

"Well it's summertime. She'll be all over the place with her friends and we don't want Ryan Baldwin loose in town, asking questions and stirring up trouble. So use that chemistry to your advantage and when you can't be with Sam, make it your business to be all over Baldwin. From what I noticed in the kitchen last night, you won't find the assignment a hardship." A smart-ass smirk was on Quinn's face while Connor was doing his best not to snicker.

Zoe strode up to the desk and leaned forward. Nose to nose, she warned him, "You keep this up and I'll tell Ari you're smoking the occasional cigar. You'll be sleeping on the couch for at least a week." Zoe stood straight, folded her arms over her chest and grinned. "We both know even one night without my sister would be a hardship."

Quinn let out a laugh. "See now this is why I agreed to this partnership. You give as good as you get and you don't get on my nerves—much," he added, with a wink. "Listen, Zoe, all kidding aside, we need you to stick close to this guy."

She nodded, understanding how serious this was. "I will."

"But watch yourself," Connor said. "There's no good outcome on this one, and if you get involved, you could end up hurt."

This time it was Zoe's turn to laugh. "Not a chance, guys. To be hurt, you have to fall for a guy and that's definitely not my MO."

Both men snorted. "Like it was either one of ours?" Connor asked.

"Hey, just because the two of you are now whipped doesn't mean I'll end up the same way."

She didn't intend to live by her parents' example. Her parents were and always had been head over heels in love, which usually meant stormy disagreements and heated apologies that ended up with them in the bedroom, locked inside for hours. She and Ari had learned to keep themselves busy during those times, though at such a young age she probably shouldn't have been aware of what the glow on her mother's face afterward really meant. But they shared a romantic, storybook kind of love.

The give and take between her parents represented the best in a relationship, but they'd married young. And the older Zoe got, the more she feared that settling down with any man after all her years alone would mean compromises that would chip away at the essence of who she was. A person that was still too undefined, she thought.

Zoe had had her share of relationships and men. If love had been in the cards, she would have definitely discovered

it by now. At the very least, she'd have been through devastating heartbreak. Instead she'd been disappointed at
times, hurt on occasion, but she'd always bounced back,
never truly having had her heart broken. Never having said,
I love you.

"I guess it's not in my genetic makeup, so I'll hang around
with Ryan Baldwin and keep a close eye on him." A very
close, admiring eye.

"Just be careful," Quinn said. "I don't want you hurt.
You're like a sister to me and if Baldwin turns out to be who
he claims he is, I'd hate like hell to have to beat the crap out
of Sam's uncle." He slammed his hand on the desk and muttered a succinct curse. "Uncle. This is going to kill everyone involved."

Connor nodded. "Let's just hope like hell we find dirt on
his family and maybe then there'll be some way Zoe's parents can keep Sam."

Zoe shuddered. The entire situation was a mess she
couldn't begin to decipher. Instead, she waved at her partners and headed home—before Ryan could show up and
possibly alert her parents or Sam to the fact that something
was wrong.

Chapter Three

AFTER THE MEETING at the office, Zoe rushed home, skipping lunch because she was determined to get there before Ryan showed up for his visit. She'd expected to find Sam cuddled up with the pig near his cage. Instead the kitchen was empty and she heard voices coming from outside.

She stepped out the sliding glass door and onto the large patio. Her mother was nowhere to be found, but Sam and Ryan were alone together in the yard. That by itself was enough to jolt her system. But when she caught sight of a shirtless Ryan digging a hole in the grass, a rush of adrenaline and desire raced through her veins.

The man was handsome in a suit, but, *thee mou,* she couldn't have imagined the body hidden beneath the well-cut material. His back was already deeply tanned from the summer sun and his muscles flexed and pulled, teasing her each time he dug into the dirt. Watching him, she couldn't stop imagining what his smooth skin would feel like beneath her hands or how his hard body would mesh perfectly with hers.

A warning voice echoed in her head, reminding her he wasn't a social worker and he was a threat to Sam's place in Zoe's well-loved family. But the truth didn't change the desire churning inside her or the need he inspired.

She'd never let her emotions take over common sense, but then she'd never met a man like Ryan.

"Zoe! Come hang with me and Ryan."

Sam's voice snapped her out of her musings and she approached warily, completely aware of the one-hundred-and-eighty-degree turn Sam's attitude toward Ryan Baldwin seemed to have taken.

"What have you and *Ryan* been talking about?" Zoe asked. *And just when had Mr. Baldwin, the social worker with the stick up his butt, become just plain Ryan?* Zoe wondered.

He dug the shovel into the dirt and leaned on the handle, his entire look and attitude providing a more rugged, outdoorsy appearance than she would have associated with him after their first meeting.

"We're discussing the finer points of raising pigs." He rubbed his sweaty hands on his khakis, leaving a trail of dirt behind.

Zoe wondered what his Boston relatives would think if they saw him now, but with Sam around she couldn't ask. She could however remark on the unusual nature of his task. "What's going on?" She pointed to the patch of dirt where grass used to be.

"It's a place for Ima to root," Sam explained. "The books Ryan brought me said that if we give Ima a place of her own to dig and play in, we'll cut down on her doing it in inappropriate places."

Zoe's gaze flew to Ryan. "You bought her books?"

"And magazines," Sam added.

"I see." Zoe nodded slowly.

"I showed up at her birthday party empty-handed. It was

the least I could do." He shrugged as if the gesture meant nothing.

Zoe knew that for him, the gift was a huge offering. Symbolic of something Sam couldn't begin to understand or comprehend. Zoe wondered if she should question his sincerity, but then decided it was a petty thought, unworthy of her.

"So I read a few pages and now we're giving Ima a place of her own." Sam grinned and gestured to the patch of dirt Ryan had created.

Zoe glanced down. "In the yard."

"Yep."

"Where Elena's daffodils bloom in the spring." She leaned closer to inspect his handiwork. "Interesting choice," she said, looking into Ryan's stunned eyes.

"Sam said that was an empty spot." He blanched. "She said that nobody would care if I dug here. In fact, young lady, you begged for me to dig in this very place." He raised his voice at Sam, obviously caught himself, then moderated his tone. "You said it would be fine."

Sam flung her arms in the air, typical teenager style. "Hey I didn't know, okay?"

The muscle in his jaw that ticked when he was agitated started up again. "Then maybe you should have asked for permission first."

"Hey—"

"Is for horses," Zoe said in an attempt to diffuse the situation.

Not that Ryan would know, but Sam wouldn't put up with yelling or discipline from a stranger. In her mind, an adult had to earn the right to reprimand her by first proving they cared. The Costas family had already been down that road. Sam had tested them, retested them and now finally believed she belonged. If they punished her, she understood it was because they loved her, not because they were worried the state would take away their monthly foster stipend.

Zoe placed a hand on his arm. She'd meant her touch to calm him, but it had the opposite effect, at least on her. His skin was hot from a combination of the sun's rays and his body heat. Heat she wanted desperately to share in the most intimate way possible, and those butterflies came to life in her stomach once more.

But she couldn't just ignore everything going on around her. "It's okay," she reassured him. "We can replant the daffodil bulbs in the fall and the flowers will bloom again next year. They'll look just as pretty over there." She pointed to a spot a few feet away.

Ryan still looked like he was about to be sick and Zoe was certain the reasons had to run deeper than the fact that he'd messed up Elena's flower garden.

Zoe glanced at Sam. "Honey, why don't you go check on Ima? Take her leash and walk her. She needs to get used to training."

"Cool! I'm gonna take her to meet old Mrs. Morton next door."

Zoe laughed. "Okay, just avoid the spa area, okay? I don't think the clients would appreciate seeing a pig during their visit."

"Okay." Sam started for the house, then turned and ran back to Zoe, throwing her arms around her neck. "This was the best birthday ever."

Zoe's heart melted a bit more and she hugged Sam tightly. Sometimes, despite that Sam was fourteen and nearly as tall as Zoe, her hugs and touches seemed younger, somehow. Sweeter. A lump rose in Zoe's throat as it did each time Sam felt comfortable enough to express her emotions.

As the young girl blossomed, Zoe came to understand just how much she valued her family and why. As a child she hadn't realized how lucky she was to have parents who loved unconditionally and she'd assumed all families were the same way. Sam's background showed just how untrue Zoe's adolescent assumptions had been. Through Sam, Zoe appreciated her clan even more.

Before Zoe could find her voice and reply, Sam continued speaking. "It's been even better than the few I remember with my mom." Her hand shifted to the necklace at her throat.

In six years, Sam's memories of her mother were faded. Because the necklace was the last link Sam had to her mother, she never took it off. Only recently had Sam admitted she'd been with her mother when she'd died from a gunshot meant for the man who'd been her father, a drug dealer Sam never asked about and refused to see. No matter how bad her own choices had been, obviously Sam's mother had done something right in raising her daughter.

Sam fingered the old-looking keys that hung from a silver chain. "Does saying that make me a bad person?" she asked softly.

Zoe shook her head. "No, honey. Just an honest one."

Sam seemed satisfied with that and stepped back, transferring her gaze to Ryan. "You're pretty cool, too, Ryan. Thanks for the books and stuff."

"You're welcome," he said gruffly.

Zoe didn't know which had affected him more, Sam's comments about her mother or the compliment she'd just directed at him.

With a wave, Sam took off for the house, leaving Zoe and Ryan alone.

She didn't know where to begin with him, so she started with the first shock of the afternoon. "You weren't supposed to be here until noon."

"I finished up early at the bookstore. I couldn't see the point in driving around in circles for an hour when I could just come by here." His gaze locked with hers. "I didn't tell her anything."

Zoe nodded. "I know." Sam's happy mood made it clear she hadn't been the recipient of Ryan's news. But that wasn't the only reason Zoe was sure Sam remained in the dark. "I guess I trust you a little," she admitted.

He raised an eyebrow. "I can tell by the way you came bar-reling out of the house that you weren't at all concerned about me being alone with her," Ryan said wryly.

She laughed at being caught red-handed. "Yeah, well, I think I decided I trusted you about the time I found out you bought Sam the book on pigs."

"If she wants to keep a pet, she should learn how to care for it properly."

Zoe had a hunch she knew where this was heading. "You mean she should follow the rules."

He nodded. "Exactly."

Zoe dug her sneakered toe into the mound of dirt and grass he'd excavated and searched for a diplomatic reply.

"Look, Ryan, I realize you mean well and everything, but you should know, the chances of that pig being well trained while living in this house are slim to none."

"That's the wrong attitude to take. You can't go into a long-term commitment like pet ownership on a negative note."

"I'm not. It's just that to train an animal, you need consistency. Everyone who has daily contact with the pig has to do the same thing and in this insane asylum, it's better not to hold out false hope." She shook her head and laughed at herself, realizing she was beating around the point she wanted to make. "Look at it this way. Ari and I turned out just fine. Ima Pig will survive, too." She gave him a direct look. "But I'm really not talking about Ima."

He met her gaze, his brown eyes serious. "I figured that."

"You need to know that Sam's not a follow-the-rules type of kid. And you need to respect who she is as a person." At that moment, Zoe realized she was, in a way, preparing Ryan in case he should end up with Sam.

The thought caused a sharp pain in her heart along with a gaping hole she couldn't cope with right now. But she'd be doing a disservice to both Sam and Ryan if she didn't face the possibility of losing her.

He walked over to a bench and sat down, leaning back against the white iron. "Five minutes alone with her and I knew she was more like her mother than I'd expected." He gazed up at the sky as if there were answers and explanations there. "My family stifled Faith."

Zoe had suspected as much. "And that can't happen to Sam."

Ryan nodded. "I know." He understood what Zoe meant, so much more than she realized.

His sister had stepped out of the bounds of what his family considered proper and she'd paid for her so-called *crime* by being disowned. Often he had wondered if his father had been glad Faith had disappeared because that way he wouldn't have to acknowledge her problems and addiction. But then he'd heard his mother's muffled crying and known he didn't comprehend as much as he'd thought.

For fear of being cut off from the only life and family he'd known, Ryan had walked the straight and narrow long after Faith had gone. Though his sister had been weak and an addict, she'd had the strength to stand on her own until the end. In an absurd way, he admired her for it.

"Ryan?" Zoe's hand on his arm and her soft voice called to him.

He knew he shouldn't be affected by her, knew he was lying to her family about being a social worker while planning to take his sister's child away with him. He didn't want to want her, yet he did. He couldn't deny the attraction and had a hunch he couldn't avoid acting on it, either.

"Ryan?" she called him again.

"Hmm?"

"I asked why you reacted so strongly to the mistake with the daffodils."

He laughed because he wasn't sure this subject was any easier to tackle than his growing desire for Zoe.

Standing, he walked back toward the patch of dirt. "My grandmother Edna grows roses. She has a garden that I suspect means more to her than any of her children."

"And heaven help the little heathen who hits a baseball into the bushes and tramples the flowers to retrieve it?" She waggled her eyebrows in an attempt to soften the blow of her words, something Zoe seemed to accomplish with ease.

"That about sums it up."

"Trust me, Elena won't bat an eyelash at her lost bulbs. In November, she'll just wake me at dawn to replant."

He grinned. "Thank you for that."

She narrowed her gaze, a small crease forming between her eyebrows. "For what?"

He shrugged. "I'm not sure. For being you maybe? Here we are, two people who couldn't have more at stake or be more at odds and yet you seem to care about my feelings, anyway."

To his surprise, she actually blushed. "It's one of my short-comings I guess. I blame those Costas genes. We're suckers for people we like."

He stepped closer. "And you like me."

Her lips curved in a reluctant smile. "Yeah. More so when you forget you're a conservative suit-and-tie kind of guy. Like now." Her gaze fell to his bare chest and remained.

Her stare was obvious and seductive, making him feel like he was bathed in light, and not because the summer sun shone hot above them. Zoe managed to brighten his life during what should be a dark time. She confused and confounded him because she was the opposite of everything he was taught to value in life.

But here they were and he wasn't walking away. Neither was she, and her approving gaze became the permission he needed to take the kiss he desired.

Ryan brought his hands up, cupping her face between his palms. "I like you, too."

"Oh." Her tongue darted out and swept across her lower lip, moistening her mouth.

Unable to resist, he lowered his head and captured her lips with his. He immediately discovered the chemistry between them from the moment they'd met paled in comparison to the passion that flared to life now. She tasted sweet and his desire for her grew. He slid his tongue over the seam of her lips and demanded she let him inside.

With a welcoming groan, she gave what he asked for, his tongue touching and tangling with hers. He wanted to possess her completely, to learn the deep secrets she kept and he explored thoroughly with his tongue to accomplish that goal. Needing to feel her against him, he moved his hands from her face, down her back, pausing on her behind as he pulled her close until her body was flush with his.

She came willingly and nestled into the V of his legs, fitting like she belonged. He was rock hard, something she clearly recognized when she shifted her hips so his erection nestled in even more snugly between her thighs.

Her heat beckoned to him, making him want to toss her onto the ground and make love to her right here, outside, damn whoever might see.

He couldn't imagine anything more out of character. He couldn't imagine anything he wanted more. Since he couldn't act on that particular desire, he groaned and deepened the kiss, using his mouth to mimic making love.

Zoe trembled and held on to Ryan's bare shoulders. Reveling in the feel of his hot skin beneath her hands, she pressed her body closer to his, his heat seeping through her clothes and into her pores. Her breasts grew full and heavy, her nipples puckering tight against his chest.

He shuddered, groaned and continued the incredible assault on her senses.

Never before had a kiss so rocked her world as this one did. The man was an expert at taking possession. Every sweep and swirl of his tongue pulled a matching whirlpool of need from deep inside her. Nor did he keep his feelings hidden as a deep groan reverberated in his chest.

The man was complex. The uptight facade he presented on first meeting was a better cover than any she'd seen. Because his cool exterior hid a powder keg of emotion, and now that she'd tapped into it, she wasn't likely to forget. She threw herself into the moment, and continued to kiss him back.

"Ahem."

Ryan jumped back immediately.

Zoe faced her twin. "Hi, Ari," she said, blinking, her voice slightly hoarse.

Her sister nodded. "Hi. Do you really think this is the right place for that?"

Zoe caught the teasing note in her sister's voice. "And who appointed you the kissing gestapo?"

Ari laughed, then leaned closer to Ryan. "I don't believe we were formally introduced yesterday." She extended her hand. "I'm Ariana Donovan."

"Ryan Baldwin. I'd shake your hand, but I've been digging in the dirt."

"If Zoe didn't mind your hands all over her, I think I can handle a simple shake."

Ryan felt a rush of heat rise to his face. "I think I'm going to make myself scarce," he muttered.

"Ryan spent the morning with Sam," Zoe told her twin. "They were making the pig feel more at home." She gestured toward the patch of dirt.

"In Mom's daffodils, I see. It's gonna be a pain replanting those."

Ryan groaned. The sisters were more alike than they realized. He grabbed his shirt, which hung over the back of the bench. "It was nice to meet you, Ari," he said.

"Same here." Ari gave him a brief nod.

"Bye, Ryan." Zoe treated him to a wave. "I'll be seeing you."

At her blatant stare at his still-bare chest, he had a hunch she meant that in a very literal sense, too.

ZOE WATCHED AS RYAN STRODE around the side of the house. He couldn't get away fast enough and she found his embarrassment endearing. His kiss, on the other hand, had been explosive.

"Well, well, well." Ari studied her twin, piercing her with a knowing stare.

Zoe shoved her hands into her front jeans pockets. "Well what?"

"I can't believe I caught you making out with the social worker," she said, laughing.

Obviously Ari hadn't seen Quinn yet today because she was acting as if everything were normal. They might keep the truth about Ryan from the rest of the family, but Quinn and Zoe wouldn't keep Ari in the dark. She'd been the only family member who'd finally known Zoe was alive back when everyone had thought she'd disappeared and had probably died. On her return, Zoe had promised herself no more lies between herself and her twin. But they couldn't talk here and run the risk of Sam overhearing.

"That social worker is hot. Or hadn't you noticed?" Zoe asked.

Focusing on the more positive aspects of Ryan wasn't difficult after that heated kiss. Of course she couldn't entirely ignore the discomfort she felt at enjoying Ryan when he didn't have her family's best interest at heart.

Ari raised an eyebrow. "I hadn't actually. I have my own guy at home, but I'm glad to see you've got *your* eyes open."

Zoe shrugged. Her feelings about Ryan and their first kiss were too new for her to want to discuss them even with her sister.

"He's definitely different than anyone you've been attracted to before."

"So I've noticed."

"He's much more… How shall I put this delicately? He's much more like me than like you. Which makes sense since opposites attract. Just look at me and Quinn."

Ari and Quinn were the ultimate in love couples. Comparing Zoe's lust for Ryan to her twin's love for her husband didn't make a lick of sense. Also not a conversation Zoe intended to have now.

"If you mean Ryan's uptight, conservative, and he loves rules and regulations, then, yes, I can definitely see why you'd think you two had something in common." Zoe met her sister's gaze and they laughed, a true testament to how far their relationship had come since Ari's return last year.

"Where're Mom and Sam?" Ari asked. "I want to drop off a blouse I borrowed."

Zoe glanced around. "Good question. My guess is that Mom has spa appointments and I know Sam went next door for a little while."

Ari shifted her purse strap higher onto her shoulder. "I left the blouse on the kitchen table. Can you just let her know?"

Zoe nodded.

"Oh and by the way, I got the guidance position at Ocean Isle High," she said casually, but Zoe knew how much she'd wanted the job.

"That's amazing!" She hugged her sister.

"The hours are perfect for me and it's so close to home."

"You don't miss Vermont at all?"

"Not at all. It was a place I ran to. It wasn't home."

Zoe stepped back and grinned. "Home is where Quinn Donovan is, huh?"

"And you, too. And Mom and Dad, and Sam and…"

"Speaking of Quinn, have you spoken with him?" Zoe asked, interrupting.

"Not since he left this morning, but he called earlier and we're meeting for lunch in a little while."

Zoe nodded. "Okay good. Good," she said, relieved all would be out in the open between them soon.

"Good? Why good? What's going on?" Ari asked, suddenly more alert.

Zoe swung her arm over her sister's shoulder. "Go talk to Quinn and we'll catch up later."

"I'm not going to like this, am I?"

Zoe shook her head and Ari shivered.

But it wasn't Ari's reaction that had Zoe the most concerned. What bothered her most was that after a lifetime of nonthreatening relationships, she was starting to fall for a man who was most definitely a threat—to the freespirited world she'd grown up in and the close-knit family she adored.

AFTER THE KISS, Ryan retreated to his hotel room. He needed a cold shower, but first he wanted to call the private investigator he'd hired and ask him to get more information on the Costas clan.

Now that he knew they were a force in Sam's life, he wanted to find out more about their background and what kind of people he was dealing with. He already knew they didn't have the money to compete with him in court, but each one of them had more heart than his family combined. And that scared him.

So did Zoe. It was one thing to be attracted to a woman, another to be *affected* and something about Zoe got to him. Her devotion to a child who wasn't a blood relative, her kindness to him despite his potential to upset her world, and her free spirit made him *feel* in a way he never had before. Not in a family that went out of their way to rein in emotion and put up barriers. When he was with Zoe, holding, kissing and laughing with her, there were no walls.

Which was why he decided to steer clear for the coming weekend. Though it would be damn difficult not to show up at the Costases' house during the next two days, he intended to stay away from the new women in his life. As far as his cover went, his decision made sense because he doubted a social worker would make house calls on Saturday or Sunday. Instead, he planned to do some work that he'd taken with him and recoup for Monday morning when he'd deal with Zoe and her family again.

Now fresh from a shower, Ryan sat on the bed in his hotel room. After ordering room service, he decided to check in with his family. He'd informed his parents he was going to New Jersey to follow up on a lead about Faith's daughter. They knew Faith had died and that they had a granddaughter out there somewhere, yet they hadn't been interested in accompanying him on his trip.

"Let sleeping dogs lie, Ryan," his father had said. "Faith's gone. No good can come of dredging up the past."

And though he'd mentioned that their granddaughter was being shuffled through foster care, his father's attitude hadn't softened. "Most probably she's stubborn and harder to handle than Faith, then." Mark Baldwin had dismissed any type of reunion, as had his mother, Vivian. But Ryan had seen a hint of emotion in her eyes and held out hope for when she met Sam.

But his father's brother, Ryan's uncle Russ, supported his quest and had from the time Ryan had told him Faith had a daughter who was alive and living in New Jersey. So it was Russ he turned to now.

Ryan reached him at work in the corporate offices of Baldwin's, New England's favorite department store and his family's dynasty, he thought wryly. Some dynasty when it excluded family at whim.

Uncle Russ had devoted his life to the business, more so after Ryan's father's heart attack and subsequent cutting back over the past couple of years. Though J.T. worked at Baldwin's, he was more a hands-on manager while Uncle Russ oversaw delivery and transport.

"Hi, Uncle Russ," he said when the other man answered his private line.

"Ryan, it's good to finally hear from you. I was beginning to think I'd have to come after you myself."

He shook his head and laughed. "Nothing that drastic is warranted, I promise you."

"Did you find the girl?" Uncle Russ asked.

"Samantha. As a matter of fact, I did."

Uncle Russ sucked in a sharp breath. "After all this time!"

"She looks exactly like Faith."

"That is remarkable. I didn't think, well I don't know what I thought you'd find."

"Have my parents given any indication of coming around?" Ryan asked.

The other man cleared his throat. "I think that like me, they didn't know what would come of this quest. In truth, they haven't discussed it with me."

"Ever the diplomat, Uncle Russ?"

He chuckled. "Well, now that you've found the young lady, I'll talk to them again." He paused. "So, what does this Sam think about having an uncle?"

Ryan winced. He'd been hoping to put off disclosing the details of Sam's situation and his agreement with Zoe.

"That's a little complicated. She doesn't know who I am just yet. The family she's staying with thinks it's best if she's eased into things."

"I see."

A knock on the door told him room service had arrived. "I need to go, but I'll call soon."

"Okay, and you take care."

Ryan hung up the phone, grateful he had at least one relative he could count on. Unlike Zoe, who had more than a
handful of strange but caring people who would always be
there for her.

Over the long, lonely weekend, Ryan watched three rental
movies in his Atlantic City hotel room. First thing Monday
morning, he took Zoe's advice and booked a room closer to
Ocean Isle, closer to Sam. And closer to Zoe. Once he got
settled, he decided that although the place wasn't five-star,
it more than suited his needs. He checked in at his office
and after speaking to his secretary, he was certain his partners were handling everything in his absence.

It was time he turned his attention to the here and now.

And now it was time to visit the Costas clan.

Chapter Four

MONDAY MORNING, Zoe left the house bright and early at 7:00 a.m. to meet with Quinn, Connor and a friend of hers who used to work with the Secret Service, but who was now a promoter with GSC Music Company. GSC needed bodyguards and security specialists for their talent performing in the area and Zoe, Quinn and Connor needed clients.

Although the hour was early for a business meeting, Zoe's friend had to be at a rehearsal this morning. Zoe was also only too happy to avoid dealing with her family on her birthday. Normally she loved birthdays, and aging didn't bother her much, but thirty was a milestone and she didn't want to hear the family grumbling about how Ari had managed to marry while Zoe was still single.

She sneaked out of the house and reached the office, which was freshly painted in a bright yellow, much to Connor and Quinn's frustration. To appease them, she'd promised masculine accessories, even if they had to be purchased secondhand, which was all they could afford.

The discussions between the parties took place around the only furniture they owned, a conference table left by the original tenant and bridge chairs donated by her family. Nobody seemed to mind as they drank coffee and hammered out an agreement, easily reached since everyone involved had an interest in working together. By 9:00 a.m., they'd decided on the preliminaries for a contract and Zoe, Quinn and Connor had officially retained their first client.

Zoe arrived home, pulling up to the house to find a police car out front. She bolted inside, her fear overwhelming. In the kitchen, her mother paced the floors, muttering in Greek. Her father stood speaking to two uniformed officers, while Aunt Dee and Uncle John, who lived across the street, had joined them still wearing their pajamas. The room was in a shambles, and Sam was nowhere to be seen.

Zoe glanced around. Finally her gaze settled on the half-open door of the pantry. A quick glance told her Sam sat huddled inside, no doubt with her new pet. The poor kid probably feared the cops would take Ima away for the same reason they'd had to find a new home for Spank the monkey. At a glance, the pig's cage looked like a puppy crate, so there were no worries there.

She winked at Sam, then stood beside her father. "What happened?"

"Someone broke in here and—how do you say—they trashed the place," her father said.

Now that she knew everyone she loved was fine, her heart rate slowed and she took in the damage for the first time. The kitchen drawers were in disarray, things had been pulled out and strewn everywhere. "What other rooms were touched?"

"Sam's room and the whole downstairs. I was sleeping in my bed so he didn't touch the master bedroom."

"And it happened this morning?"

"It was sometime after you left for work and your mother went for her daily walk," her father said.

"Without his hearing aids, he doesn't hear anything," Elena paused her pacing long enough to chime in.

Nicholas shot her a scowl. He hated any reference to the devices even though they made a huge difference in his hearing.

"Where was Sam during all this?" Zoe asked.

"She was asleep, too," her mother said too quickly, her gaze darting away, a sure sign she was lying.

Elena was protecting Sam. *Had the young girl heard or seen something?* Zoe wondered.

"Has anyone called Quinn?" Zoe wouldn't bring Sam and Ima out now in front of the police, but as soon as Quinn arrived, they'd sort things out.

"Detective Donovan is on his way," the youngest officer assured Zoe.

"And we've gotten statements from Mr. and Mrs. Costas," the other uniformed man said. "At first glance nothing seems to be missing, but let us know if you realize differently. In the meantime, we've dusted for prints and will keep you posted if anything comes up."

"Thank you," Elena said.

"And Detective Donovan will talk to the girl?" He glanced down at his notepad. "Samantha."

Elena nodded. "Not that I see why," she muttered.

By not insisting they speak to Sam now, the officers were obviously extending a courtesy to Quinn, an ex-detective, and Zoe was grateful they didn't insist and traumatize her in the process.

"Who is this?" the second officer, one who couldn't be older than his early twenties, asked, pointing to Zoe.

Nicholas wrapped an arm around her shoulder. "This is our daughter, Zoe."

"She lives here?"

Zoe nodded. "I do."

"I'm going to need to know where you were this morning and if anyone can vouch for your whereabouts."

"That's enough," her father bellowed.

"Of all the outrageous things!" Elena said, also clearly affronted.

"They're just doing their jobs," Zoe reassured her parents. "Relax." Zoe supplied the officer with all the pertinent information and after they spoke with Aunt Dee and Uncle John, who hadn't seen or heard a thing, they took off.

Zoe sighed. "It's okay, Sam. You can come out now."

"The cops are gone?" Her voice sounded muffled.

Zoe pulled the pantry door open wide and Sam stepped out, the pig in her arms.

"Yes, they're gone, but that isn't the question. Why would you hide from the police?"

Elena pulled Sam into her arms. "My poor baby." She squeezed the girl tight so her face was smashed into her chest.

"I mmmbrrsffft."

"What?" Elena asked.

"She probably said something like, she can't breathe." Zoe released her mother's grip and Sam ducked out from under her.

"Exactly." Sam gulped in a breath of air. "I didn't want them to tell me I have to give Ima away like we did with Spank."

Zoe nodded. "I thought so. Don't worry. The laws about

pigs are more lenient around here. Now tell me what you heard and saw and don't leave out a thing."

Sam rubbed her hands up and down her bare arms. "I got up and was coming out of the bathroom when I heard a noise in my room. I knew Elena was taking her morning meditative walk, and you said you had an early appointment."

"How'd you know it wasn't Dad?"

Sam rolled her eyes. "He was snoring and the sound shook the walls."

Zoe tried not to laugh. "I see. What happened next?"

"I peeked into my room and saw a guy snooping around." She shuddered, then began to skulk around giving them an exaggerated, charadelike description. "He opened the drawers, tossed things around, and then he started coming toward the door so I ducked back into the bathroom. I hid in the tub like this." She crouched down, hands over her head like in an emergency drill. "So if he looked in, he wouldn't see me."

Like most of the Costases' relatives, Sam had a knack for the dramatic and despite her fear, which was evident in her wide eyes, she was still milking her moment now.

"Looks like the kid's got a future career as a spy." Quinn walked into the room. A complete air of authority surrounded him as all eyes looked his way, and Sam beamed at what she took as a compliment.

Quinn forced a smile and though Zoe could read the concern on his face, she admired his self-restraint in not shaking Sam to get the facts out of her faster.

"Keep talking, squirt," Quinn said.

"Quit calling me that. Anyway, I finally heard him going

down the stairs. I hung out at the top and watched him toss
the kitchen and family room next. I was going to wake
Nicholas up, but I got scared. I was too afraid to move because I might make noise. Then all of a sudden, Ima
squealed from her crate in the kitchen and I guess he got
nervous and thought someone might come down to check
the pig and find him there. He left out the back door to the
kitchen." She finished out of breath.

The door between the kitchen and family room banged
open wide and Ryan Baldwin, the "social worker," strode inside. "What the hell happened? The police were driving away
as I pulled up and this place looks like a tornado hit it."

Zoe let out a groan. As an admiring female, she couldn't
stop staring at him after two days of drought, but as a member of a family who didn't need to give him any ammunition
to take Sam from this home, she wished he'd stayed away.

"We wuz robbed!" Sam jumped up and down, her fear
giving way to an obvious adrenaline rush now that the danger was over.

"Not robbed," Zoe was quick to assure Ryan. "Nothing
was taken."

"Which means whoever broke in here was looking for
something." Quinn, the ex-cop, said, his focus on Sam.

Zoe swallowed hard. "I suppose that's a possibility." She
forced herself to focus on what she'd been thinking before
Ryan's arrival, and glanced at Sam. "When did you hide in
the pantry?"

"Elena came home and started yelling, Nicholas came
running, and they were trying to figure out what happened.
Next thing I know the police are banging on the door and

all I could think of was saving the bacon. So I grabbed Ima and ducked back into the pantry. Smart hiding place if I do say so myself."

Ryan began to pace. "Am I to understand Sam was here when someone broke in?"

Zoe stepped forward and placed a hand on his arm. The last thing she wanted was for him to find out that the intruder had been in Sam's bedroom. "I'll explain everything in a few minutes. I promise. Let's just let Quinn get a few more facts from Sam first, okay?"

He gritted his teeth. "Okay."

"Did you see the guy's face?" Quinn asked her.

"For a second. He was real ugly and he had dark hair."

"Tall or short?"

"Medium."

Quinn shook his head, probably at the vague description. "How'd he get in? What did the cops find? Picked or jimmied lock?"

"Nothing. He just walked right in since I left the door open when I went out for a walk." Elena stepped forward. In black leggings that ended below her knees and an oversize white tank top, and with her hair in a ponytail, she looked younger than her years. But when she dropped her head in shame, she aged before Zoe's eyes. "Quinn, I'm sorry. I know you put in a security system and that Medici lock."

"Medeco."

Elena nodded. "The point is, I was trusting. And I'm sorry. I never meant to put anyone at risk. Especially Samantha."

Zoe realized the moment it dawned on her mother that

Ryan, *the social worker,* was here witnessing her admission. She lifted her head and met Ryan's gaze head-on. Then she dropped to her knees and somehow shuffled her way over to where Ryan stood, concern etched all over his handsome face.

Elena grabbed his hand. "It was a lapse. A stupid one. One that'll never happen again, so please don't report us. Don't snitch. Don't take Samantha away," she wailed.

Over her mother's bent head, Zoe met Ryan's gaze. He was upset and he feared for Sam, but still she could see him biting back a grin because despite the seriousness of the moment, her mother's theatrics were way over the top. Zoe was just surprised Ryan realized it, too.

Ryan forced himself to stay calm. He focused on Elena's dramatics as he tried to regain the ability to breathe. He'd driven up to the house to find the police leaving. He'd walked in to see the place in shambles, obviously ransacked. And Sam was regaling the family with tales of what she'd seen.

His fear for Sam and Zoe had receded as soon as he'd seen them standing in the kitchen, unhurt. But his stomach churned as he'd listened to the end of Sam's story and now witnessed the unorthodox way the family handled the crisis. They were upset, yes, but the break-in seemed more a cause for drama than concern.

Even Sam seemed to revel in her role in the escapade.

"Mama, I'm going to take Ryan for breakfast and explain everything." Zoe placed an arm around her mother's shoulder and helped her rise to her feet.

"You go to Paradeisos, yes?" Elena asked. "Aunt Kassie will take good care of you."

"Okay. You take care of Dad and Sam, okay?"

Elena nodded. "You're a good girl, Zoe." She kissed her daughter's cheek and whispered something in her ear.

"I love you." Zoe hugged her mother tight.

Watching the interaction, a lump of emotion swelled in Ryan's chest and he wondered if his sister would still be alive had she experienced even one tenth of the love so freely given in this family. No judgments were made, no life-altering repercussions came as a result of bad behavior. Quite simply, this family was as foreign to Ryan as any distant country or culture.

Zoe walked up beside him. "Let's go."

He shot a glance Sam's way. "Are you okay?" he asked the young girl in the calm, steady voice expected of a foster-care worker. Inside, Ryan struggled with his emotions and was frustrated by his inability to express them.

"I'm cool." But she held tightly onto Ima and, despite her outward bravado, he sensed she wasn't as fearless as she wanted him to believe.

"And I'm serious. If you need anything—"

"She knows who to turn to." Zoe prodded him in the back. "Come."

He narrowed his gaze. She was a damn pushy woman, but he couldn't deny he was glad to see her after the weekend apart. Just knowing Zoe was a member of this family eased Ryan's mind about Sam's safety. Zoe could be trusted to take good care of her.

"Elena, you *will* use the locks in the future," he stated, not asked.

"Yes."

"I will see to it, Mr. Baldwin." Nicholas held his hand up in the air. "I promise you Samantha is safe with us."

Ryan merely nodded and this time allowed Zoe to practically shove him out of the kitchen, then the family room and finally the house.

Once they were in the sunshine, she pasted a bright smile on her face and asked, "My car or yours? Actually why don't I drive since you don't know your way around here and I go to the diner all the time. This way we won't get lost and we'll be eating in no time."

He already knew Zoe rambled when she was worried and now was no different.

He remained quiet on the way to wherever the restaurant was and let Zoe point out sights and continue to talk. He liked listening to her voice and despite their odd circumstances, she soothed his nerves.

Too much, considering everything that lay between them.

AFTER ZOE PARKED in the graveled lot, Ryan followed her into the local diner. "So your aunt Kassie owns this place?" he asked.

Zoe nodded. "She's my father's sister."

"I met her that first night."

He settled into a seat across from Zoe in a tight booth with an individual coin-operated jukebox on the wall by the window. "They don't have anything quite like this in Boston." He glanced around at the linoleum floors, the blue vinyl seats and paper place mats printed with various advertisements.

She tipped her head to the side and those long, dark

strands brushed her shoulders. "Oh really? Because they aren't upscale?"

He read the wariness in her tone. "No, because from my understanding, a traditional diner is a New York/New Jersey thing."

"We're Greek. Diners are our heritage," a female voice said.

He glanced up to see a dark-haired woman standing by the table.

"Hi, Daph. Meet Sam's social worker, Ryan Baldwin. Daphne's my first cousin," Zoe explained.

"Nice to meet you, Daphne." Ryan shook the other woman's hand, but his mind was on how seamlessly Zoe had lied to yet another family member and he shifted uncomfortably in his seat.

"Need menus?"

Zoe waved a hand, indicating she didn't. "But I'm sure Ryan does seeing as how he's never been to a diner before."

He caught the snicker in her voice and shot her a scowl. "I'd appreciate a menu," he told Daphne.

The waitress handed him what felt more like a pile of laminated lead. "Take your time," she said, but continued to stand over him.

He glanced from Daphne, who was beautiful in a more made-up way than her cousin, back to Zoe again.

Zoe let out an exaggerated sigh. "You can go now, Daph."

"Are you sure he's just the social worker?" She leaned down, giving him a gratuitous view of her cleavage.

"I'm sure he's just the social worker." Zoe shook her head and laughed. "Daphne loves to snoop into her cousins' lives because she doesn't have a love life of her own."

"Aha! So you admit he's more than a social worker."

Zoe turned beet red. "I admit no such thing."

"You just did by the color in your cheeks."

Ryan had never been around this kind of family teasing and he took pity on Zoe. "I'll have eggs over easy and white toast with butter," he said hoping to distract Daphne from the more personal issues.

"Tsk-tsk, cholesterol heaven. I'll tell Dad to make it egg whites so you'll live a long, healthy life." She snatched his menu. "You'll have the usual, Zoe?"

She nodded and Daphne finally left them alone.

"So what's the usual?" he asked.

"Old-fashioned French toast."

"What makes it old-fashioned?"

She raised her eyebrows, obviously surprised. "Old-fashioned is made on regular bread, not the extrathick kind."

"Aha." He glanced over his shoulder in time to see their waitress enter the swinging kitchen doors, then turned back to Zoe. "So what do you do for a living?" he asked now that he was certain Cousin Daphne had disappeared.

Zoe leaned both elbows on the table and edged forward. "So what makes you ask?" She knew Ryan had given her more information about himself than she'd reciprocated, yet this sudden question took her by surprise.

He shrugged. "I'm not sure. You don't seem to be having much trouble helping me act the social worker role in front of your family. I mean look how easily you just lied to Daphne."

She narrowed her gaze. "So?"

"So lying comes easily to you. I read about your family's

cons. I've seen the old newspaper articles. The 'Alien Twins Invade New Jersey' photograph in *The National Enquirer*—"

"Hey just because my mother put self-tanning lotion on us and we turned orange—"

"A normal family wouldn't have leveraged it into a national spectacle."

Zoe rolled her eyes and laughed at the memory. "'All the news that's fit to print.'"

"That particular slogan belongs to *The New York Times*."

Daphne arrived with their coffees, placing their cups on the table. Before Zoe could send her on her way, she said, "I know, I know, I'm going. I'll give you privacy." Shaking her head, she walked away, her heels clicking.

"So besides finding sensationalism amusing and protecting my family, what else am I doing wrong in your eyes?" Zoe asked.

He ran his hand through his hair, messing up that always perfect coif. "It isn't wrong, it's different. And I'm allowing for it," he admitted. "All of you just take some getting used to."

She grinned. "We do tend to grow on you. Oh, and to get back to your original question, I used to be a Secret Service agent."

"Wow." He leaned closer, staring at her intently. "What made you choose the Secret Service?"

"Hmm. I'd have to say the excitement of the training is what lured me into the FBI initially. Later I chose Secret Service because I loved meeting new people. And since I was in the lower echelons of government protection, I didn't have to leave my family." She spread her hands wide. "For the most part it was a win-win situation."

"But?"

"What?"

"You said for the most part it was win-win. What didn't you like?"

She grinned. "As you might guess, the strict rules and regulations didn't agree with me. I mean after I had to be forced into a safe house and my family thought I was dead, the agency ripped into me but good. Of course, I did it *for* my family, but did anyone understand? Nope." She paused for a sip of coffee. "Forced confinement can really make a person evaluate what's important and I wanted more out of my career than a strict, by-the-book environment."

He looked at her for a moment as though to take in all of what she'd revealed. "Not a shock," he finally said and he laughed, and Zoe realized exactly what she found most attractive about him.

The dimples he showed when he smiled. Really smiled, not the forced kind when he was trying to figure her family out or pretend to like a situation when he was really confused. The dimples that didn't seem to go with the Italian-cut suits he favored, like the navy one he wore today. Also appealing was the way he kissed, something she hadn't been able to get out of her mind all weekend.

"Am I that predictable?" she asked.

"I definitely hadn't pegged you for an agent of any kind, but now that I know you, I'm sure the rules made you insane. But at least I understand how you hold on to a poker face so easily. So, what are you doing now that your federal career is behind you?"

She rubbed her hands together, the excitement she felt in

talking about her new business growing. "I'm in business with Quinn and Connor. We're going to provide protection for movie stars and musicians coming to entertain in Atlantic City. In fact, we just took on our first official client this morning. GSC Music."

He nodded and she could see from his expression that she'd impressed him.

"Congratulations."

"Thank you."

"I need to ask another question."

She laughed. "Anyone tell you you're nosy?"

"Only when it comes to you," he said, sounding a bit stunned by the admission. "What did your mother whisper to you before we left the house?"

She hadn't realized he was paying attention. "She asked me to stick close to Sam's social worker."

He reached for the centerpiece on the table and rolled it between his palms. "And you didn't feel guilty?"

"Of course I did, but let me tell you something. I'd feel guiltier if I told her the truth before I knew enough about you and your family. I need time with you. You need time with Sam. I think we both understand and agree on that, don't we?"

He nodded slowly. "I do. And I think you're an incredible woman, Zoe Costas."

Something about the way he said her name sent tremors of awareness down her spine. Again. The man was amazing, from his caring nature to his potent sex appeal. Her fingers itched with the uncontrollable urge to touch his hand. A simple touch, though the feelings he evoked were much more complex than simple.

She glanced down at his hands, in which he still held the infamous Paradeisos centerpiece. Zoe immediately realized what anatomy part he held in his hand and the sensuality surrounding her evaporated in favor of a fit of laughter. She knew the moment he noticed it, too, because he dropped the centerpiece, a naked Greek god with flowers nestled in his—

"And they call this a family restaurant?" Ryan asked, clearly in shock.

"Yep." Daphne replied as she placed their meals on the table. "Normal doesn't exist in our family or hadn't you noticed?" She laughed, stopping when Zoe stretched a leg out and blatantly kicked her in the shin.

"Right. Social worker. Got it. I'm going. Enjoy your food."

Zoe laughed as her cousin departed again. "Usually she's the hostess, but Gus is out sick, so she's filling in waiting on tables." She poured some syrup over her French toast. "So you haven't asked about the break-in."

He placed his fork down and met her stare. "I figured you'd fill me in when you were ready. I take it you're ready now?"

She shrugged. "No time like the present. I don't know all that much. Mom forgot to set the alarm when she went for her walk, I'd already left for work and Dad was sleeping without his hearing aids in. Sam stepped out of the bathroom and heard noises coming from her room. With my father snoring in his bed, she knew something was wrong and remained out of sight until he left."

"I didn't realize he was in Sam's room," he said, a muscle ticking in his jaw. "And you said nothing was taken?"

"That's right. I mean it's too soon to know for sure, but at first glance everything looked messed up but nothing more."

"Any chance this man was looking for something because someone in your family was up to something?"

"Such as?" She batted her eyelashes at him too innocently, she knew.

He rolled his eyes. "Come on, Zoe. You have to know I'm aware that your family hasn't always been on the up-and-up."

"Hey no one's ever been arrested."

"So, they skate the perimeters of the law." He sliced his hand through the air. "That's semantics. You even said yourself that you were involved in something that landed you in protective custody. So I'm asking, could someone in your family be involved in something that led to today's break-in?"

He'd leaned forward in his seat so she couldn't mistake his serious expression, and his intense stare would brook no jokes or lies.

"I don't know." She'd lost her appetite and she pushed her plate away.

"I'm sorry," he said in a gruff voice.

"For pointing out the obvious? Don't be. After we eat, I need to go take care of some things." Make some phone calls, she thought. Talk to Quinn. The police. Find out what was really going on in her own home.

He ate his food in silence and she sat stiffly, keeping him company, until finally he spoke. "I'd like to spend time with Sam this afternoon."

She coughed. "Excuse me. Spend time with Sam…how?"

"I don't know. Take her for ice cream. Just get to know her a little. Under the guise of a final interview type of situation."

Zoe shivered, her nerves completely on edge. "I don't know.…"

"When I look at her, I see my sister, but I don't know who Sam is as a person."

"And that matters to you." She said it as a definitive statement, not a question.

He obviously cared. Sam was more than a blood tie to Ryan and now Zoe realized that Sam was also more than just a connection to his deceased sister. He recognized Sam as a person with likes and dislikes, needs and desires of her own. He was everything Zoe could hope for in a blood relative for Samantha and everything she could hope for in a man. Too bad once this charade was over, he'd be the cause of so much pain for her family, she reminded herself forcefully.

"Of course who Sam is matters to me." He didn't seem angered by her statement. "Look." He reached into his pocket and pulled out a single photograph in old plastic. "This is Faith."

Zoe accepted the picture and glanced down at the photo of the teenager, frozen in time at around the same age as Sam. Zoe sucked in a startled breath. "Wow," she said, staring at the eerily familiar features and blond hair. "You weren't kidding."

He shook his head. "Startling resemblance, isn't it?"

"My thoughts exactly," she said, placing her hand over his. "I'm so sorry."

He met her gaze, his eyes warm and grateful. "I appreciate that."

"Why didn't you show this photograph to me before?"

He shrugged as he placed the picture back into his pocket. "You didn't ask."

She shifted uncomfortably in her seat. "You should know I have Quinn digging for info on your family," she admitted.

"Would it make you feel any better if I told you I was doing some more investigating of the Costas clan on my own?"

She burst out laughing. "Not really, but I'm glad to see we think alike."

"Because we both have Sam's best interest at heart, which leads me back to my original point. I'd like to spend time with Sam."

"Do you promise not to reveal the truth?"

He covered her hand. Warmth surged through her at his touch, heating her body inside and out.

"I promise. When that time comes for honesty, we'll tell Sam in the most painless way possible."

She inhaled and forced herself to agree. Coming from a family of loving con artists, Zoe didn't normally trust outsiders easily. Which made her feelings for Ryan all the more complicated.

ZOE DROPPED RYAN OFF back at the house where he'd left his car. He stood and watched as she drove off for parts unknown. Probably to look into whether her family's dealings had any relation to the break-in this morning. Only a few hours had passed, but by the time he knocked on the door and Elena let him in, there was no sign of turmoil, except for a few pieces of furniture out of place. The rooms had been cleaned and the mess put away.

"I take it everyone's calmed down?" Ryan asked as Elena fussed over him, handing him an unasked for glass of water.

She nodded. "We're fine. Fine. Help me move this chair, please."

He assisted her with order after order, putting the pieces of furniture back where they belonged.

Elena was in a frenzy, issuing directives and speaking a mile a minute.

A tornado, he thought to himself again.

"Anyway," she continued. "Sam helped us clean the little things around the house so we can pull off the surprise party tonight. Quinn's going to bring Ari and I was hoping you'd bring Zoe."

"What party?" he asked.

Elena paused. "What party?" she repeated and stared as if he ought to know the answer. "Zoe and Ari are turning thirty today. Tonight we're throwing a surprise party at Paradeisos."

"We need you to be the decoy," Sam said, bouncing down the stairs and joining them. Her eyes were bright and happy, no sign of trauma from the incident earlier.

"Decoy, huh? How do I do that?"

She tossed her long ponytail over one shoulder. "I told you he's dense," she muttered, and then before anyone could reprimand her, she continued. "You call Zoe, on the phone. You know, a tel-e-phone. Ask her on a date—"

"And then bring her to her aunt's diner again? Somehow I don't think she'd buy that as a real date," he said laughing. "Now who's dense?" he asked, proud he'd one-upped Sam.

The young girl blinked. "Uh, the answer to that is still *you.* Because what happens is that you're going to take her to this very fancy restaurant where you've made a reservation, and then on the way, Zoe'll get a frantic call from Elena at Paradeisos and then Zoe'll beg you to turn around and come see what's wrong with *me.*"

"Then hopefully Quinn will get Ari there at the same

time and everyone will yell *surprise!*" Elena said with a grand sweep of her arm.

"And if Ari gets there first? Or later?" he couldn't stop himself from asking.

"Then we yell surprise twice, of course."

"Of course."

"So now that you've helped with the furniture, what can we do for you, Mr. Baldwin?" Elena asked.

He cleared his throat. "First, please call me Ryan. And second, I was wondering if I could steal Sam for an hour."

Sam stiffened her shoulders. "Why? I didn't do anything wrong. The pig's allowed to stay. Zoe said so." She uttered Zoe's name with reverence and awe. The big sister Sam probably had never thought she'd have.

Meanwhile she stared at *him* as if he were the pond scum who wanted to steal everything she held dear. Which, he thought, wasn't far from the truth.

He drew a deep breath. "The pig's fine. I just thought that we could go for ice cream and I could ask you some questions." Deceit wasn't a comfortable fit for him and he tried to keep his answers as honest as possible.

Elena nodded. "That's a wonderful idea."

Sam merely glared. "No matter what you say to me, I still want to be adopted and live here forever."

A slicing pain ripped through his gut. "I understand what you want, Sam. I just want to get to know you better. That's all."

"Can I get a sundae?" she asked.

"If I say yes, will you come with me?"

Sam walked over to the phone, picked up the receiver

and handed it to him. "After you ask Zoe for a date tonight."

Ryan shook his head and laughed because if he hadn't known that they needed him to get Zoe to her party, he'd think the kid and Elena were actually matchmaking.

Chapter Five

AFTER SPENDING A FEW HOURS in a shopping mall with a four-teen-year-old, Ryan had been spent. First he'd taken Sam for ice cream as promised, where she'd ducked behind him every time she'd seen a boy she knew from school. Then he'd had what he thought was a brainstorm and he'd asked her to help him shop for a birthday gift for Zoe.

Sam had dragged him into an all-natural beauty store that smelled ultrafeminine and too seductive for his peace of mind. Clenching his mouth shut tight, he'd stood back as Sam had chosen Zoe's favorite scents in body scrub, body wash, body splash and he was sure there were more items he couldn't remember. He couldn't very well tell the kid that they were in way too intimate territory when she was so pleased with her selections, so he'd gone ahead and pur-chased her choices.

The store clerk had insisted on wrapping them in a gift basket with some courtesy products, including a loofah sponge he couldn't stop envisioning running over every part of Zoe's body, inch by tantalizing inch. His desire for her grew each time he saw her. His need to taste her again, to possess her body and learn her secrets, was with him day and night.

Now hours later, he was driving Zoe to a surprise destination for their date. His nerves were on edge as he waited for the phone call redirecting them to her aunt's diner. Each time he inhaled, he took in her fresh-like-summer scent, forcing him to shake his head in an attempt to stop thinking about Zoe and sex. Sleeping with her would compromise his emotions, he knew, and in turn he'd jeopardize his goal to take Sam to Boston with him.

Instead he focused on the trip he'd made after taking Sam back to Elena's. He'd gone back to the mall to purchase another, more practical gift for Zoe. One that had a purpose, but wasn't in the least bit romantic. Though he knew he'd have to give both wrapped packages in order to protect Sam's feelings, he hoped the more simple one would take away from the innuendo implied by the bath and body basket—even if his skin were tingling as if she'd used that loofah sponge on *him,* then followed it up with her hands, and then those luscious lips he'd tasted the other day.

Zoe placed a hand on his shoulder, her soft touch doing nothing to help him repress his desire to sleep with her as soon as possible.

"It was so nice of you to ask me out for my birthday, even if I'm certain Sam put you up to it," she said, laughing.

He grinned. "The kid has a way about her, that's for sure. It's true she might have told me it was your birthday, but I would have asked you out, anyway."

"Really?"

"Eventually," he admitted. "When these things between us got more settled." When there was no agenda between them.

Which might be never, he thought to himself.

She raised an eyebrow, her understanding as strong as his.

"Settled isn't necessarily going to be a good thing, so let's just enjoy now, why don't we?"

He nodded. "Good thinking."

A glance at the road signs told him they were only five minutes away from the restaurant Elena had suggested for their "date" and he wondered when the hell Zoe's cell phone would ring and put the real plan into motion.

As if by command, he heard the distinctive sound of a cell-phone ring coming from her bag. She answered, spoke to the person on the other end, argued some and then finally agreed to do whatever was being asked of her.

"I said I'll be right there," she grumbled before she hung up and looked over at Ryan.

"Something wrong?" he asked.

"Only adolescent angst."

He glanced at her questioningly.

"We call it the old *stomp, stomp, slam*. In other words, something set Sam off and she stormed into another room and slammed the door."

He pulled into the parking lot of the restaurant, which faced the water and where they supposedly had an outdoor table reserved.

"I'm sure she'll come out of her room eventually." He put the car into park and turned toward her.

Zoe sighed. "She's not in her room, she's at Aunt Kassie's restaurant. Apparently, she's locked herself in the ladies' room and won't come out."

Ryan tried not to laugh at Sam's shenanigans to get Zoe to her surprise party. "Is this normal behavior for her?" he asked, playing along.

To his shock, she nodded. "It's normal teenage, hormonal behavior. That's why we call it *stomp, stomp, slam,* as in, stomp out of the room, then stomp down the hall and finally slam the door shut behind her."

"I have vague recollections of my sister acting the same way."

"So you understand why we have to head on over there?" She sounded truly disappointed and something inside him lifted with the knowledge that she really had wanted to go out on a date with him.

"Your parents can't handle it?"

She shook her head. "Sam yelled through the closed door that she'd only talk to me."

"You think it's a good idea to indulge her tantrums?" Although Ryan knew this particular episode was faked, he wondered how often Sam pulled such extreme stunts to get attention.

"I'll explain on the way, okay?"

Feigning resignation, he placed the car into reverse and pulled out of the parking spot. "I need directions, though. It was enough of a challenge memorizing the way to this place from the map." He treated her to what he hoped looked like a forced smile, doing his bit for the charade.

"Make a left out of here and get back onto the Garden State."

As he followed her directions, he listened to her insight into his niece. "We don't indulge Sam. It's just that we're aware of how hard she's had it, and we do our best to balance discipline and understanding. Sam responds best to a reaction from us that acknowledges her behavior."

"Why is that?"

"Because in her experience, if she ran away or did some-thing wrong, the family she was living with wouldn't report it to Social Services, not because they were being compas-sionate, but because they were afraid if Sam was taken away, they'd lose their monthly stipend from the state."

Her distaste for those past foster families and the system was evident in her tone. His heart squeezed tight as he ac-knowledged the difficult life Sam had led since her mother's traumatic death.

"This is the exit." She pointed and he followed her direc-tions to her aunt Kassie's restaurant.

The teenager was fortunate she had the Costas family in her corner and no matter what happened, Ryan would never cut these people out of her life completely, he thought. He could never be that cruel.

"I really admire how well you understand what Sam has been through and what she needs now."

"I can't take the credit. Ari's the one with the psychology degree. She met Sam first and they just bonded."

"Sam obviously adores you, too."

Zoe grinned. "That's because I'm the more unorthodox sister. Also, I live at home with her, at least for now."

He raised an eyebrow. "Moving somewhere?"

"I think it's about time I got a place of my own, but I haven't started looking yet. I need to get the business off the ground first."

"I can understand wanting to stand on your own."

"I've always done that," she said somewhat defensively. "I just haven't…" She shook her head. "Whatever. Sam loves both me and Ari," she said, picking up the original thread of conversation.

Because he'd touched a nerve about her standing on her own? he wondered. He didn't know, but he'd let her change the subject since he was equally interested in what she had to say about Sam.

"I do think it was Ari's psych background that helped her to realize that Sam liked to test my parents. It was Sam's way of finding out what would happen. She wanted to know that even if she misbehaved, they wouldn't give her away."

He groaned. "She's really had it tough." And he was determined to make it better for her.

The challenge would be in accomplishing his goal without hurting this incredible woman in the process.

THE PARKING LOT to Paradeisos was less crowded than usual, Zoe thought as she stepped out of the car. She planned on talking Sam out of her snit and the restroom and then returning to her date as soon as possible. With Ryan right behind her, she pushed through the glass doors. Her mother was waiting for her in the vestibule.

"What happened?" Zoe asked. "Did it have something to do with the pig?" She couldn't imagine anything else that would set Sam off so badly.

"Ask her yourself." Her mother waved a hand and Zoe walked farther inside.

"Surprise!" The entire Costas clan from up and down the Jersey Shore greeted her in an excited frenzy and she stepped back in shock.

This morning, she'd attributed the fact that everyone had

forgotten her birthday to the fear and commotion over the break-in. She'd called Ari and they'd wished each other a happy birthday, promising to exchange gifts during the week. Ari was supposed to be going out for dinner with Quinn tonight, while Zoe hadn't had any special plans until Ryan had called earlier today. She didn't believe in playing hard to get, not when she really had wanted to go out with him. And, she admitted, she hadn't wanted to be alone on her thirtieth birthday.

Once in the car with Ryan, she'd enjoyed his company despite the sometimes serious conversation. In truth, she'd been so enticed by his cologne and swept away by thoughts of kissing him again that by the time they'd arrived at the exclusive restaurant he'd chosen, she'd put the birthday out of her mind completely. Then when her mother had called, she'd turned her focus to more important concerns, like Sam.

But she should have known she couldn't escape a celebration. In her family, every birthday was a big event. Turning thirty was a milestone, more for Zoe than for Ari because Ari was thirty and married. Zoe was the proverbial old maid—something her relatives reminded her with every kiss on the forehead and every loving slap on the cheek, each accompanied by a birthday wish for a handsome young man.

Meddling and all, Zoe loved these people. She hugged the last of her cousins, Daphne who'd stood last in line.

"Happy big one, Zoe."

She squeezed her cousin tight. "Thanks, Daph," she said, then glanced around, looking for her twin. No way would the family throw a party for just one of them.

"Where's Ari?" Zoe asked.

"Right here waiting for my hug." Ari grinned.

Zoe turned, happy to see her twin and share the party with her. Gone were the days when a little voice in her head wished that just once she could be the center of attention without splitting it with her sister. Those had been her teenage years, but once Ari had left for Vermont, Zoe had come to realize just how much she hated having that particular wish come true.

It wasn't a birthday if she didn't celebrate with her twin, Zoe realized now and met her sister's gaze. "So they ambushed you first?" Zoe asked.

Ari nodded. "Five minutes before you. They wanted to try and manage the surprise at the same time, but Quinn got me here early, just in time to share your surprise. I'm so glad I'm home to celebrate this birthday with you."

"I was just thinking the same thing." Zoe's heart filled as she looked at her twin. If not for Zoe's fake death last year, Ari might not have come home and healed old wounds at all, Ari might not have met Quinn, Quinn wouldn't have introduced them to Sam....

Apparently Zoe's troublemaking had led to many positive things, she thought with amusement. "None of our birthdays were the same while you were gone."

"Mine were so lonely," Ari said softly, then shook her head as if ridding her mind of the past. "But no longer." She stepped back and grinned. "I've got my family, I've got you, and I've got Quinn. And you've got the hottie social worker who isn't a social worker," she said, lowering her voice. "Be careful, Zoe."

She nodded, appreciating her twin's concern. Despite

their time apart, Ari still knew Zoe well and she obviously sensed the truth—that her attraction to Ryan was potent and overwhelming, even though the fact of his presence alone could have a negative effect on the family.

Zoe drew her tongue over her lower lip. "I'll watch myself. I have to." She only hoped she'd heed her words when faced with temptation, she thought, glancing at the man himself.

He waited off to one side, standing by himself, a man alone in a crowd of people. Not an easy feat in her family. Just watching his solitary presence caused her heart to skip a beat. She wanted to help ease his discomfort and assimilation into the clan. The attraction was strong, but so was the emotional pull.

Unable to explain it and unable to ignore him and leave him suffering alone, Zoe told Ari she'd catch up with her later and headed to join Ryan.

"Hi there," she said, coming up beside him.

"Hi." He shoved his hands into his pants pocket.

Sexy khakis that, although neatly pressed and probably expensive, still gave him a more casual look than usual and she couldn't help but admire the fit. Wondering if his thighs were as strong as she thought or how they would feel pressed hard against her own.

At her thoughts, she didn't just swallow hard, she gulped. "I guess some thanks are in order," she said, opting for the safe subject of his role in bringing her to the party.

Though aware all prying eyes of her family were on them, she stepped closer, anyway. His musky scent enveloped her, reminding her of the sensual dreams he'd inspired lately.

He grinned. "If you want to say a proper thanks, I can't say I'd stop you," he said, his voice husky and deep.

Zoe was so far gone with thoughts of being alone with Ryan that she immediately took his words as sexually charged innuendo and her body responded. Heat spread through her belly, and dampness pooled between her thighs.

"You're cute, Baldwin, but I'm not dumb enough to make out with you in front of the whole clan."

"Not even a quick peck on the cheek?" he asked.

"How about later?" She spoke quickly, before she could think it through or change her mind.

"Be sure," he warned her, sounding like a man on the edge.

"I am." The man might be trouble of the deepest kind. He might represent a heartbreak to her family. Yet Zoe was so drawn to him, so mentally involved already, she couldn't control what she now believed was inevitable.

In her mind, she was making a promise she absolutely intended to keep.

At her reply, a low groan reverberated from deep in his throat, cut off because at that moment the jukebox began to play and her family began to clap and dance, drowning out any chance at conversation.

She exhaled hard, aware of the break they'd just been given, knowing it was just a temporary reprieve. Still, she wasn't about to let the relatives separate her from Ryan. He'd asked her out on a date and she wanted to spend the evening with him. Before one of her cousins could drag her off, she grabbed Ryan's hand. They spent the night in true Costas style, eating, dancing and eating some more.

Her male relatives pulled Ryan aside and although she pitied him, she decided to let them have some fun. Ryan could handle any question they threw at him and since they believed him to be Sam's social worker, he wouldn't be subjected to questions about his manliness, as Zoe's and Ari's past boyfriends had been, she thought wryly.

Stifling a laugh, she turned to find her mother standing by her side.

"It's so good to see you happy," Elena said.

Zoe shot her mother a sideways glance. "I'm always happy." She paused. "Aren't I?"

Her mother shrugged. "I suppose, but you have a light in your eyes I haven't seen in quite some time. Maybe never. I like to see it and I bet that nice Mr. Baldwin has something to do with putting it there."

Zoe shuffled her feet and did her best not to look around for Ryan, lest she give credence to her mother's innuendo. "Maybe it's just turning thirty. It's a good age."

"Ha." Elena waved a hand dismissively. "Now come with me. I have something special for your birthday."

She followed her mother to the back of the restaurant where there was a small party room. "What's going on?" Zoe asked.

"Just a game to make the party more fun."

Zoe rolled her eyes. "Ari and I are too old for games."

"Not this kind." Elena held a scarf in front of Zoe's face.

"Isn't that from Sam's party? Orlando Bloom's not quite my speed, Mom."

"That's because he was too flat." Her mother wrapped the scarf around Zoe's eyes. "Your surprise is real."

Zoe tried to pull the scarf off, but her mother slapped her hands, then turned her around three times, making her dizzy by the time she stopped.

"Okay, now go." Elena kissed Zoe's cheek and pushed her forward.

From behind her, Zoe could have sworn she heard Elena tell her to "Go pin the hard-on Ryan Baldwin."

Zoe's aunt Kassie had walked Ryan into the back room in the guise of showing him the rest of the restaurant. She left him there and asked him to wait a minute and she'd be right back because she needed his help with Zoe's birthday gift. Enough time had gone by that he figured he'd been had, when a blindfolded Zoe stumbled inside and the door slammed shut behind her.

He grabbed Zoe before she could fall, then he heard Elena and Kassie's voices beyond the door. And finally, one of them opened the door, flipped off the light and closed them inside once more.

He shook his head and laughed. "They can't be serious."

"Oh you don't know the half of it," Zoe said as she pulled the blindfold off and shook out her hair. "They're over the top to begin with, but add me turning thirty to the mix and I think they've lost their collective minds."

"Don't they realize that the light switch is inside the room so we can turn it on ourselves?"

She laughed.

"Or that it's not quite dark out yet and there's light coming through the window?"

She laughed again. "You don't get my family, Ryan. They

really just want you and me together. Scratch that. Me and anybody together."

"Now that hurts my feelings."

She stepped closer, her body language and sultry tone making it clear she was fully aware of the sexually charged air around them. They had been set up by her family yet Zoe obviously didn't mind.

"I wouldn't want you to feel insulted," she murmured. "Especially when you could be *feeling* so much more."

She had a point and the bulge in his pants and desire pulsing through him proved it.

He met her gaze and let his hand caress the soft skin of her cheek. "I think we should get out of here."

"You're reading my mind." Her gorgeous green eyes sparkled with desire, but her serious expression indicated the time for jokes was over. "Unfortunately I live with my parents. The same people we're looking to avoid."

He chuckled at the reminder. "Fortunately I've got a motel room," he said, knowing full well the step they were about to take. Zoe Costas was many things, but a one-night stand wasn't one of them.

"You know you're the first guy who could use that line on me and not end up flat on his back."

"Can I take that to mean you're sure about this?" There were too many issues and feelings for either of them to take this lightly.

She nodded and he released the breath he hadn't been aware of holding. "Think we can get out the front door without too much of a fuss made by the posse?" he asked.

"No chance in hell." She stepped on the chair and then

climbed onto the tabletop and unlocked the window. "I know you're a by-the-book kind of guy, but how would you feel about sneaking out the back way instead?"

ZOE COULDN'T REMEMBER the last time she'd had to sneak around with a guy in order to avoid her family, but she didn't want an audience nor did she want to provide more ammunition for their questions tomorrow. She'd have enough questions for herself come morning.

Somehow they made it out of the restaurant, through the parking lot and into Ryan's car without being seen. He drove to his motel like someone who knew the area, already comfortable with the New Jersey highways and cloverleaf turns. And now, holding hands, they made their way along the catwalk to his small motel room.

Her heart pounded hard in her chest, her desire for him as strong as her determination to be with him tonight. She just didn't understand how a man like this affected her so deeply. She didn't get how she felt so good around a guy who represented the opposite of the unstructured life she enjoyed. Oh she knew he was sexy, but that wasn't enough to explain the reason she'd come to his motel room after knowing him such a short time.

It was the combination of all of Ryan's decent qualities that attracted her. Like how he tried his best to understand Sam, a kid who meant nothing to him except a continuation of bloodlines. He treated Zoe's whole nutty family with respect, when in reality, he probably had every right just to pick up Sam and walk out, and would likely win against the Costas clan in any court. And then there was the tenderness and desire she saw in his gaze each time he looked at her. The same way he was looking at her now.

She sat on the edge of the bed and watched as he pulled off his jacket and shut off the overhead lights, leaving on only one bedside lamp. She swallowed hard and extended one hand toward him.

Ryan strode forward, tall, imposing and breathtakingly male. When he pushed her onto the bed and came down over her, she appreciated the breadth of his shoulders and the strength in the muscles normally hidden beneath his suit jacket. And when his lips came down hard on hers, all the pent-up passion they'd held in check since their first meeting rose to the surface.

Her entire body trembled as she returned his kiss. Letting her eyes shut and her mind go blank, she focused on feeling—his lips nibbling at hers, his tongue tangling and swirling inside the deep recesses of her mouth, and his teeth taking light nips as he devoured her every way he could.

She worked at the buttons on his shirt with shaking hands, eager to get him naked as soon as possible. Apparently he shared a similar goal because at the same time he pulled her shirt upward. She sat back and helped, lifting her top over her head and tossing it to the floor.

Within minutes they were both free of clothing and once more his body covered hers. "Damn but you feel good."

He nipped at her earlobe and tremors shot straight to her core. Liquid heat trickled between her legs, making her even hotter for him than she already had been.

"You're pretty impressive yourself. Who knew you hid such a fantastic body beneath those fancy suits," she said.

He chuckled, then taking her off guard, he rolled so he was on his back and she lay atop him, her breasts heavy against his chest and their lower bodies perfectly entwined.

Skin against skin, his heat seeped into her pores and as he laced his fingers through hers and raised her arms above her head, she suddenly became aware of the intimacy of the moment—the intensity, which she'd never experienced to this degree with another man. Something else she just couldn't explain away as pure physical attraction.

"Can I ask you something?"

"I don't see why not," he said, his breath against her ear.

"Does your need to follow the rules extend to the bedroom?" As she asked, she rose until she straddled his hips, wanting to see his face during this particular conversation.

He burst out laughing, his grin causing somersaults in her stomach. "Are you trying to tell me you're kinky?"

She shook her head, hoping her cheeks weren't bright red by now. "I just want to know whether I need to be…restrained."

A part of her worried that his more conservative past would lead him to want a sedate woman in bed, yet she had a feeling that sex with Ryan would be nothing short of mind-blowing. If so, there was no way she'd be able to maintain any type of pretense. Nor did she want to. With the emotions this man aroused, she needed him to accept her for the expressive, open woman she was.

His warm gaze held hers. "Aah, Zoe, I think I'd be disappointed if you were restrained." He cupped her breasts with his hands and her nipples grew hard beneath his touch. "In fact, if I didn't hear loud moans, I'd worry that I wasn't pleasing you."

His seductive stare never wavered as he began to slowly massage both nipples between his thumb and forefingers, teasing and arousing her with his deft touch. The desire he built traveled directly from her breasts straight to the damp place between her thighs, making her want to clench her legs together until the sensations built higher and higher. She had to force her eyelids to remain open so she could see his face and absorb his eager expression as he worked his magic on her.

He leaned up on his elbows until his face was level with her chest and without warning, he tasted her breast. His tongue swept over her nipple in luxurious laps, ending with him suckling her until a low purring sound rose from the back of her throat.

"I take it I have nothing to worry about?" he asked in a raspy, but certain voice.

Though she didn't want him to think she was *that* easy or he was *that* good, they both had their answers. She didn't need to concern herself with covering her reactions or not being herself. He truly did accept her and the relief she felt knowing that was huge. And more emotionally frightening than she'd bargained for.

"Well?" he asked, still grinning.

She focused on the ceiling as she replied. "Arrogant as you may be, no, you have nothing to worry about."

"Then I think it's time we stop talking, don't you?" He leaned back against the pillows.

She followed so she could kiss him, taking unbelievable

pleasure in the taste, texture and feel of his mouth. He kissed her back, tangling his hands in her hair and running his fingers through the long strands. The tugging sensation at her scalp had a rippling, erotic effect in her body. Her throat swelled and her back arched of its own volition, her body seeking deeper contact with his hard erection.

"I want you, Ryan Baldwin." Her hand snaked between them, slowly trailing down his chest and stomach, ending at his groin. Her fingertips gently teased the head of his erection.

He clenched his jaw and fought not to allow the physical need pummeling him to become overpowering. No woman had ever made him come so close to losing control.

She did. He wondered if it was because she openly challenged every notion of propriety and behavior that had been ingrained in him since childhood or because she wanted him despite it all.

Yet he was going to have to be that by-the-rules man she'd mentioned earlier. "As much as I hate bringing up reality, I don't have protection. I wasn't prepared for this." He should have stopped at a drugstore on the way back here.

She brushed his hair off his forehead. "Not a Boy Scout, huh?" she asked, laughing. "Would you settle for the fact that I'm on the pill and I've been tested annually? I'm safe."

She was hardly that, Ryan thought as he looked into her green eyes. "It works for me if you can accept my word that I'm safe, too." Never in his past had he had sex without a condom.

He wasn't lacking for women when he needed a date for an occasion and he knew who to turn to when he desired sexual release. But no woman had ever become a priority in his life, made him shift his focus from his work. No woman had made him stop and take notice.

Then there was this one, who'd caught his eye despite that she stood between him and the end of a long journey—his search for Sam, the young girl who was the answer to his long-held dreams of family.

Zoe threaded her fingers through his. "I accept."

Which was all he needed to hear. The time for foreplay and talk was over. He eased his hand between her legs, feeling the slick wetness and damp heat that moistened his fingertips. She moaned and clenched her thighs around his hand.

She trembled and sighed, her need aching and obvious. Somehow he managed to roll her onto the mattress and continue what he started, caressing her slick outer folds as she writhed beside him. He came over her and spread her thighs, his thick, hot erection poised at her dewy entrance. Then, placing his hands on her thighs, he locked his gaze with hers and thrust deep inside her waiting body.

She gasped and let out a load moan of satisfaction, tightening around him. He found her slick, warm and snug, everything he'd dreamed of even when he hadn't known her at all. Unable to wait, he began to move, sliding in and out, a motion she met by grinding her pelvis into him, hard. Her inner walls contracted, milking him with every thrust of his body into hers. They were in sync and each motion brought him closer and closer to release. Zoe's vocal moans told him she was right there with him.

Seconds before he reached his peak, she locked her legs around his back, bringing him so deeply into her body, he thought he saw heaven. Then he exploded, his orgasm more powerful than he'd expected and lasting longer than he thought possible.

Zoe came at the same time with a succession of cries that ended with her calling out his name and pulling every last bit of energy and emotion from him, as well.

He collapsed on top of her, completely spent and satisfied in a soul-deep way.

"Wow," she said, her voice muffled beneath him.

"Yeah." He couldn't manage more than one word in agreement.

They lay that way for what felt like a long while until the jarring ring of the motel telephone broke into the sound of their heavy breathing.

"Who could that be?" he muttered.

"There's only one way to find out."

With a groan of complete regret, he rolled off her to the cold side of the bed and answered the phone. He spoke to the motel operator, trying like hell to suppress a laugh at what the person said on the other end.

"I'm sorry and it won't happen again." He somehow spoke in a serious tone. Hanging up, he turned to Zoe.

She lay on her side, spent and still breathing deeply. Her dark hair tangled around her face in stark contrast to the standard white sheets. She was so damn beautiful. He reached down for the blanket they'd somehow kicked off the bed and pulled it over her in case she was cold.

"Everything okay?" she asked.

He looked into her eyes as he explained. "The front desk said the people in the next room would appreciate it if we'd keep the noise level down and be a bit... How did the man put it? A bit more *restrained*." This time Ryan burst out laughing.

"I'm mortified." Zoe's cheeks turned a deep shade of pink and she smothered her face in a pillow.

He propped himself up on his side with one arm. "Yeah? You could have fooled me." He pulled the pillow off and tossed it onto the floor.

"That phone call doesn't bother you?"

He shook his head.

She raised an eyebrow and studied him in a way that made him look deep inside himself. At any other time, under any other circumstances, being chastised for inappropriate behavior would have put him on edge, but not here. Not with Zoe. She helped him to loosen up.

To his never-ending surprise, the change didn't upset him as much as it should have.

 *Chapter Six*

Zoe hadn't meant to fall asleep. In fact she'd planned on leaving Ryan's motel and spending the night in her own bed. For one thing, she didn't want to set a bad example for Sam and for another, she didn't want to create even more memories with Ryan and forge yet another bond between them. In her mind, there was enough binding them already.

But something about being in his arms had felt so darn good, she'd let herself relax and the next thing she knew, the sun was streaming through the window. Since he'd driven her here, there was no way to sneak out and avoid an awkward morning after.

She rolled over and found Ryan sitting on a chair near the small wooden desk, reading over papers. She sat up against the pillows, pulling the covers up with her.

A little late for modesty, but what the hell. "Morning," she mumbled.

"Morning." He dropped the pen and pushed the papers aside, then stood and walked over to the bed. Leaning down, he planted a long, thorough kiss on her lips.

Nothing awkward or hesitant about it, she thought, and all her anxieties fled. "That was nice," she said softly.

He grinned. "Want breakfast?" He pointed to a Dunkin' Donuts bag waiting on the table.

"You managed to go out, pick up breakfast *and* get work done, all while I slept?" She glanced at the digital clock, which read 9:07 a.m.

"You were out cold."

"Because someone wore me out last night." Her skin tingled with the memory.

He met and held her gaze, warmth and desire evident in his eyes. "Someone wants to wear you out again," he said, slipping a hand beneath the sheet so he could cup and fondle her breast, arousing her with his touch.

She moaned, making sure to keep her noises more quiet this morning. "I need to get home though."

"Sam?" he guessed correctly.

"Yep. I never meant to spend the night." She flipped the covers off and began to scramble for her clothes.

"Why don't you shower first and then I'll take a quick one and drive you home?" he asked.

She glanced up, last night's clothing hanging from her arms. Just looking at the man made her hungry for him all over again. "Wouldn't it be quicker if we showered together?" She fluttered her lashes at him too innocently, her suggestive tone all too obvious.

Zoe didn't know how much time they would have together once his secret was revealed. Once he ripped Sam from their lives. She didn't know how to cope with all her conflicting emotions and yet somehow she managed to focus only on the here and now. On Ryan and this moment in time.

He obviously felt the same way because he laughed and they did as she suggested. Then they drove back to Zoe's house, where despite her protests, Ryan walked her to the front door.

Even if she wouldn't admit it aloud to him, she appreciated that he was brought up to be a gentleman because she was grateful for the few extra minutes alone with him. Unfortunately, she had something to tell him before they parted that would definitely kill the mood.

"Zoe…"

"Ryan…"

They spoke at the same time and she laughed.

"Ladies first."

She hugged her arms close to her chest. "I really don't deserve for you to be so nice to me."

He raised an eyebrow in surprise. "I'm not sure what you're getting at, but if you're feeling insecure, I can assure you that you were amazing in bed." A teasing grin twitched at his lips, his dimples showing when he allowed a full-blown smile.

She flushed hot, remembering the feeling of making love with him, his body buried deep inside hers, filling her completely.

"Did you know you're adorable when you blush? Which I've managed to get you to do quite often." He brushed her cheek with the back of his hand.

"I'm very anti-Mediterranean that way. My olive complexion should protect me from giving myself away," she muttered.

"Well I wouldn't want you to be able hide your real feelings from me. Now what's on your mind?"

She shifted on her feet. The summer sun had yet to reach its peak, yet she was blistering hot, both from nerves and from being around Ryan.

When it came to a guy or a relationship, she was usually the one in control. But she couldn't get a handle on her feelings for this man. "I… We… Last night was amazing," she said first, not wanting to gloss over something so important to them both.

"Yes, it was." His voice dropped an octave. "But I hear a *but* coming."

She shook her head. "Not a typical *but*."

"What then?"

"Look…" She exhaled hard and forced her gaze up from her shoes to his face. "We met because of Sam. Because you're her uncle and you want her in your life. And we didn't tell her about you because I needed to be sure of you and your character."

He propped his shoulder against the screen door. "And now you are?"

"Unfortunately, I am." He was a good man. The best kind, really. She reached for his hand, holding it tight. "We need to tell Sam the truth." Her stomach hurt just saying the words.

She couldn't begin to imagine the fallout from the actual revelation. But it was time. She no longer had any justification to keep the truth from her family and Sam. They all had to stop living a lie, especially Zoe herself. She had to stop pretending Ryan could actually be a part of her life. She was becoming too attached to a man who was just passing through and who would leave nothing but spiraling upheaval in his wake.

Ryan glanced down at their intertwined hands. He opened and closed his mouth, unsure of what to say. He'd been so focused on last night and on Zoe, he hadn't seen this one coming. True, he wanted Sam to know he was her uncle, but he'd been content to wait until the time was right. He and Zoe had been so close, the last thing he'd considered doing was putting a wedge between them.

Which made him wonder about her motives for doing so now. Could she be using his relationship with Sam to keep him at a distance? It was possible. After all, he'd seen her wariness this morning. He'd watched her wake up, stiffen and take too long to figure out how to handle the situation. No doubt, if she'd awakened before him, she would have bolted. For reasons he didn't yet understand, he sensed Zoe was afraid.

He wanted more time to figure her out. To figure *them* out.

Yet she'd offered him the opportunity he'd come for and he couldn't turn her down. "You're sure the time is right?" he asked.

Zoe dropped his hand, putting physical and emotional distance between them. She tipped her head to one side and sighed. "As sure as I'll ever be. I just need a chance to break it to my parents first."

"Of course. And then what?" He flexed and unflexed his hands, nerves taking over.

Questions raced through his mind. Was she going to talk her parents into just letting him take Sam home, once they got through the New Jersey red tape, or did she plan to have him stay in town awhile longer? And how would Sam react to discovering she had family after all this time?

"I don't—" Zoe started to speak.

"Elena, they're back!" Sam's voice struck him in his gut, and prevented Zoe from revealing her thoughts.

Zoe shot him a suddenly frightened look. He understood and wondered if Sam had overheard any part of their conversation.

The young girl fumbled with the lock on the screen door, but finally worked the catch, opened the door and waved them inside. "Come in! You left so early you never opened your presents," she said to Zoe.

Sam didn't meet Ryan's gaze, but that wasn't unusual and once he saw her excitement and smiles, his concern eased. She was too happy to have heard a thing. Now all he had to worry about was Zoe viewing his embarrassing gifts.

"Do you want to help me unwrap them?" Zoe asked Sam.

"Already done." The young girl grabbed Zoe's hand and they walked into the family room.

Ryan followed and seated himself on a chair across from them so he could watch.

Sam shook her head, her ponytail flipping behind her. "Elena said if you were gonna be rude and leave, we could still enjoy the traditional parts of a party, so I already opened the presents, well all except for the ones from Ryan," Sam explained in a rush, as only a teenager could.

"I see. And what did I get?" Zoe asked, laughing.

"Aunt Dee and Uncle John bought you a subscription to an online dating service that lets you pick out whatever traits you want in a guy. They said you'd better make sure he's Greek."

Ryan didn't have to glance at Zoe to know she was blushing. He also didn't have to look down at his clenched fists to realize the thought of her with any other man didn't sit well with him at all.

Sam ran through a litany of other gifts until she reached the end. "And Elena and Aunt Kassie said you already got your gift from them, not that I know what they mean."

Ryan did and his gaze met Zoe's, every moment of last night passing between them in that one look.

"And this is from me." Sam pulled out a pillow that she'd been hiding behind her back. "I made it myself," she said softly, suddenly shy. "Since you have one that Ari made you, I wanted you to have one from me, too. So I could be a real sister, too."

"Oh, Sam." Zoe pulled her into a huge hug and over her shoulder, Sam met Ryan's gaze with a pleading one of her own. One that begged him, the "social worker," not to take her away from these special people.

If only Sam knew the real damage he could do. He glanced from the hugging women to the hook-rug type pillow that said Sisters & Best Friends 4 Ever. A wave of nausea swept through him as he realized that in telling Sam the truth, he'd be depriving her of the security she had finally achieved in her otherwise unsettled life.

How could he do that to her? Ryan wondered.

Yet how could he not?

Sam pulled out of Zoe's grasp. "It's Ryan's turn to give you his presents." She stepped back to reveal the wrapped packages on the table behind the sofa. "We bought one of them yesterday when we went shopping, but there's an extra thing here and I don't know what it is. But I helped him pick out the big one." She pointed to the larger gift as she practically hopped from foot to foot in eager anticipation of the big reveal.

Zoe's eyes narrowed as she took in the presents. "Hmmm.

What could Ryan have bought me? I think I'll open this one first." Zoe winked at Sam and started peeling the wrapping off the larger present.

"Oh I can't wait to see," Elena said from the doorway, joining them in time for Ryan's mortification.

"Same here." Nicholas strode in and seated himself in the large recliner chair.

"Oh man," he muttered aloud.

Zoe pulled away the last of the wrapping. "These are wonderful," Zoe exclaimed as she examined each fruit-scented item in the basket, from bath gel, foot cream, hand cream, body lotion, to the different textured sponges.

Ryan would rather die than look at her parents now, though a covert glance showed him that Nicholas was indeed scowling at him. No doubt the man also knew his daughter hadn't come home last night and it was obvious she still wore last evening's clothes.

Well, hell, was it his fault she was thirty and living at home? Still, he cringed.

"Sam, thank you for helping Ryan pick out my favorite scents." Zoe's soft voice interrupted his thoughts.

"It's okay. You know I love you." Sam sounded a little more subdued, Ryan figured because the excitement of giving her gift was over.

"How about opening Ryan's other one?" Elena asked.

Now that he'd seen Zoe's pleased reaction to the bath-shop gift, he wanted to take his more practical one and shove it into his pocket. But that wouldn't be happening.

Elena, Nicholas and Sam crowded around as Zoe ripped apart the paper and pulled out the present he'd purchased to minimize the impact of the first. No chance of that happening, he thought. Now that they'd made love, and now that her family knew they'd spent last night together, he couldn't win with either gift.

He forced himself to look at Zoe. She stared at the Montblanc pen in the black box for so long, he thought he might puke.

"To sign your first contract with," he said, his voice sounding as lame as he felt.

She met his gaze, her eyes filled with warmth, gratitude and, he thought, a hell of a lot more. "That's the most thoughtful thing I've ever heard," she said.

"And the most dorky and lame." Sam grunted and rose from the couch. "I'm going to Michelle's." She was clearly as unimpressed with Ryan's additional birthday present as she was with him.

"Be back for us to go shopping around three," Elena called to Sam.

"Thanks, Sam. Everyone," Zoe said. "I should put all this in my room." Without looking at Ryan, she gathered her gifts in her arms.

He wondered what had her spooked this time. Either it was the knowledge that her parents *knew* about their relationship or she just wanted to run from last night as fast as she could. He'd been able to stop her this morning, when he'd kissed her senseless and reminded her of why she shouldn't panic. He couldn't do the same thing now.

In the silence, he heard Nicholas whisper to Elena in a not-so-quiet voice, "Another one that isn't Greek."

Elena laid her head on his shoulder and spoke into his

ear. "As long as she's happy, Nicky. She should have what we share, no?"

With those comments, Zoe bolted for the stairs leading to her room.

As Ryan rose to leave and said his goodbyes to Zoe's parents, he was struck by the warmth between them. A love and under-standing he'd never seen between his parents, growing up. In their home, formality ruled, even in personal, intimate relation-ships. Elena and Nicholas apparently adhered to no such rules of decorum. The family had told him last night that the couple's fights contained fireworks that were something to see. So, too, did their making up.

He glanced at Elena and Nicholas again. Zoe couldn't possibly fear relationships based on what she'd seen at home. Which meant she feared something about *him*.

All of which convinced him that his hunch about Zoe's sudden wariness now was correct. She wanted to put space between them and telling Sam the truth would help accom-plish her goal.

IN THE NEW OFFICES, Ari paced the linoleum floor that Zoe had just mopped clean. "A pen? The man bought you a pen for your birthday?" Ari asked, clearly in shock.

"Isn't it the most honest gift you've ever heard of?" Zoe rolled the pen between her palms, the gift reminding her so much of Ryan and his contradictions. The hard exterior and the gentle man beneath. When she closed her eyes, she saw his face, warm and caring, and the gift cemented those emotions.

"Well at least you didn't say it's the most romantic present you ever received. What's going on with you, anyway?" Ari asked.

Zoe lifted her gaze. "I'm going to try to explain this, but you may not get it," she warned her sister.

"Well, try me."

"This is a guy who was brought up in an uptight environment—that's all he's ever known and yet he doesn't mind our family. The more time he spends with us, the more he loosens up."

"Which explains the bath basket?" Ari guessed.

Zoe shook her head. "No, Sam explains the bath basket. Ryan bought the pen himself. It's conservative, just like he is."

"But you don't like conservative," Ari said, tossing her hands in the air in frustration.

"Exactly. If he'd bought the pen because it was the right thing to do, I'd hate it. But he picked it so I'd have something special to mark signing the contract with our first real client. He *gets* how excited I am about the business." Which was why she had to pull back from him now, before anyone really got hurt.

"Aaah." Ari nodded slowly. "I'm beginning to understand. The man gets you. And you're going to repay him by handing over Sam?"

"Good question." Quinn strode into the room and gave his wife a kiss on the cheek. "By the way, can we go with a darker yellow on the walls? This color is so cheery I may walk in and vomit every morning."

Zoe rolled her eyes. "No. And no I am not just handing over Sam. Quinn, did you find out anything about the break-in? Like why the burglar would be in Sam's room at all?"

He shook his head. "I haven't a clue what Sam has that could possibly interest someone enough to break in and ransack the house."

"Start with anyone in our family," Ari said, obviously resigned to the fact that someone could be involved in a con of some kind.

She wasn't wrong. Zoe knew firsthand that their scheming could lead to anything. Lord knew she'd ended up in a safe house, thanks to a simple matchmaking scheme.

Quinn eyed his wife with wariness and concern. "You know I checked up on them?"

She and Quinn glanced over, but Ari showed no signs of distress. Not long ago, just the mere mention of an old family prank or oddity caused Ariana to withdraw, if not as far as Vermont, then deep inside herself where she didn't have to deal with the family's oddities. Quinn had accepted the family right away and he'd helped Ari learn to value her close-knit clan.

Ari nodded. "Of course."

Apparently her twin had come to terms with who and what the Costas family was. Zoe was grateful because it helped strengthen their relationship, too.

"And?" Zoe asked.

He groaned. "Well, let's see. There have been some complaints about the new skin-care cream Elena created and the fishy smell, but as far as I can tell from the bookkeeper, those people have been reimbursed."

"She's working on finding a scent to cover the fish oil," Zoe offered helpfully and grinned. "Anything else?"

"Elena had been giving massages to men and women, but

after one male patron lodged a complaint about wandering hands, your mother instituted a policy that men work on men, and women on women."

Zoe shook her head. "Makes no sense considering someone could just as easily lodge a complaint against the same sex."

"When did any of Mom's actions need to make sense to anyone but her?" Ari asked.

"Good point." Zoe settled into a desk chair and began spinning back and forth. "Is that it?" she asked Quinn.

"Except the one person who claims they had something stolen from their wallet during a facial session."

Zoe frowned. "Is there any reason we're just hearing about this now?"

Quinn shrugged. "I don't know. All I had to do was talk to the receptionist and she spilled all. I think your parents just want to succeed and don't want you or Ari to worry about anything."

Ari blew out a frustrated breath. "Just because of who they are, I'll always worry. So there've been some complaints."

"The police were only called in about the stealing issue, but the client decided not to press charges. Everything else was settled in-house and amicably. No reason for anyone to trash the house," Quinn said, his frustration obvious.

Zoe stopped spinning herself and waited till the dizzying sensation subsided. "Quinn, the person who declined to press charges, could she have sent someone to break in to look for what she claims was taken? Maybe they thought it could be stashed in an un-obvious place, like Sam's room."

"It's something to consider and we'll look into it."

Ari nodded. "I think you should."

"Now how about Ryan's family?" Zoe asked. "What did you find out about them?" She hated that she was prying into things she'd rather hear from Ryan himself, but desperate times and Sam's welfare called for desperate measures.

Quinn pulled a pad out of the back pocket of his jeans. "They own Baldwin's Department Stores, a ritzy chain scattered throughout New England's wealthiest areas." He glanced at his notes. "Baldwin himself is a lawyer and has no part in the family business. It's mainly run by his father's brother, Russell. The family's fairly conservative, which means boarding schools and country clubs and the like."

Ari rubbed her hands up and down her arms. "Sam will die in that kind of environment."

Zoe nodded. "From what I've got on paper, I agree. We're going to have to see what happens beyond the basic introductions. Ryan understands she's a sensitive kid despite her tough exterior. Once she knows the truth, he's going to have to spend more time with her here. Then we'll have to talk about what comes next."

"I hate it," Quinn muttered.

Zoe nodded. "Join the club."

"When do we break the news to Mom and Dad?" Ari asked, resigned.

"Sam has plans to sleep at her friend's tonight. We'll double-check and if Mom and Dad are home alone, we'll fill them in then." Zoe laid her head in her hands, not wanting to face her parents with the dreaded news.

Especially after she'd spent the night with the man who could take Sam away. And what a night it had been. She still recalled every intimate moment, each sensual touch.

Zoe groaned. Quinn had suggested she stick close to Ryan as a means of measuring him as a person and keeping him from revealing all to Sam. Her mother had suggested the same, her motive being for Zoe to cozy up to the so-called social worker who'd ultimately determine Sam's placement. Although Zoe had gone along with their suggestions, she'd never fooled herself into believing she'd been with Ryan for completely selfless reasons.

The attraction had been potent from day one and had exploded between them last night. So had emotions she had no business feeling. Even if she put his relationship to Sam aside, that didn't change her reservations.

She and Ryan couldn't be more different. He was a conservative man with a life and expectations far removed from her own. He lived in a city that was a solid four hours away. And he evoked an intensity of feeling that could cause untold upheaval in a life she was just beginning to reclaim.

Heaven only knew what kind of damage he could cause if she let him into her heart.

RYAN WALKED BAREFOOT DOWN to the beach, wishing he could share the gorgeous night with Zoe. Instead, he found himself alone. Because it was early evening, the sun lovers had headed inside, but there were still large groups of people hanging out by the water. The frothy waves hit the shore and rolled back, relaxed and easy—unlike how Ryan was feeling at the moment. He rolled his shoulders, but the tension remained.

He was a short time away from achieving everything he'd come to New Jersey for and yet the victory was bittersweet.

In getting what he desired, he'd be hurting people he'd come to like and respect. Worse, he was falling hard for a woman who had every right to want distance between them.

He kicked at the sand in disgust and when his cell phone rang, he was grateful for the distraction.

He pulled the phone out of his pocket and flipped it open. "Hello?"

"Ryan, how are you?"

"Uncle Russ. I'm fine."

"You don't sound fine."

Ryan could picture the scowl on his uncle's face. "I never could put one over on you, could I?"

His uncle chuckled. "That's because I'm older and wiser. Now talk to me."

He told his uncle about Sam, about how much her attitude reminded him of his sister, about how she tried to act tough, but had a soft heart for animals and about her relationship with her foster family. "She's a great kid," he summed up, knowing that *great* didn't nearly cover all Sam's attributes.

"Of course she's great. She's got Baldwin blood running through her veins," Uncle Russ said, chuckling.

"I suspect she's great in spite of that fact," Ryan said bluntly.

His uncle cleared his throat. "Well don't you worry. I'll make her feel like she's part of the family and who knows? Perhaps your parents will come around. Does she know who you are yet?"

"Good question."

Ryan glanced at his watch. Zoe had called him earlier to

say she planned to gather her parents and give them the news. Telling Sam could come later. On the phone, Zoe had been cool and distant, something he both understood and hated at the same time. Though he had no idea whether she'd be in touch with him after she delivered the blow to her parents, his stomach rolled in anticipation.

"Sam should be told soon," he informed his uncle, taking no pleasure in his own words.

After Sam knew, then the real challenge would begin. Trying to convince her of his sincerity. Trying to get her to appreciate his position as family not enemy.

"Do you need me? I can come down, you know." Uncle Russ had always been there to offer his support.

The gesture brought a lump to Ryan's throat. He might not have much of an immediate family to speak of, but he'd always had Uncle Russ. He hadn't realized how much he needed to hear a friendly, familiar voice from home, but speaking to his uncle now helped him feel more grounded and cemented to the life he'd temporarily left behind.

He glanced up at the setting sun and closed his eyes, grateful for what he did have and determined to let Sam share in the same things.

"Ryan, are you there?"

"I'm here. No need to visit just yet. Maybe when the initial shock blows over. We'll see."

"Well, I've got to run. My dinner date is here," his uncle said.

Ryan grinned. The consummate bachelor, Uncle Russ never had the same dinner date more than a few times, and he wondered who the lucky woman was this evening.

"Have a good time." Ryan paused, unsure of how to speak

his feelings after a lifetime spent keeping them inside. "Before I hang up—"

"Yes?"

"Thanks for being there."

Silence followed for a moment before Uncle Russ spoke. "You're the son I never had, Ryan. Always remember that."

His uncle's declaration was welcome at a time when Ryan felt adrift from everyone and everything. He hung up and settled into the sand to watch the last of the sun set on the horizon.

He needed time to think about the fallout sure to come, and mentally say goodbye to Zoe, the woman he felt certain he was about to lose.

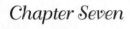

Chapter Seven

WITH ALL THE FAMILY CHANGES on the horizon, Zoe was lured to the wall of photographs going up the stairs in her parents' home. Though unorthodox, her own childhood had been a happy one, as documented by the assorted pictures facing her. Part of the reason she'd never moved out of her parents' house was the feeling of warmth and security she found here, something she never thought she could find anywhere else.

Since her old job had kept her on the road sometimes for days on end, she hadn't missed having a place of her own until recently. And, she admitted, it helped that her parents no longer kept tabs on her, and that she liked their unstructured life.

Was there also an element of inability to commit to anyone or anything, as her father said? She shivered and, instead of dealing with the present, she focused on the wall that showed off her past.

The most recent photo added to the collection caught her eye. The picture showed Sam, Spank the monkey, Ari and Zoe together at Zoe's welcome-home party after she'd returned from her enforced confinement last year. The three of them looked like real sisters. And her parents truly did treat Sam like one of their own children. They'd even become more structured since Sam had come into their lives. Dinner was served at six and they all ate seated as a family. Sam's homework had to be completed before television was allowed, and she had a strict curfew.

Though Zoe wouldn't call her mother June Cleaver, Elena had become more regimented with Sam around because she understood what the child needed. Despite the fact that Elena had become a certified masseuse, she never scheduled a spa appointment after three and she was home every afternoon when Sam returned from school. All these changes had been made because the entire Costas family loved Sam and wanted her to have as close to a perfect childhood as possible.

"Looking at the wall of shame?" Ari asked.

Zoe felt her twin's hand on her shoulder and covered it with her own. "That always was your description." But Zoe knew that Ari had come to terms with her difficulties within their family. "I was just thinking what a great childhood we had."

"We did. Even I can see that now, especially compared to Sam's journey through the foster-care system," Ari said.

"I wanted the same thing for Sam," Zoe said.

"Maybe Ryan Baldwin can provide it for her. You like him and that's no small feat."

Zoe turned toward her twin. "He's a good man, but do you know what his family's kind of life would do to Sam? The rules, the regulations, the criticism that drove her mother to run away." Zoe shivered, mentally placing herself in that same position of being judged.

Thinking along those lines always sent her into an emotional freeze. Her relationship with Ryan worked only because she knew he would return to Boston and there was no chance of a long-term relationship between them. If not for that assurance, she'd run far and fast to escape, just as his sister had.

"You ready to talk to Mom and Dad?" Ari asked. "Quinn's waiting with them in the family room."

Zoe inclined her head. "Let's do it."

Less than ten minutes later, the truth had been revealed. Elena sat on the couch, her head bent, and Zoe knelt down beside her mother, holding her hand. Zoe's stomach was twisted in knots and she hated herself for putting her parents through so much pain.

"So to be clear, this Ryan Baldwin isn't a social worker?" her father asked.

Ari shook her head.

"He's Sam's mother's brother," Quinn explained again.

"Which makes him a liar," Nicholas snapped.

Zoe cringed. "Papa," she said, using the nickname she'd called him as a child. "The lie was my fault. Mom mistook Ryan for a social worker the day of Sam's party and yes, he went along with it in the beginning, but I found out that day…and I convinced him to stay quiet."

While her mother remained uncharacteristically silent, Nicholas let out a litany of Greek profanity that singed her ears. "Why?" he asked. "Why would you do this to your own family?"

Her throat tightened. She rose to face her father in order to explain. "At first I needed to check out if he was who he claimed to be. And then I wanted to make sure he was a decent guy before I revealed anything."

"And then you fell for the man." Elena lifted her head from her kimono sleeve for the first time since hearing the news.

Her mother's words slammed into Zoe with the force of a Mack truck. "Untrue," Zoe protested too quickly. "I just didn't want to cause complete panic until I had more facts. You know how much I love you all. You know I adore Sam. I had everyone's best interests at heart."

Her father strode forward and claimed her in a reassuring bear hug. "You, I have faith in. That man, him I don't trust."

Despite understanding her father's side, Zoe wanted to defend Ryan. She told herself it was for Sam's sake that she needed to redeem him in her parents' eyes, but her rapidly beating heart and the wave of emotions sweeping through her told her that her motives were more self-serving.

"Ryan's a decent man, Papa."

"Bah." Nicholas folded his arms across his chest.

"Ari? Quinn? What do you think of Ryan?" her mother asked.

"You don't need to ask them." Zoe's voice rose, this time in her own defense. "I'm the one who's spent time with him and can judge his character. And I can tell you that he's as much a victim of circumstance as we are. Ryan loved Sam before he ever met her. He came here with the best intentions, to find his niece and give her a good life."

"She already has a good life," her father said, gesturing with his hands to the four walls of the home he'd provided for his family.

"But he didn't know that!" Zoe clenched her fists in frustration.

"Everyone needs to calm down," Quinn said, stepping between them. "This is a shock, so let's take some time to let it sink in before we tell Sam."

"Sam already knows." The object of their discussion walked in from the kitchen, pig in her arms, eyes wide with shock. "That stuffed shirt is my uncle?" she asked, her voice shaking.

Zoe had no words to reassure her. Sam was a smart kid and she'd probably already assessed the situation and realized the possibility of yet another upheaval in her life.

"What are you doing back from Michelle's?" Elena strode forward, taking control while everyone else stared in mute shock.

"She got sick and her mom dropped me off on the way to the pharmacy."

Elena wrapped an arm around Sam's stiff shoulders, but the young girl remained remote and withdrawn.

Watching them, Zoe's heart was close to breaking.

"Don't jump to any conclusions or panic, squirt. We'll get this figured out, okay?" As always, Quinn attempted to be the voice of reason.

"Yeah, sure. Whatever." Obviously not even Quinn's strong presence seemed to reassure Sam. She snuggled the pig tighter against her chest, ignoring Ima's squeals of protest.

Then, without meeting anyone's gaze, Sam stormed out of the room. Nobody dared call Sam on breaking the rules of bringing the pig upstairs. The teen deserved some form of comfort, something nobody else seemed able to give.

Stomp, stomp, slam, Zoe thought, echoing Sam's actions in her mind. The walls shook when she slammed the door, leaving the adults to stare helplessly at one another.

What could they say? There was so much more at stake than just the possibility of Ryan taking Sam back to Boston. Sam's actions proved it. She'd already begun the process of withdrawing emotionally to protect herself from being hurt. Not only had she been handed unexpected and painful information, but she'd heard it through eavesdropping. By the family holding this meeting without her and getting caught, they'd reinforced her biggest insecurity—that she wasn't wanted here, anyway.

And Zoe feared that reaching past Sam's defenses this time would be not just difficult, but impossible.

A FEW HOURS LATER, Ari and Quinn had gone home, while her mother and father had retreated to their bedroom to discuss and absorb the news. Zoe had heard her mother knock on Sam's door and the loud *go away* she'd received in response. She guessed Elena hadn't pushed the issue because she wanted to let Sam settle for a bit before she forced her to talk.

Zoe figured she'd try and see Sam before she turned in for the night. She paused outside her closed door and knocked lightly. "Sam? It's me."

"Go away."

"No. I'm coming in," she warned. She knew better than to leave Sam alone for too long. With her active adolescent mind, she'd conjure up all sorts of proof that the Costases wanted her gone, anyway.

No, Sam needed to feel the love.

Zoe walked inside. She glanced around, taking in the touches Sam had added that marked the room as hers. The Orlando Bloom stand-up poster from the party, the stuffed animals and the typical clutter accumulated over time. Except in Sam's case, all the *stuff* had been gathered over the short period during which she'd lived with Zoe's parents.

She'd arrived from her last foster home with little in the way of personal items except for the keys around her neck and she seemed surprised each time someone—Ari, Zoe, Elena, Nicholas or even one of the aunts—bought her something just because they wanted to see her smile.

Sam sat on her bed.

Zoe joined her. "You can't keep your feelings inside." Counseling was Ari's forte, but Zoe tried, anyway, for Sam's sake.

Sam pulled her knees up to her chest and leaned back against the headboard. "I'm not. Ryan Baldwin is a liar and I don't want to be related to him. You knew about the lie, so you were probably helping him to get close to me so you could get me out of your house and have your parents back all to yourself."

Zoe rolled her eyes. "I'm thirty years old. What makes you think I want my parents' attention all on me? I saw this one coming, but I thought you'd come up with a better story than that lame one." She nudged Sam's leg with her elbow.

And got a grudging half smile in return. "Okay, then why did you lie?" Sam asked.

"Because I needed time to find out if Ryan was telling the truth. I wanted to know what kind of man he really was before turning everyone's lives upside down. Can you try to understand?"

Sam shrugged. "Maybe."

She was trying valiantly to show no fear, but Zoe saw her trembling lips and wide eyes, the scared little girl beneath the facade.

Since nothing could make this nightmare go away, Zoe opted to try and make it easier. "And maybe you can find out a little about your uncle? Maybe Ryan can tell you some more about your mom." Zoe prodded her softly, wanting Sam to realize there were benefits to having Ryan in her life.

Sam fingered the keys around her neck, but said nothing.

Zoe tilted her head and scooted a little closer. "You never talked about her. Do you want to? With me?"

Sam shook her head. "I just want to go to sleep." A single tear dripped down her cheek. She ignored it, didn't bother to wipe it away.

Zoe desperately wanted to pull Sam into her arms, but she sensed how much the teen valued her composure. Even at this young age, Sam knew how to keep it together, a function of growing up in foster homes with no one who truly cared.

In her heart, Sam had to know everyone in the Costas family loved and respected her. Enough to give her the space she needed.

"I'd just like you to remember one thing," Zoe said.

Sam reluctantly lifted her gaze. "What's that?"

"We love you, whatever happens." Some words had to be said, Zoe thought, in order to be both felt and remembered.

And then, though Sam had curled into a ball, Zoe pressed a kiss to the top of her head before slipping out the door.

She leaned back, hands flat against the wall and exhaled hard. Despite it all, she felt torn. On the one hand, she wanted to kill Ryan for putting Sam through this pain and on the other hand, she wanted to show up on his doorstep and fill him in on everything that had happened tonight. And then she wanted to let him hold her, make love to her, and ease the pain. She felt that close to him.

What irony. Because if not for Ryan, she wouldn't feel so gut-wrenchingly bad right now.

THE SUN PEEKED through the curtains on the window, but Ryan didn't need daylight to tell him it was morning. He hadn't slept a wink all night.

When he hadn't heard from Zoe by midnight, he resigned himself to not hearing from her at all. Unable to sit still in his small motel room, he'd headed out to a local bar and nursed a couple of drinks. He'd thought he'd consumed enough to put him out for the night, but instead, he'd stared at the ceiling, tortured by the memory of Zoe's enthusiastic moans, groans and earth-shattering climax. A climax she'd had at the same moment he'd come inside her.

He felt as though those memories were some kind of punishment, though he hadn't done a damn thing wrong except be related to Sam. He ran a hand through his hair and rose from the bed, determined to take his and Sam's fate into his own hands.

After a quick shower and shave, he dressed, ready to head over to the Costas home and have this discussion with all interested parties present.

He stepped out of his room onto the catwalk and was greeted by a warm breeze. And then by his uncle Russell walking toward him.

"Well this is a surprise." Ryan strode forward and by habit, held out his hand.

"A good one I hope." His uncle grabbed his hand and pulled him into a hug.

The man always had provided the affection his parents failed to give and he was grateful. But he couldn't afford to have him here now, messing up any headway he might have made with the Costas family. Or more important, with Sam.

Ryan stepped back. "It's always nice to see you, but I thought we agreed you'd wait till I told you it was a good idea to come here."

The other man leaned against the railing overlooking the parking lot. "You seemed down when we spoke last night and I thought you could use the moral support."

"So you drove all this way in the middle of the night?"

His uncle inclined his head. "I told you. You're the son I never had."

"And I appreciate the support." More than he was able to express at the moment, despite his mixed feelings about Uncle Russ joining him here.

"I intend to be here for you every step of the way."

Ryan glanced at the sky, wondering when the hell his life had gotten so damn complicated. Then, resigned to the in-evitable, Ryan turned to his uncle. "Want to go meet your niece?"

His uncle's face lit up in a way Ryan hadn't seen in years. "Just lead the way, son."

ZOE PACED THE FAMILY ROOM, angry at Sam and furious with herself. Early that morning, the family discovered Sam was gone, missing from her bedroom and nowhere else in the house. No matter how many alternatives they discussed, they could come to no other conclusion than she had run away from home. Common sense told them that Sam had bolted the same way she'd done before, to test the family's loyalty and desire to have her around.

Normally they'd wait her out, give her some time to think, and then find her in an obvious place. She'd be lectured, then grounded, just as Ari or Zoe had been as children—proof to Sam that she was one of them. But in this case, her fear of being taken away was valid, and nobody had wanted to give her too much headway in her escape.

Zoe had anticipated the teenager withdrawing, so why hadn't she insisted on sleeping in her room last night instead of leaving her alone? She slammed her palm against the table in frustration, then shook the sting from her hand.

She hated being the one home waiting in case Sam called or showed up, but her parents had gone knocking on her friends' doors, Quinn and Ari were checking other places Sam might go, like the youth center around the corner, and Connor was asking around at local hospitals.

Zoe walked to the window and glanced out to the street in time to see Ryan pull up in his fancy BMW. God, he was the last thing she needed now. He was also the one person she wanted desperately. It would help to have his shoulder to cry on because despite that they each wanted Sam in their family, they both had her welfare at heart. She needed to share her fear with him now.

She opened the door and watched Ryan…and an older man she didn't recognize as they strode together up her front walk.

The stranger's presence prevented her from acting on her stupid impulse to fling herself into Ryan's arms for comfort and reassurance. Odd things to expect or desire from the man whose very presence had caused the upheaval.

He strode forward with confidence, wearing the suit he'd had on the first day they'd met. He was clean shaven and his hair was neatly combed. His appearance made him look more like the uptight man she'd met at the birthday party than the relaxed guy she'd spent time with lately. Yet his appeal was certain and unnerving and not even the ultra-conservative look changed the fact that the man was drop-dead gorgeous and caused Zoe's awareness levels to soar.

"Zoe? What's wrong?" he asked.

She pulled her thoughts together and forced a smile. "What makes you think anything's wrong?"

He stepped closer, so he could speak directly to her, whispering for her ears alone. "Because I know you and while your smile might say one thing, I see something else entirely in your eyes."

Her internal radar went on the fritz when he stepped closer and she smelled his familiar, sexy cologne, while her stomach churned, warmed by his concern and understanding. Still, he hadn't introduced her to his companion and he held himself apart from her in a way that told her their intimacy seemed to be in the past. Reminding herself that she'd pulled away from him first didn't ease the sting.

"You told her, didn't you?" he asked, guessing accurately.

"Come on in and I'll explain." She pushed the front door open wide and gestured inside.

When they were all seated, she inclined her head toward

the older gentleman. His salt-and-pepper hair gave him a distinguished air. "And who is this?" she asked.

Ryan shook his head. "Sorry, my manners seem to have failed me," he said rather formally. "Uncle Russell, meet Zoe Costas. Uncle Russell came down because… He…"

Ryan's voice trailed off and Zoe understood the reason for his sudden discomfort. "He wanted to meet Sam," she finished for him. "Odd considering nobody but you has seemed interested in Sam in years." Zoe lashed out, refusing to hold her feelings back, but unable to meet Ryan's gaze as she did so.

Beside Ryan, his uncle stiffened.

"That was completely uncalled for," Ryan said as he turned suddenly judgmental before her eyes.

"The young lady has gumption," his uncle said in an equally formal voice.

She couldn't tell if his comment was meant as a compliment or an insult. Between the New England accent and the haughty attitude, he hid his true feelings well.

"I always have gumption, especially when I'm protecting family. And Sam is already family. She's my sister. Signing adoption papers is just a formality," she said, forcing herself to speak aloud a conviction she no longer believed was so simple and straightforward.

Ryan set his jaw. "We'll see about that."

She narrowed her gaze. Never in all the time they'd been together, first as adversaries and later as lovers, had this subject come up. They'd each trodden carefully around the other's feelings, wanting what was best for the teenager, and respecting the other's position and desires. Yet in front of his uncle, Ryan took a definitive stand that froze Zoe inside and out.

But she'd started it by mentioning the adoption and suddenly she knew why, just as she knew what was different about Ryan now. His demeanor had changed. Though he'd only been in New Jersey a short time, in the past few days he'd relaxed around Zoe and her family. He'd accepted their outspokenness and come to enjoy their uniqueness, like Elena's kimonos and Sam's pet pig. All things that would never be accepted in his Boston home.

Yet sitting sandwiched between Zoe and his uncle, he was faced with two disparate choices. The Costases' eccentricity versus the values of his conservative relatives. Any feelings he might have developed for Zoe versus his loyalty to his own family.

His worst nightmare had come to life, Zoe thought. As had hers, since it was obvious whom he would choose. Ryan's aloofness and the clothes he'd chosen all put a barrier between himself and Zoe, and proved her gut instinct had been correct all along. More than the physical distance between New Jersey and Massachusetts separated her from Ryan. More separated them than even their desire to claim Sam.

The emotional gulf between them couldn't be greater. Heaven help her when he discovered Sam had run away.

RYAN WAS FURIOUS. He couldn't look at Zoe without wanting to strangle her. *Signing adoption papers was just a formality?* Since when had she deleted him from the equation, without a thought? That lack of thought was the key to his anger. Throughout this painful process, they'd developed a respect for one another that she'd completely trashed in one split second.

He clenched his fists, then turned to his uncle. "Excuse

us for a minute, won't you?" Ryan stood, grasped Zoe's hand and pulled her into the kitchen.

The door swung shut behind them and he immediately turned, backing her toward the counter. He stared into the green eyes capable of bringing him to his knees.

He couldn't afford to lose focus now. "Care to tell me what that was all about back there?"

"What was what all about?" She braced her hands against the Formica and leaned back. Away from him.

"That nonsense about Sam. The cold way you're deliberately distancing yourself from me. When we need to help each other most."

She blinked. "Are you for real? You show up on my doorstep right after I had to break my parents' hearts, wearing your stuffy suit and bringing your equally stuffy uncle in what has to be a show of power and—"

Ryan didn't know what possessed him, but one minute she was hurling accusations that clearly told him how scared and hurt she really was, and the next minute all he could think about was kissing her. He watched those full, sensual lips moving and all he could hear was the blood pounding in his ears propelled by the desire coursing through his veins.

He'd missed her and now he had to taste her or go completely insane. He grabbed her forearms and pulled her close, then pressed his lips against hers. He was hard and demanded everything and she immediately responded, kissing him back, her mouth willing and open, all the pent-up passion and desire and need spilling forth.

He tangled his hands in her hair and angled her head so

he could get deeper access into the warm, wet recesses of her mouth. She trembled under his assault and he turned his head so he could trail moist kisses down her cheek and slender neck, inhaling her fragrant scent.

Zoe loved the taste and feel of him. Sensually he lit her on fire, and emotionally he filled the cold, scared places. The intensity between them grew stronger each time they laid eyes on one another. Not even distance or anger could remain between them for long.

His impulsive, take-charge kiss was obviously meant to be a resolution of sorts. She'd seen it with her parents too often to be wrong, and she reluctantly pulled out of his embrace.

"We can't do this." Shaking, she rubbed her hands up and down her arms. "Especially not now."

"Because?" He inclined his head, obviously confused.

She combed her fingers through her hair, trying to smooth the messy strands. "A kiss can't fix our problems. There's too much between us."

A muscle ticked in his jaw and she had to stifle the urge to stroke his skin. "It's a start."

"Sam ran away."

He reared back, her words obviously hitting him hard. "Dammit," he growled, his initial shock giving way to palpable anger.

He swung around and walked toward the kitchen sink. Bracing his hands on the counter, he glanced out the window overlooking the yard. "Because she found out the truth?"

"Yes. She came home unexpectedly and overheard us talking. She stormed off to her room. She was there at bed-time—I know because I checked on her—but this morning she was gone."

"What about that state-of-the-art alarm system your mother promised she'd use?"

Zoe touched his shoulder lightly when she really wanted to grab him and pound him for his innuendo.

He swiveled around to face her.

"Sam likes cool air when she sleeps so my mother by-passes her window so she can open it at night. Would you like to arrest her for making Sam more comfortable?" she asked, her sarcasm deliberately biting.

"I didn't mean it that way."

"The hell you didn't."

"I don't think your fighting is going to help find Samantha."

Zoe turned, shocked to see Ryan's uncle standing in the kitchen doorway. She wondered how much he'd witnessed, then decided she didn't care.

"He's right." Ryan threaded his fingers through his hair.

"My family's out looking for Sam." Zoe didn't want either of these men thinking her family wasn't worried about the teen, or worse, that they were neglectful in caring for her.

"I'm sure they are. Tell me, has anyone checked her room for clues to her whereabouts?" Uncle Russ asked.

Zoe narrowed her gaze. "Well, no. We immediately spread out to check places she's gone to before or might be likely to go to now." Zoe hated that this smug man thought of something her family, including Quinn, had missed. But he had a good point. "I'll go up to Sam's room now."

At that moment, the telephone rang and Zoe jumped to grab it, in case someone had found Sam. "Hello?"

"Hi, Zoe. It's Connor."

"Hey. Any news?" Since Connor had the emergency rooms on his list, she fervently hoped not.

"Not a thing."

Zoe let out a deep breath of air. Covering the phone, she glanced at Ryan. "She's not in any of the local hospitals," she reassured him.

"Thank God." He lowered himself into the nearest chair, looking too pale for her peace of mind.

"Would it help if I gave her room a cursory glance?" Uncle Russ asked.

Zoe waved him away. Let him do whatever he wanted as long as he stayed out of her way. "Connor, thank you for calling. Let me know if you hear from Quinn."

"Will do."

"Thanks." Zoe hung up the phone and strode over to where Ryan sat. "Are you okay?" She was hesitant to touch him in a way that offered support or comfort.

One minute they were adversaries, the next desperate lovers and after that uncertain allies, both concerned about Sam. Zoe wasn't certain what category they fell into right now.

"Did I ever tell you about the day Faith ran away?" Ryan asked, taking her by surprise.

Zoe shook her head. Until this moment, the parallels hadn't occurred to her. But Zoe understood now that Ryan was reliving a painful time in his life.

She pulled a chair up beside him and covered his hand with hers. "I'm listening." Not only because she relished details of his life, but because it gave her something to focus on while she manned the house.

"Faith was a typical older sister. She rarely wanted me around. That is, until the night before she left." His eyes clouded over and Zoe could tell he was remembering vividly.

"Ari and I were twins and sometimes we didn't want each other around," she said, laughing.

"That's what made that last night so strange. But I didn't know it at the time. She called me into her room and I hung out with her awhile. She paced around the room, talking quickly. I don't know if she was high at the time or completely lucid and just excited, knowing she planned to run away the next day."

He would never know, but Zoe wasn't about to say so aloud.

"The only thing I really remember was that she kept talking to me about staying true to myself. Being myself. Doing what I wanted with my life and not what was expected of me."

"She cared."

He swallowed hard, his eyes damp, visibly shaken by the memories. "It was probably the only time she showed it. The rest of my memories revolve around her fights with my parents, slamming doors to get away from them."

"Like mother like daughter." Zoe shook her head. "But it's typical teenage behavior. We expect it."

"My parents didn't." His fist clenched at his side. "Whoever told them to expect perfection from children had definitely steered them wrong," he muttered.

"What happened the morning Faith left?"

"I can answer that."

Zoe stiffened as Uncle Russ, a man she'd come to view as

an intruder, walked back into the room. She wanted time alone with Ryan and he'd taken that from her.

Zoe wondered what else Ryan's family would take away.

Chapter Eight

ZOE WAITED FOR RYAN'S UNCLE to speak. The muscles in the back of her neck hurt from nerves and stress and she rolled her head from side to side, trying to ease the tension.

"Faith liked to stir things up," Russ said at last. "She had obviously planned to run away because she knew I kept petty cash in my briefcase and she stole that money before she took off."

"From the business?" Zoe asked, surprised any teenager would take that kind of risk.

Russ shook his head. "She stole money from the home office, actually."

"Uncle Russ lives in a gatehouse on the property," Ryan explained. "He and my father have an office there. Wasn't that also during the days when there were mob-related truck hijackings?" Ryan asked his uncle. "I remember Dad talking about those days when J.T. was ready to come into the business."

His uncle nodded slowly. "Yes, yes. Those were chaotic times in every sense of the word," he said.

"And why is it you never tried to find Faith?" she asked, turning the subject back to what was important. She met the older man's gaze and waited for an answer.

He cleared his throat. "I beg to differ, young lady. I did

try to find my niece. Unfortunately her trail grew cold rather quickly."

Ryan rose from his seat. "Uncle Russ is my main ally and supporter. I've seen his paperwork and the detective I hired worked off of any trail he'd managed to find."

Zoe glanced at the older man. "Speaking of trails, did you find anything in her room?"

"Beyond all those candles, stuffed animals, magazines and books?" He shook his head laughing softly. "She's obviously been treated well."

"Here," Zoe reminded him. "She's been treated well here." She pointed to the floor of her home. "Before that it was the foster-care shuffle and nobody bought her a damn thing unless she absolutely needed it."

Ryan placed a calming hand on her arm. "Let's try to hold it together until she comes home, okay?"

Zoe nodded. Another half an hour passed during which she thought she'd go mad, mostly from the feeling that Ryan's uncle was watching her and her actions around his nephew. She hated being under a microscope and this man made studying and examining an art form.

Ryan and his uncle spoke in hushed tones in the corner of the family room, yet every so often she'd catch Ryan's compelling gaze on her and she'd heat up, knowing they still had unspoken feelings and desires between them.

Zoe was lying on the couch nearby with one arm covering her eyes when the phone finally rang. She jumped up and grabbed the receiver. "Hello?"

"Hello, this is Francesca at the spa. I think I have someone here you might be looking for," the woman said in a lowered voice.

Zoe swallowed hard, her relief so profound her legs began to shake. "How long has Sam been there?"

"I found her outside the entrance this morning and she followed me inside. She said she was wondering if I could fit her in for a manicure."

She'd been right next door the entire time? Good Lord.

Nobody had thought to check the spa because since they'd opened, Sam had never once shown an interest in beauty treatments of any kind. Manicures, pedicures and facials weren't her thing, she'd often said. Sam was more of a tomboy, so looking for her at the spa had never dawned on any of them who knew her well.

So much still didn't make sense. Even if Sam had changed her mind about more girlie things, why not just ask Elena for an appointment? Why sneak out the window for something so innocent? Especially the morning after she'd received devastating news.

Zoe shook her head. There was much more going on, of that Zoe was certain. "What happened next?" she asked Francesca.

"I told her I was booked for the early appointment, but if she didn't mind waiting an hour or so I could fit her in. She sat and watched me most of the morning. But just now, when I said I needed to check on Elena and see why she hadn't come in today, she freaked out. She begged me not to call and it was obvious something was going on. She thinks I'm in the ladies' room now."

"Keep her there for me. I'll be right over. And thank you so much for calling."

Zoe exhaled a huge breath of air.

"Well?" Ryan stood towering over her.

"She's at the spa and please don't ask why we didn't realize it before now. I don't have time to explain."

"Thank God," he muttered. "Thank God."

She wanted to hug him and join in his relief, but she had to stay focused on Sam. Zoe grabbed a pad and jotted down a bunch of cell-phone numbers. "Please call my parents, Quinn and Ari, and Connor, with the news." She handed the pad to Ryan.

"Sure thing."

"I'm going next door to get her. And Ryan?"

"Yes?" He gazed at her with those gorgeous brown eyes.

Zoe paused, knowing her next words would sound cruel. She truly wasn't looking to hurt Ryan; she just wanted to look out for Sam. "Could you...could you not be here when we get back? I promise to call you this afternoon. Just let me get Sam here and talk—"

"No."

Zoe blinked. "Excuse me?" She thought he'd be understanding. Reasonable.

"No, I won't disappear. We'll all deal with Sam together, your family and mine," he said, his gaze encompassing both Zoe and his uncle.

She could see from his clenched jaw that he wouldn't budge on this issue. Apparently, she didn't know Ryan as well as she'd thought.

IN THE SPA, ZOE FOUND Sam having a grand old time. She sat with her bare feet in a pedicure tub full of bubbling water.

Her nails had been freshly done. She had a mud pack spread across her face and she was currently applying the same salve to Ima Pig's skin. When she finished, she lifted the animal's hooves and held them under the dryer along with her own nails.

Zoe stepped closer. Sure enough, Ima's nails, or whatever they were called on a pig, had a bold red color that matched Sam's.

Zoe cleared her throat.

Sam glanced up, saw Zoe and jumped. Her nails hit the fans. She put Ima on the floor, then glanced at her hands and frowned. "You made me mess my manicure."

"I'm going to mess more than that. Do you realize that everyone in the family is out looking for you? Connor checked all the hospital emergency rooms. Mom and Dad and Ari and Quinn are driving all over creation, knocking on your friends' doors, and you're here having a pampering session!" Zoe yelled, not caring about disturbing other customers.

Sam glanced down, obviously duly chastised. Then without warning, she threw herself at Zoe, sobbing like crazy. "I'm sorry. I was going to run away. I was. And then when I got down the tree by my window, I saw that guy."

Zoe's nerves went on alert. "What guy?"

"The guy that was in my room the other day. He was lurking in the shadows by the house. Right beneath my window," she said, eyes wide.

Theatrics aside, Sam had obviously been spooked.

"Are you sure he was the same person?" Zoe asked, then shivered. Because if Sam was right, they'd been searching for

someone with a beef against her parents, but maybe someone wanted something from Sam.

"I'm sure. He had dark hair like the guy who was in the
kitchen that morning, ugly face with big teeth and everything. I got scared and I hid behind the tree. Even if I wanted
to go back, I couldn't. I'm good, but not even I could climb
back up that tree as easily as I got down. And I didn't want
him to see me and end up following me. I could end up like
someone on those *Without a Trace* or *CSI* shows, you know?"

"Heaven forbid!" Zoe said.

"Well there was no place for me to go even if I changed
my mind. The alarm was set and I'd forgotten my key, and
I couldn't just ring the doorbell and tell you all I was going
to run away again, so I just hid, praying that man wouldn't
see me," she said, her voice rising.

"Slow down, okay?"

"Okay." Sam sniffed and drew a deep breath. "When I
looked out from around the tree again, I didn't see him
there. So I started to walk, sticking close to the house, and
then I saw Francesca opening up the spa and I thought,
safety in numbers."

"So you told her you wanted a manicure."

Sam nodded. "Besides I didn't want to leave you guys. I
really didn't. So I thought I'd hang out with Francesca and
maybe by the time Elena came to work, I'd have figured out
some story and wouldn't get in any trouble."

Zoe rolled her eyes. "Trouble is your middle name, missy.
Go wash the mud pack off your face. By then let's hope
everyone will be back and we can deal with all this." She
prodded Sam's back.

"I'm going," she muttered. She picked up Ima and they started for the bathroom. Five minutes later, Sam and Ima returned, all cleaned up.

Zoe ushered them to the door, pausing at the front desk where Francesca sat. "Don't you have something to say?" Zoe asked Sam.

"Thanks for this morning," Sam said. "And I'm sorry that I lied."

Francesca smiled. "You're a good girl, Samantha. You take care of yourself and that piglet."

"I will."

They traipsed back to the house, Sam dragging her feet as they walked. "You called everyone and told them I'm okay?" she asked in a low voice.

Oh boy, Zoe thought. Now came the fun part. "I didn't call. I came right over to get you. Ryan made the calls for me."

As Zoe had expected, Sam dug in her heels. "If he's there, I'm not going back."

"Something tells me you're in no position to be making demands right now. Besides, you can't hate Ryan just because he's related to you."

"Well where has he been up until now?" Sam pouted like a little girl, but in her eyes Zoe saw the ache deep in her heart.

"I'm sure he can answer that better than I can." Zoe met Sam's gaze. "But my understanding is that when your mom ran away, he was young, about your age. And by the time he was able to start looking, she'd managed to make herself hard to find. He just found out his sister had a child and he came to find you right away." Again, she found herself defending Ryan at the expense of her own interests.

"So maybe he can come visit once a year at Christmas," Sam muttered.

Out of the mouths of babes, Zoe thought and she couldn't help but laugh dryly.

WHILE ZOE HAD GONE to pick up Sam from the spa, Ryan had talked his uncle into taking his car and making himself scarce. Ryan would have liked him to stay, but the family didn't need an unfamiliar face and more important, neither did Sam.

When she'd returned, he'd waited while Sam had had her reunion with everyone and then sat through the Costases' lectures about running away and letting everyone worry about her. Then Sam had gone to her room while the family had excused themselves to meet alone in the kitchen.

Now Ryan sat with them in the den. Actually, he sat apart from them, as nobody wanted to get within inches of him. They stood united on one side of the room protectively huddled around Sam who'd stomped down from her room. All except Zoe eyed him with distrust and Ryan shifted uncomfortably in his chair.

"We found footprints near the tree where Sam said she saw the intruder," Quinn said.

"I told you!" Sam raised a victory hand in the air.

Zoe sighed, grabbed Sam's wrist and pulled her arm back down. "Go on," she said to Quinn.

"We have nothing specific to tell us that this person is targeting Sam, but it's the only conclusion since he was in her room the first time and beneath her window this morning. Add to that she's seen his face and can identify him. If you ask me, Sam's definitely at risk."

Each family member murmured in agreement, and then Quinn continued. "We talked in the kitchen and we agree that Sam needs to get out of here for a while."

Ryan hadn't been included in the family discussion, but he remained silent as he listened to their concerns.

Elena rose from her seat. "I'll take her to Greece." She nodded and folded her arms in front of her, the long flowing sleeves of her outfit hitting Nicholas in the face as she moved.

Ryan stiffened at the suggestion, but before he could react, Quinn shook his head. "Nothing that drastic is necessary and it wouldn't work, anyway. First, you won't get Social Services to approve the trip and second, you can't run away from the other problem." With that pronouncement, his dark gaze settled on Ryan.

He took that as his cue. Rising from his seat, Ryan faced the family. Their angry stares and hurt gazes weren't easy for him to bear. Zoe and her feelings would be even more of a challenge, but he would have to deal with them later.

"I apologize for lying to you all. The first time was a misunderstanding and after that...well all I can say is that it seemed like the right thing to do." He was careful not to lay blame at Zoe's feet since he'd started the charade and had chosen to let it continue. "I wanted you to know and like me before I gave you the news about who I was."

Zoe shot him a quick smile of gratitude and, dare he hope, respect? But in the silence that followed, Ryan couldn't begin to judge the rest of the family's true feelings or reaction to his confession.

"What is it you want from us?" Nicholas asked, his hands firmly on Sam's shoulders.

Ryan wasn't ready to answer that and start a war, not when they had so much to deal with, beginning with the break-in and, most important, Sam's welfare. "I want time to get to know Sam and for her to know me. I'm willing to start with that."

"I already know all I need to about—"

Zoe slapped a hand across Sam's mouth before she could insult him and it was his turn to shoot her a grateful look.

"Wanting to get to know each other sounds reasonable enough," Zoe said.

"I agree," Quinn said, seeming to be the spokesperson for Zoe's parents. "What's your situation in Boston?"

Ryan let out a laugh. "Something tells me you can answer that as well or better than I can. I'm sure you've dug deep into my history."

Quinn inclined his head. "True. So let's cut to the chase. After your sister ran away, your parents didn't go out looking for her. They were glad to be rid of the problem, weren't they?"

Ryan's stomach cramped at the harsh reminder. "It's more complicated than that, but they didn't do much more than report her disappearance and let the police handle things. By the time Faith ran away, they'd lost their ability to handle her and didn't know what more they could do to bring her in line."

"Children have wills and minds of their own," Ari, the psych professor, chimed in.

"And my parents failed to respect that. Why are we even discussing this?" The last thing Ryan wanted was to showcase his family's shortcomings when Sam was in the room, and when it would do nothing to strengthen his claim to having her in his life.

"Because Sam needs to get out of New Jersey until we figure out who wants something from her and why. And though you've been careful not to say it, obviously you're contemplating asking for custody of Sam and bringing her home to Boston with you." Quinn stepped between Ryan and the group across the room, obviously sensing they'd take issue with his words.

"The hell I'll go—" Zoe again shut Sam up with a hand across her mouth.

"I think we can accomplish dual goals if Sam takes a short trip with you. I just want to make sure that the atmosphere there isn't hostile, that your parents won't make her feel unwelcome or traumatize her in any way."

Ryan was still reeling from Quinn's words. They were letting him take Sam to Boston without him having to ask? He glanced down and realized his hands were shaking.

"She's perfectly safe with me."

Nicholas eyed him warily, but obviously had agreed to defer to Quinn.

Quinn nodded. "Okay, then. You should know that Elena and Nicholas have agreed to let Social Services know about you and your relationship to Sam. But they aren't giving up their rights as foster parents or their adoption desires. Not yet. We'll have to fully discuss everything over time. But for now, you have the right to get to know your niece and, for her safety, she needs to get out of town."

Ryan stepped forward, gratitude welling in his throat, almost choking him. They could have fought him. They could have engaged him in a prolonged fight for Sam. Hell, they still could.

But for now the Costas family was obviously willing to make him a part of Sam's life and have him help them in protecting his niece. "I don't know what to say. I'll take good care of her."

"Damn right, you will," Nicholas said. "And Zoe will go along to make sure you and your family don't misbehave."

"Or stifle Sam's individuality," Elena added.

Ryan opened his mouth, then shut it again, the shock of it all making him mute. Sam *and* Zoe were going home with him?

Obviously this had been the focus of their discussion in the kitchen earlier. Just as obviously she'd agreed.

He glanced at Zoe, meeting her gaze. Her cheeks were flushed pink, but she didn't say a word nor could he decipher from her expression how she felt about this turn of events. But no matter how Zoe viewed things, Ryan felt as if he'd been given a second chance with her and with Sam.

And this time they'd be on his turf. Though normally advantage went to the home team, the old adage didn't apply here and Ryan knew he'd have to work extra hard to win Sam over. And not to lose Zoe at the same time.

ZOE SHIFTED in the passenger seat of Ryan's car. With every breath she took, she inhaled his cologne and her insides cramped with a burning need she couldn't suppress no matter how much practicality dictated she ought to.

She still didn't know how she'd ended up accompanying Sam to Boston with Ryan. She'd fought the good fight with her parents and Quinn, but even she'd agreed Sam needed to get out of town. And everyone including Zoe felt that Sam couldn't go alone with Ryan.

For his part, Ryan had been understanding of Sam's feelings. He'd even shocked Zoe by convincing his uncle that meeting Sam right now would be too traumatic. So after staying one night with Ryan, Russ had gone home and neither Zoe nor her family had had to deal with him just yet.

Just when she thought she'd pegged Ryan, a conservative man with whom she had nothing in common, he went and did something that put him back into high esteem, leaving her confused about her feelings. She shook her head, knowing she'd lied. She wasn't confused. She desired Ryan Baldwin. She liked the man a whole lot. Unless he morphed into the uptight man she'd first met. *Then* he scared her. And now they were heading to his territory, a place where she had no bearings and where she feared he'd definitely become a man she couldn't understand.

For now she sat in the middle of a mini war zone with Sam having entrenched herself in the back, determined not to like Ryan. She'd wanted to bring Ima and though Zoe had agreed, she'd had a gut feeling Ryan would not. So she'd instructed Sam to put Ima in the dog tote they'd bought for her until she became too big to be a lap pet, and Zoe had placed the covered bag in the back with Sam when Ryan wasn't looking. Sam had already learned how to keep the pig happy and relatively quiet and each bathroom trip Sam made, she took Ima with her so the pig could relieve herself somewhere besides the car or the carrier.

Unfortunately, taking along Ima hadn't appeased Sam. She'd spent their first hour on the road sulking in the back seat. Ryan had long since stopped trying to make conversation with her and after a short talk about the Red Sox and

Yankees, in which Zoe discovered that being a Mets fan made her rise further in Ryan's estimation, they'd reverted to a silence that included Sam's prolonged sighs and groans.

For her part, Zoe tried not to stare at Ryan's handsome profile or reach out and touch his hand to reassure him that in time he *would* win Sam over.

"I have to pee," Sam said from behind them.

Ryan glanced in the rearview mirror. "I just stopped for you not fifteen minutes ago."

"Yeah, well, I have to pee again."

Zoe shook her head. Between Sam's language and rest stop commands, she was sorely testing Ryan's patience. Not even Ima, who'd already begun to train, needed to relieve herself that often.

"I'll make you a deal. You watch your mouth, especially when we hit Boston, and I'll stop as many times as you need without complaining." Despite his dark sunglasses, Zoe could tell he was watching in the mirror for a reaction from the teen.

Zoe turned toward the back seat in time to see Sam shrug, but she didn't volunteer a yes or no answer.

Although Zoe agreed that Sam needed to refine her choice of words, she couldn't help but fear that Ryan's demand had more ominous undertones, ones that had roots in his late sister's behavior and the reasons she'd run away from home. Zoe didn't want to see Ryan, the relaxed man she'd come to enjoy in New Jersey, revert to the stuffier man she'd first met. The one she'd seen again when his uncle had arrived.

"I'm waiting for an answer," Ryan said.

Zoe shivered and pushed up the air-conditioning vents so they pointed away from her, but the chill remained.

"I don't see that I have a choice but to follow your rules unless I want a flood back here," Sam muttered.

A muscle twitched in Ryan's cheek. "You just reminded me of my next condition. No more soda until we get there."

Sam started to stick out her tongue, then obviously thought better of it and whipped her head around to the side, glancing out the window. "Whatever you say, oh great one," Sam muttered.

Ryan raised an eyebrow Zoe's way. "Is she always this pleasant?"

Zoe couldn't help but stifle a chuckle. "I have to say she reserves her best behavior for you."

"I feel so privileged." Ryan grinned and they shared their first easy laugh of the day.

True to his word, he pulled off at the next rest stop and drove up to the entrance of a small mini-mart with bath-rooms around the side.

Sam yanked on the handle, obviously intent on storming out of the car.

"Come right back," he called after her.

She saluted and marched out of the car, slamming the door behind her.

Zoe rolled her eyes and leaned back in her seat. "I hope you don't think you've won this round."

"What does that mean?"

"Just that I expect Sam will stop ordering you to pull over now that you promised her that her demand for pit stops won't bother you."

He lowered his sunglasses. "And wasn't that the point?" he asked with all the confusion of a man unfamiliar with children.

His puzzled expression was endearing, showing her yet another side of this multifaceted man. She shook her head and laughed. "Ryan, you have a lot to learn when it comes to teens. I mean, just don't think she's letting up because you put one over on her or because she's found some sort of respect for you. You just took the fun out of her game. She'll find another way to torture you instead."

He turned in his seat. "Well I'll call it a draw, then."

She inclined her head, giving him this one. Heaven knew Sam would find enough ways to challenge him in the days ahead. But without the frequent pit stops now, Zoe knew they might not have another chance to talk alone.

"Ryan, something you just said bothers me," she stated bluntly. She bent one knee beneath her, accidentally brushing her leg against his thigh. She sucked in a deep breath and tried to focus.

He whipped off his eyeglasses, placing them in the empty cup holder, and his deep gaze bored into hers—so warm, so darn sexy, she thought she'd melt right then and there. She flipped the vents again so the cool air blew directly onto her skin.

"What's wrong?" he asked, sounding as if he truly cared.

She badly wanted to believe that he did. "We already talked about you not trying to mold Sam into some perfect child your family will accept."

He opened his mouth to speak, but she held up a hand, forestalling him. "I'm not suggesting her current language is appropriate or even acceptable. She needs discipline and I agree with how you're handling her."

"Thank you for that." He tipped his head to one side. "Then I don't see what the problem is."

She sighed. How to explain and not insult him at the same time? "The problem is you need to accept her for the free spirit she is. So does your family. Otherwise not only will they have learned nothing from your sister's running away and subsequent death, but you'll end up running Sam off, too."

Despite Sam's frequent over-the-top behavior, Zoe had seen firsthand the fun and joy he experienced watching her just be herself. That was the man Zoe enjoyed, too, and she didn't want to lose him when they reached Boston.

Her fingers twitched with the desire to reach out to him, her emotions warring with her mind. Her emotions won. She placed a hand over his warmer, more roughened one. "Am I making any sense to you?"

Ryan nodded. Her soft fingers wrapped around his hand and the heat shot straight through to his heart. This woman affected him. She made him want to please her in ways he'd never thought or cared about with any woman who'd come before. For that reason he was listening to her concerns and honestly trying to keep an open mind. But the truth was that coming home would mean a reversion of sorts and that included a stricter code of behavior. Especially if he was going to convince his parents to accept Sam, as they hadn't accepted their own daughter.

Ryan had never faced a greater challenge. Except for keeping Zoe happy. He had no idea how he'd accomplish both goals.

"I'll try to be more understanding," he promised, not just for Sam's sake, but for his and Zoe's. The key to any kind of future with this woman lay in her believing in him.

She nodded. "That's all I can ask for."

Her hand still lay on top of his, and as gestures went, he knew it was a big one.

They waited five minutes more, but there was no sign of Sam. "Want to go in after her?" he asked.

"I guess I'd better." Zoe reached for her seat belt buckle when a piercing scream shattered the silence.

Both Ryan and Zoe darted out of the car.

He ran to the end of the small building in time to see Sam running and shrieking.

"Come back!" she yelled and began to run toward the patch of grass on the boulevard.

In that instant, Ryan somehow knew exactly what was going on and he sprinted past Sam, determined to stop the wandering pig. Unfortunately Ima had other ideas and the little runt continued to bolt toward the grass. The highway lay just beyond.

He managed to step on the leash, which gave him a chance to reach for the pig, but she was more than an arm's length away. He stumbled and she scooted ahead, giving him no choice but to dive into the grass and grab her leash just in time.

He rose to his feet, trembling pig in hand, to find Sam and Zoe staring at him with wide, frightened eyes.

"Your stowaway, I presume?" He held Ima out for Sam.

She grabbed her pet, first wrapping her hand around and around the leash so the animal couldn't run away again. "You saved her from becoming roadkill," Sam said, obviously grateful he'd shown up when he had.

Zoe cleared her throat loudly.

"Thank you," Sam added.

"You're welcome." He met her gaze and for a brief moment, all her teenage anger and resentment disappeared.

Only gratitude and pleasure shone in her blue eyes and Ryan warmed, happy to be the recipient of something other than her disgust.

"What happened?" Zoe asked.

Sam shrugged. "It was so fast, I'm not sure. I used the bathroom and then I took Ima out so she could do the same thing. Somehow the leash slipped out of my hands and she bolted. I was so scared when she started running for the highway." She shivered. "I didn't want some car makin' bacon out of her."

Ryan shook his head and tried not to laugh at her description. "You should have told me you wanted to bring her along. Then you wouldn't have had to sneak her out for walks behind my back."

"We were afraid you'd say no," Sam said.

"*We* were afraid?" He glanced Zoe's way.

She clasped her hands behind her back and began whistling, deliberately not meeting his gaze.

She definitely wasn't innocent. "You didn't have much faith in me, did you?" he asked her.

She looked away. "I guess not."

The admission hit him in the gut and hurt more than it should have. He wasn't sure what disappointed him more, her lack of trust or himself and what he'd done to bring it on.

In silence, the three of them walked back to the car. Before getting in he paused to brush the dirt off his arms and khaki slacks, figuring he resembled a major-league ball player after a long skid home.

Unable to help himself, he glanced up at the sky and laughed.

SINCE RYAN WOULDN'T HEAR of Sam staying in a hotel and Sam wouldn't remain at Ryan's without Zoe, Zoe found herself unpacking clothing in one of the two extra rooms in Ryan's townhome in downtown Boston.

The condo was an old brownstone duplex apartment that had been renovated inside with gorgeous crown moldings and auburn-colored wood floors. Although the apartment had obviously been decorated by a professional, Zoe couldn't fault Ryan for going to excesses. Every piece in the apartment served a purpose or looked as if it belonged.

For warmth and personal touches, on the shelves she'd passed in the living room he'd placed photographs—Ryan and a couple that had to be his parents, Ryan and his uncle, whom Zoe hoped to avoid on this trip because he made her uncomfortable, and a photo of his sister, Faith, at Sam's age. Forever young because of her untimely death.

Zoe liked Ryan's home, and the fact that it lacked the up-tight, artificial feeling she'd feared she'd find here, gave her hope. Hope that Ryan had more of the man she liked inside him.

It had been a day of contrasts, she thought. Her mind strayed back to the incident at the rest stop with the pig. He'd thought nothing of his own safety or his good clothing, as he'd dived into the dirt to save Ima because he knew how much the animal meant to Sam. And because he knew his life wouldn't be worth squat if Sam lost her pet.

His expression when he'd handed the pig back to Sam had been priceless, a man so proud of his accomplishment—until he'd realized even Zoe hadn't trusted him enough to ask permission to take Ima along. The hurt and desolation in his gaze stayed with her even now.

But then there was the moment at the car when he'd brushed off his filthy pants and arms. He'd been dirty, disheveled and sexy. A man comfortable in his own skin. And when he'd laughed—oh, when he'd looked up and flashed those dimples—Zoe could have sworn the sun shone more brightly in the sky. She'd felt the heat and happiness and wished it could always be that way between them.

"I'm unpacked!" Sam bounced into the room and onto the bed.

"Someone's in a good mood."

"Yeah well you-know-who said Ima could stay with me in my room."

"No kidding? Well make sure you keep her in her crate so she doesn't mess the floors," Zoe warned.

"Yeah, yeah. So how long do we have to stay here before we can go back home?" Sam asked.

Zoe shivered, not wanting to admit to Sam that for all they knew, *this* would be her home.

Chapter Nine

TO ZOE'S SURPRISE, they spent the next few days having a lot
of fun. Ryan took them to Faneuil Hall, on the Duck Tour,
and they hit many historical landmarks. They had dinner
at Legal Seafoods one night and at Union Oyster Bar the
next, and Davio's, an Italian restaurant in the North End on
the third evening.

Now they found themselves at Ryan's office where he
proudly showed off the brownstone where he and his partners worked. He'd wanted Sam to meet his associates and
the rest of the staff, and perhaps because she was still ex-
periencing twinges of gratitude over his saving Ima, Sam
went without argument. For Zoe, it was a chance to see Ryan
in his own environment without his family pulling at him
and without hers changing him.

Zoe waited until Sam headed off to get something to eat
with Ryan's secretary before she inclined her head toward
his office, indicating she wanted to talk to him alone.

He gestured for her to go on in and he followed, shutting
the door behind them. "Like it?" he asked.

She glanced around at the typical attorney's surroundings,
dark wood desk, bookshelves, diplomas and a row of windows with a view of the cloudless blue sky. Clearly, Ryan did
well for himself and he cared about what she thought.

"It's perfect," she said, stepping toward the plate-glass windows.

"Meaning?"

She sensed him come up behind her, his body heat warmer than that of the sun shining through the glass. Ignoring her awareness of him in his apartment was getting more and more difficult, especially since her bedroom shared a wall with his. She knew when he woke up and when he went to sleep—and when he tossed and turned as fitfully as she.

She turned now to find him closer than she'd realized and she stepped back toward the window. He came forward.

Zoe sucked in a breath and exhaled slowly. "We need to talk," she told him.

"We damn well do." He reached up and loosened his tie.

The effect of him looking so relaxed and slightly rumpled in his power suit was devastating to her senses. Her knees shook as though she was a schoolgirl on her first date.

"I need to hold you or I'm going to go insane." His deep gaze burned into hers. "I have to taste you." His hands came to rest on the window above her shoulders, as he dipped his head closer. His determined expression told her he wasn't about to be deterred.

She trembled, wanting the same things. "That's not what I wanted to talk about," she managed to say, despite being breathless with anticipation.

He lowered his head, his forehead touching hers. "What is it?" He sounded resigned to listening first and kissing second.

Disappointment filled her nonpractical side, while her rational side applauded her self-restraint. "This is our fourth day here and you haven't mentioned taking Sam to see your family at all."

She voiced the concern that enveloped her constantly. How would his relatives treat the teenager who was just coming to trust Ryan a little bit more each day?

Zoe refused to factor her own feelings into meeting his family, telling herself that what they thought of her didn't matter. Yet she couldn't deny that if and when they were introduced, she wanted smoother sailing than she'd had with Uncle Russ. The thought of his parents judging and finding her lacking turned her stomach, because despite everything, she cared how it might affect what Ryan thought of her.

"We're going to my parents' house for dinner tonight," he said, finally.

"Let me guess. You were going to spring it on us at the last minute." She tried for a teasing tone, but Ryan had tensed up and he wasn't relaxing or laughing at her joke.

"Do you blame me?" he asked instead. "Sam doesn't need another excuse to run away and as for you—"

"Afraid I'll embarrass you in front of your parents?" Again she tried for a laugh, but she also averted her gaze, not wanting him to see how serious her question actually was.

Ryan knew Zoe well enough by now to get when she was feeling vulnerable and, despite the jokes, the idea of meeting his family obviously scared her. Hell, there were times his parents scared him, too.

He placed his hand beneath her chin and lifted her gaze. "They will adore you," he said, knowing in his heart every word was a lie.

They'd find her short skirts and high heels as offensive as they'd found his sister's tube tops and ripped denim shorts way back when. Hell, Uncle Russ had already expressed his shock after meeting Zoe and catching the obvious undercurrents between them. Though Russ was a ladies' man and he dated all types, it didn't matter since he was determined never to settle down.

But Ryan was different. His uncle knew that Ryan wanted to have the kind of family he'd lacked growing up. Unfortunately, for all that Uncle Russ supported Ryan, he also had enough of the Baldwin genes to want Ryan to find the proper wife to carry on the Baldwin name. "Proper" meaning correct bloodlines, manners and breeding.

"Ryan?" Zoe's voice startled him. "Where'd you go?" she asked of the mental break he'd just taken.

He met her wide-eyed gaze and refused to acknowledge aloud that Zoe Costas and her con-artist, day-spa, pig-owning family didn't fit with the Baldwin family lineage—something Ryan hadn't wanted to think about or deal with during his time in New Jersey. He'd blocked out everything he could about home and focused on nothing but getting to know Sam. And his growing feelings for Zoe.

"I was just thinking about this." He leaned forward and captured her lips in a kiss. A hot, devouring kiss filled with all the desire that had kept him awake nights and the yearning he experienced each time he looked at her.

Apparently she felt the same way and missed him just as much because she wound her arms around his neck, pulled him close, and thrust her tongue inside his mouth in a clear act of desire and possession.

He groaned and pulled her tightly against him, his groin thrusting against the barrier of his pants, eager to escape confinement and sink deep inside her moist heat. It'd been too damn long, he thought. Her hips swayed from side to side, seeking more intimate contact, and he was happy to oblige. He widened his stance and let his aching member settle between her legs so they could grind against each other, mimicking the act of making love as best they could.

Only the window seemed to support them now. Zoe's breath came faster and she breathed hot and heavy in his ear. He couldn't remember any woman who made him want so much. Need so much. And wish to give back as generously as she gave to him. In the back of his mind, he understood that more than his body was engaged with Zoe and he'd have to deal with that soon.

But first he'd handle the woman writhing against him, almost ready to come apart in his arms. He was damn close himself and every ounce of self-control went into keeping himself in check while bringing her closer and closer to what he hoped would be a mind-blowing orgasm.

He'd already caught her rhythm with his hips and pelvis and it wasn't long before he thrust upward one last time and she shook, groaned and came, calling out his name.

Only when she finally caught her breath did he step back. He took in her flushed cheeks and the way she attempted to straighten her clothing and grinned.

"I'm sure this isn't appropriate behavior for a partner," she said wryly.

He raised an eyebrow. "Who knows? There is a reason we

partners have private bathrooms in our offices, you know." He pointed to the door in the back corner of the room.

She blushed and in a very un-Zoelike way, ran to the restroom to pull herself together. Still, she had a point. He'd never brought a woman he was seeing to his office, let alone made one come behind the closed door.

Shaking his head at how different he was around Zoe, he adjusted himself, and while he waited for his most obvious reaction to Zoe to subside, he seated himself behind his desk.

Zoe stepped out of the bathroom at the same time Sam came barging into the office, barreling through like a tornado.

"Shouldn't you knock before you just run into Ryan's office?" Zoe asked. "What if he'd been having an important phone call?"

Zoe's gaze never met his, but he noticed her non-Mediterranean blush remained.

"Yeah, well this is important." Sam paused at the foot of his desk, obviously unnerved and out of breath.

"What's wrong?"

"I'm being followed," Sam said.

Ryan sat up quickly in his seat while Zoe grabbed for Sam's hand. "What do you mean?"

He had no doubt they were both thinking about the two incidents in New Jersey. Could this be a third?

"The child has an active imagination, Mr. Baldwin," Ryan's secretary, Nadine, an attractive brunette, said from where she stood in the doorway. "We went to Burger King and she kept looking over her shoulder, sure someone was behind us."

"But you didn't see anyone?" Ryan asked.

"Not till I went to the bathroom," Sam said. "When I came out, he was standing outside the men's room right opposite me."

Nadine's mouth dropped open. "I had no idea."

"Did he touch you? Try to grab you?" Zoe asked.

Sam shook her head. "He didn't have the chance. A woman was walking out with her kids and I latched on to the little one's hand and pretended I was with them. Then as soon as we were out of the hallway, I ran to the table."

"I didn't know. She just said she wanted to leave and only mentioned being followed in a general sense." Nadine glanced down. "I let her go alone," she admitted. "Sam said it would be okay. I don't have kids. I didn't realize."

Ryan nodded. "It's okay, Nadine." Hell, he didn't know how to handle a teenager yet, either. Both he and Zoe had let her go to the rest stop bathroom alone. "Don't worry about a thing," he told the other woman. "Go relax and I'll take it from here."

She nodded. "Thank you." She left them alone and shut the door behind her.

"What's going on?" Zoe asked. "Was it the same man who broke into the house back home?"

Sam nodded. "I think so. He had the same dark hair and his face was familiar. It can't be my imagination," she insisted. "And the whole time we were walking down the street, it felt like someone was watching me."

Ryan exhaled a sharp breath. "You were scared, I bet."

"Which is completely understandable considering all you've been through lately," Zoe added, exchanging a worried glance with him.

"We'll call Quinn and see how the investigation's progressing. In the meantime, how about we go back home for a while before dinner?" he asked, changing the subject.

Sam nodded. "Good idea. What's on the menu tonight? I was thinking maybe Chinese food."

"Actually..." Ryan began, then glanced at Zoe for help. After today's incident, he was sure Sam was even more fragile, although she'd never show it. After all the progress he'd made with her over the last few days, his next announcement could bring back the Arctic chill.

"I asked Ryan if we could meet his family tonight," Zoe said, unexpectedly taking the heat off him.

Sam narrowed her gaze. "How could you do something like that? I don't want to meet his stinking parents!"

"Samantha!" Zoe said, clearly appalled.

"Well I don't. They hated my mother. I remember her telling me we only had each other because they didn't want her around. So why would you want to go there?" Her voice rose with all the anger and fear of a child who'd lost the mother she loved.

By meeting two people who might paint a negative picture of her mother, Sam obviously feared those good memories being erased and her mother being taken from her again in a different way than before.

Ryan stood and walked out from behind the desk. As grateful as he was that Zoe would put herself in Sam's line of fire to protect him, he couldn't let her shoulder this burden.

"Zoe isn't the one who asked for this dinner. I did. It's time you meet your family."

Sam rolled her eyes. "Don't go defending her. She probably figures that she can dump me in that big old mausoleum I saw pictures of and go back home without me."

The tears in Sam's eyes and quiver in her voice excused anything she said to him, Ryan thought. Still Zoe deserved better. "Zoe and her family took you in when you had no one. They've treated you like you were one of them."

Sam sniffed and turned away so she could wipe her arm across her face. "So?"

"So she deserves an apology now."

Sam hiccupped and then she ran straight into Zoe's arms, shaking and sobbing, her muffled words tearing his heart in two. "I love *you*. I want to be with you and Elena and Nicholas and Ari and…" She rhymed off the names of the Costas clan while Zoe stroked her long hair hanging down her back.

"I love you, too," she said to Sam. But her eyes were on Ryan, both of them painfully aware that Zoe couldn't offer Sam the reassurance she wanted most. She couldn't promise that Sam could go back to the house she called home. Not as long as Ryan was in the picture, wanting something from this child, too.

They talked in hushed tones. Zoe handed Sam a tissue and helped her pat her cheeks and dry her tears, which had quickly turned embarrassing to the teenager.

Watching Zoe comfort Sam, Ryan's chest squeezed tight and he had trouble catching his breath. The realization hit him out of the blue. Not only was he fascinated with this woman, but he was falling for her, too. Enough that he needed time to learn even more about the raven-haired woman whose life he had turned upside down.

ZOE CLOSED HERSELF in her guest room at Ryan's and called Quinn as soon as they returned home. He cursed and muttered a few choice words about his own stupidity for not considering the possibility that whoever seemed to be after Sam would follow them to Boston. Until now, the notion that the guy was after Sam had been pure conjecture. He could have been after something in the house. Now it seemed clear he was specifically after Sam. Unless of course, he was looking to scare or punish the family and was using Sam to accomplish his goal. Until they caught the guy, they were in the dark as to his motives or what he actually wanted.

Zoe shivered. Quinn promised to call a friend of his to arrange covert protection for Sam while they were in town.

In the afternoon, she and Sam watched television, relaxing together and avoiding the topic of what had occurred earlier in the day.

Later that evening, they dressed and headed to Ryan's parents' home where Zoe and Sam suffered through stiff hellos and predinner drinks. She took in the mausoleum in which he'd grown up and realized the difference between her parents' small Jersey Shore home and this mansion couldn't be more extreme. Small versus big. Warm versus cold. She shuddered, grateful they'd finally ended up in the dining room for dinner because it meant the evening was progressing, however slowly.

Sam had been quiet during the introductions and Zoe had stayed by her side, offering silent security. Now she discovered that dinner at the Baldwins' was a formal affair, complete with too many plates, forks, knives and spoons for Zoe to handle, never mind a young girl like Sam. Zoe wondered if the place settings were so intricate on purpose, to test Zoe's breeding and Sam's place within this family. She chided herself for thinking the worst and plastered a smile on her face for Sam's sake.

"Zoe's an unusual name," Vivian, Ryan's mother said.

Zoe waited for the help to serve their salads before replying. "It's Greek," she explained.

"Her sister's name is Ariana," Uncle Russ said, surprising Zoe.

That he remembered her sister's name was a shock. A sign that he'd been interested enough to take note of it.

"That's right," she said, forcing a smile. For Ryan's sake she wanted to give the man a chance.

"Which fork do I use?" Sam whispered.

In reply, Zoe picked up her outside utensil on the left and Sam followed suit.

"I guess your family doesn't dine together often?" his mother continued.

"We eat as a family every night," Sam chimed in. "Elena makes the best mousse cocka in the world."

"Heavens!" Ryan's grandmother, who sat at the head of the table, turned pale beneath her heavily caked foundation.

Ryan coughed and Zoe tried not to laugh. "She means moussaka," Zoe said. "If you saw the movie *My Big Fat Greek Wedding*, you'd understand the joke."

"Well I'd prefer we don't speak that way at the table." Ryan's mother shot Sam a stern glare.

"Sam's got a great sense of humor. Don't you, Sam?" Ryan defended his niece for the umpteenth time tonight, regardless of her outrageous words or shocking behavior, Zoe thought approvingly.

Unfortunately, each time he sided with Sam against his family, Zoe fell a little harder for the man.

Sam grinned. "I sure do. Bet I can tell you where you got them shoes," she said, falling back on the old boardwalk joke.

Everyone around the table looked at one another with blank expressions, except for Ryan's grandmother who frowned and mumbled something about the child's deplorable grammar.

"I give up," Uncle Russ said.

Zoe sensed he sought to make Sam more comfortable and she silently applauded his attempt.

"Where'd I get my shoes?" Russ prodded Sam.

"You got 'em on your feet!" Sam laughed and slammed her hand on the table for emphasis, knocking over Zoe's glass of red wine by mistake.

Zoe jumped up to avoid being soaked by the liquid, but the white tailored blouse she wore had already taken the worst of the spill.

"Oh jeez!" Sam grabbed for her napkin and helping Zoe, they began to blot the mess.

Suddenly Ryan's grandmother yelled at them both. "Stop!"

They paused.

"Those napkins were stitched by my mother and aren't meant to be used as dishrags."

"But they're napkins," Sam said. She looked at Ryan, who also stood. He surveyed the table and the situation, his cheeks turning a ruddy color.

"Then pardon me, ma'am, but why put them on a table where there's food, drink, and their designated use is for cleaning?" Zoe asked with the same mock sweetness she'd been treated to all evening.

"Clearly we're going to have to teach the young lady table manners if she's going to fit in." Ryan's mother picked up a bell Zoe hadn't noticed before and rang for the help to clean up.

Zoe clenched her jaw. "I wonder what good table manners will do her in a house when all other form of manners are missing."

Ryan placed a hand on her shoulder. "Relax," he said softly.

She couldn't begin to know how after all she'd endured.

"I'll handle this," he promised both with his words and his touch.

"Ryan, there's no need to handle anything. I understand Samantha hasn't been raised in the best of homes, so rest assured we'll cut her some slack," his mother said.

Zoe's temper flared. "How dare you insult my family and my home—"

Ryan's easy touch turned harsher, cutting her off. "This was a mistake." He strode over to Sam and Zoe. "I wanted you to meet each other," he said, facing the table. "You've done that. Now we're leaving."

His dark eyes flashed angry sparks. He was obviously pained with emotions Zoe had never seen in him before.

Without realizing her intent, she reached up and covered his hand with her own, offering him the only support she could.

As they turned to leave, Uncle Russ spoke. "Wait. This situation has been difficult on all of us, can we at least agree on that?"

"He's got a point," Ryan's father said.

The older women, Ryan's mother and grandmother, nodded their agreement.

"Zoe?" Uncle Russ asked.

She pivoted, met the older man's gaze and forced herself to nod as well.

"Samantha?"

"It bites," she muttered, only to receive an elbow on either side from both Zoe and Ryan.

"The kid does have a point, albeit a colorful one," Uncle Russ conceded with a smile. He gestured to their empty chairs.

For the sake of Ryan's relationship with his family, Zoe decided to follow Uncle Russ's lead, and grabbing Sam's hand, she sat back down.

"I think we need to start over," Uncle Russ said, his pointed gaze settling on his nephew. "Tonight we get through this meal and as a thank-you, tomorrow we do something Samantha would enjoy more."

Although Zoe hadn't liked Russ upon meeting him, she admitted that it was because she'd feared his effect on his nephew. Instead, he'd proven to be an unlikely ally and she admired how he pulled the family together, forcing her to reassess her opinion of the man. Besides if Ryan liked him, Zoe was determined to give him a chance.

"You always were the voice of reason, Russ." Ryan's elderly grandmother smiled. "Ryan, please sit."

Ryan stiffly and warily took his seat.

While they had been arguing, Zoe realized, the help had cleaned up the mess and replaced everything like new.

"So, Samantha, that's an interesting necklace you're wearing. Care to tell us about it?" Uncle Russ strove for a non-threatening topic and Zoe was grateful.

"It was my mom's," Sam said, her fingers playing with the keys that always dangled around her neck.

"Why, I don't think Faith would wear something so—"

Ryan coughed loudly, clearly warning his mother to tread lightly or they were leaving for good this time.

The other woman flushed and said, "I meant, I don't remember Faith owning those."

Sam shrugged. "It's all they let me keep of hers when I went to my first foster family." She glanced down, picked up the proper fork, and began to eat her salad.

The rest of the family did the same. Somehow disaster had been averted for tonight, but Zoe's stomach was in complete knots when it came to the notion of Sam coping with these people on a daily basis.

She glanced at Ryan's strong profile, the mask behind which he hid his pain. Zoe knew he'd placed unspoken hope in his parents' ability to come around and they'd disappointed him. Meanwhile she'd placed no faith in Ryan's ability to stand up to his parents. If he knew that, he'd be disappointed in her, as well. Heaven knew she was disappointed in herself. She shouldn't have needed to see evidence of where his loyalties would lie.

Ryan had proven himself tonight and the thought ought to give Zoe pure joy. Instead she was forced to acknowledge that it brought her and her family closer than ever to losing Sam for good.

Chapter Ten

IT WAS MIDNIGHT and Ryan lay in his bed, channel surfing because he couldn't sleep. Couldn't forget the awful night in his stifling childhood home. He'd disappointed the new women in his life, two amazing women who he realized had come to mean more to him than the family who'd raised him.

From the minute Ryan had walked into the house and seen the formality he'd tried to forget, he knew things wouldn't go well. Still, he'd tried to let both Sam and his parents be themselves and hoped that the adults would have learned from their past mistakes. Clearly that hadn't been the case and there were only two reasons he hadn't made good on his threat to walk out—his uncle and Zoe.

Zoe hated his family and all they stood for. He'd seen it in her eyes, her expression and he'd heard it in her tone and hurt voice, when she'd defended her parents. Yet she'd backed down and she'd done it for him.

When he heard the soft knock on his bedroom door, he thought he'd imagined it until he heard it again and the door slowly swung wide. He supposed he should have been surprised to see Zoe standing there, but he wasn't. Not when she was the answer to his dreams and prayers.

He pushed himself up in bed and crooked a finger her way.

She shut the door behind her and leaned back against it. "You don't mind my being here?"

"Why should I?"

She shrugged. "Sam's down the hall, for one thing."

"After three nights I've learned the kid sleeps like the dead."

Zoe laughed. "Isn't that the truth. I can't remember the last time I crashed that hard."

"You haven't slept well since you've been here, that much I know."

She tipped her head to one side, her dark hair falling over the white satin of her robe. "Snooping on me?"

"No more than you've been doing to me, I'm sure. These walls aren't that thick. So are you going to stand there and make small talk all night?"

She laughed and strode forward, sitting on the end of his double bed. "Can I ask you something?"

"Of course."

"How'd you grow up like that?"

He'd wondered the same thing himself. "I guess I was just lucky I survived it and came out sane."

She nodded. "Well you were amazing tonight," she said, taking him by surprise.

He laced his fingers behind his head and studied her. "You expected me to let my folks get away with belittling you and being so hard on Sam?"

"Let's say I wasn't sure what to expect, but…you impressed me, Ryan." Her voice dropped an octave when she said his name.

The desire that he'd managed to hold at bay washed over him with desperate force.

"Weren't you afraid?" she asked, pegging his deepest emotions, the ones he'd thought were so well hidden.

Obviously they weren't and he wasn't about to explain it to her from a distance. He patted the empty space next to him and without hesitating, she scooted closer, curling up beside him. Only the glow of the television provided light in the room and they lay together comfortably.

"What could I be afraid of?" he asked lightly.

She reached out and caressed his cheek. "Losing your family the way Faith lost her family."

He shut his eyes, unable to believe this woman understood him so well. "My whole life I lived with this double message that always tested me. In my heart I knew what my parents did to my sister was dead wrong and the only way I could make it right was to search for her. Every birthday of mine that passed marked another year closer to finding Faith."

"You're a good man," she murmured, as her soft fingers stroked his skin, encouraging him to continue.

"But I also knew the consequences for stepping out of those boundaries my parents set for us kids. I could lose my family and everything that was familiar to me if I misbehaved. Toeing the line was second nature."

Zoe leaned her head against his shoulder, her breath soft on his neck. "Yet you became a lawyer and didn't go into the family business."

"Only because J.T. did and because being an attorney would help me if they suddenly decreed it was time I helped run Baldwin's, too." He'd just never faced the possibility that that day might arise.

"You became your own man," Zoe insisted and he laughed at her determination to make him see himself the way she viewed him.

"Still, my sister no longer existed for them and I knew… heck, I *know* that if I cross them, I may no longer exist, either." Despite himself, he shivered at the prospect.

"Yet you stood up to them tonight, and you did it for Sam."

"And for you."

She narrowed her gaze.

"You doubt me?" he asked. "Or do you just want to make believe what I said isn't true?"

"Why would I do that?"

"I don't know. Every time things get intense between us, you back off in some way."

A smile teased her lips, but it wasn't a happy one, more like an acknowledgment of his words.

"Care to tell me why?" he asked.

"If you want honesty, I'll give you honesty. You're a threat to me, Ryan. An honest-to-goodness threat."

Her admission let him know that her feelings for him ran as deeply as his did for her. The difference was, he refused to run away.

"I'm a threat? Or your own feelings are?"

She breathed in deep and he felt the tremors wracking her body. "A little of both, I suppose."

He narrowed his gaze, not surprised and yet confused at the same time. "You come from an open, loving family. One that isn't afraid of expressing their feelings, good or bad. You can't possibly be afraid of falling in love."

Love? Not yet, but the possibility wasn't completely incomprehensible. Still, he couldn't believe he'd said the word out loud.

Neither could she. Her eyes opened wide, but to her credit, she held on to her composure as she tried to explain. "I'm thirty and I've never fallen in love. Never said the words to a man who wasn't a family member. I've watched my parents live the emotion and saw my sister fall firsthand. I've long since accepted that it isn't going to happen for me. And it definitely can't happen between two people as different as us."

Well, he'd asked. Now he knew. And his stomach cramped as he realized how tightly she held on to her notions.

"Differences aren't always a bad thing," he reminded her.

She shook her head and laughed. "You're determined to make this difficult, aren't you?"

"Not at all." He reached out and stroked her cheek. "You're scared of feelings you never thought you'd have. Join the club, sweetheart. I'm thirty and I've never been in love. Never said the words or even thought I'd fallen hard." And he wouldn't say them outright just yet, either. "It's something we *do* have in common."

She glanced down at the comforter. "My life is at a crossroads. Surely you see that. I'm still living at home. My business, which doesn't even have a name, is barely up and running and I've already had to put it on hold to come up here."

"To be with Sam. Who needs you. You didn't hesitate to drop everything for her and she's not even your flesh and blood. Compare that to the situation she's got waiting for her here and you're miles ahead of us."

She laughed. "Looks like neither of us gives ourselves enough credit."

"So isn't it great that we've got each other cheering us on? You know you're the first woman I've ever known who's truly an individual. You have drive, direction—"

"Ryan, don't." She shook her head and didn't meet his gaze. "I need to resettle before I can consider myself a part of a couple or even seriously consider a relationship."

He nodded in understanding, telling himself she hadn't completely closed herself off to the notion of *them*. She needed time to adjust to her feelings, which gave him time to confront her fears and find solutions. He needed to be able to deal with each point on a rational level or he'd never change her mind. A possibility he couldn't begin to contemplate.

She shut her eyes and leaned back, closing him out.

But this time he wasn't unnerved by her need to pull away because he understood now that she was scared. Scared of how an emotion as intense as love could change her life and threaten the freedom she held so dear.

He'd just have to take her fears as a challenge to overcome.

ZOE STRETCHED OUT on the lounge chair by the pool at Ryan's parents' house. She couldn't say she was comfortable with his mother and grandmother sitting beneath an umbrella on the opposite side of the patio, alternately staring and whispering. She felt like a pariah at a party.

But then she'd turned and looked at Ryan, who lay beside her in swimming trunks, and decided life could be much, much worse. His tanned chest was a magnet for her hungry gaze and she devoured him from behind her sunglasses.

Only she knew she'd spent the night in his bed. He'd managed to coax her into forgetting their intense conversation and making love, not once, but twice last night and then again this morning. Each time he'd come inside her, he'd shuddered and whispered her name, soft and low in her ear. He'd made her insides turn to mush, made liquid trickle between her thighs so she could clasp him in moist heat. Zoe crossed her legs and felt that sensitive spot tingle and shoot desire straight to her core.

As a distraction, she tried to focus on the afternoon sun, which beat down hard, but her mind strayed back to their too-serious conversation last night. What he was coming to mean to her, and her to him. And why she needed to back off.

Zoe shivered despite the hot sun. She grabbed for the sunscreen and slathered lotion on her arms and chest. All the while, she felt Ryan watching her, too.

"Hey, Zoe!" Sam yelled.

She glanced up, shielding her eyes with her hand so she could better see the teenager's antics.

"Cannonball!" Sam yelled and jumped, grabbing her knees midair prior to hitting the water, which splashed over all the chairs drenching everything in sight.

Thanks to the heat Ryan generated, Zoe didn't mind the cold shower. His mother, on the other hand, rose from her seat and shook her arms in fury.

"Samantha, there are other people in the vicinity!" Vivian chided.

"Sorry, Mrs. Baldwin." Sam said the words in a singsong voice that failed to sound sincere.

The older woman, clad in a too-formal summer dress, glanced at Ryan. "Does the child have to call me that? I sound like a stranger."

"You are," Zoe muttered beneath her breath.

"What would you like Sam to call you?" Ryan asked.

That question seemed to stump his mother and she grew oddly quiet.

"How 'bout I call you Grandma?" Sam asked, stepping out of the pool.

Zoe chuckled. The kid might not want anything to do with Ryan's family, but she definitely knew how to push all the right buttons to annoy them.

"Why don't you just call her Vivian?" Ryan suggested.

Any replies were interrupted by shrieks from the side of the house.

"Oh, no." Zoe ran, Ryan ahead of her, and the others followed.

They rounded the corner and Zoe nearly barreled into Ryan who'd stopped short. His grandmother stood on a white wrought-iron bench, pointing at the ground and shrieking.

"Mother, what's wrong?" Vivian asked.

"It's…it's…there's a *rat* in my roses," she screamed loudly. "Call Hilton," she said. Hilton, Zoe now knew, was the butler.

Nobody pointed out that, even in her panicked state, Grandma Edna directed that the butler be called to help when there were perfectly capable family members standing around uselessly. Meanwhile, Grandma Edna still gesticulated wildly with her hands.

"Have him call a terminator," the older woman shouted.

"I think you mean an exterminator."

Zoe turned to see Uncle Russ had joined the fray.

"I'm sure it's not a rat," Vivian said, calming her mother and helping her down from the bench.

Zoe met Ryan's gaze.

"I'm quite sure it isn't," he said, somehow keeping a straight face.

Despite the insanity around them, they shared intimate eye contact, causing her insides to curl with warmth.

"I thought we told you to keep the pig caged in the shade on the other side of the house," Zoe whispered to Sam who stood wrapped in a towel behind her.

"I dunno what happened. Maybe I didn't lock the cage good enough," she said, too innocently.

Zoe cringed and waited for the fallout while Ryan dug around the garden for the pig. Zoe vividly recalled the moment in her own mother's garden when he'd described the prized roses, and decided all hope of keeping the peace, and Ryan on their side, was lost.

He might have found the situation amusing at first, but he couldn't possibly find humor in the repercussions. *So much for attempting a pleasant afternoon that would please Sam,* Zoe thought.

"There it is!" Grandma Edna yelled and pointed to the ground just as Ima made her escape from the roses and ran across the lawn, Sam in hot pursuit.

Vivian reached into her pocket for a vial that Grandma Edna referred to as her smelling salts, though Zoe didn't see why she needed them when she hadn't passed out.

Ryan rose and brushed off his hands, then bent to check on his grandmother.

"Care to explain that, that *thing?*" Vivian asked through tightly clenched teeth.

"That's Sam's pet," Ryan explained.

"If it wasn't a rat, then what was it?" Grandma Edna asked as she fanned herself with a magazine Uncle Russ had held in his hand.

"Could I convince you it was a dog, ma'am?" Zoe pasted on her broadest smile.

Nobody laughed, especially after Zoe launched into an explanation of the Vietnamese potbellied pig.

As a group, they trudged back to the pool area. Although Ryan wanted to pack up and leave and Zoe was all too happy to agree, Uncle Russ insisted they stay. He'd just returned from the Boston store. An emergency, he'd said, and he wanted his share of time with both Ryan and Sam.

Zoe couldn't help but feel excluded, but she reminded herself it was an omen of things to come. She'd better get used to it now. She wasn't a member of this family, didn't want to be, and would never fit in, anyway. She was here for Sam and when Sam no longer needed her for the transition, and it was safe back home, they'd have to talk to Social Services, say their goodbyes and…

And would Sam return here? Zoe's insides roiled.

"So I thought that since you're a member of this family, you would want the same piece of jewelry both Vivian and Grandmother Edna have," Uncle Russ was saying to Sam.

Zoe hadn't realized the teen had returned from rescuing Ima, but she had the pig packed safely in her carrier.

Russ held out a small jewelry box with the word *Baldwin's* inscribed on top and Sam accepted the gift.

"What is it?" she asked.

"Take a look."

"I can't believe he bought Sam a gift," Ryan said under his

breath in awe. For all Uncle Russ's support, even he hadn't yet shown this kind of compassion for Faith's child.

With cautious excitement and shaking hands, Sam opened the gray box. "It's a B," she said slowly. "A necklace." Her voice dropped, the enthusiasm gone.

"I thought having it would make you feel more a part of us," Uncle Russ said.

"I already have a necklace," Sam said dully.

Ryan's mouth grew dry.

"'Thank you' would be more appropriate," Zoe coached her and Ryan nodded in appreciation.

"I already have a necklace." Sam's fists gripped the oxidized keys that had once belonged to her mother.

Uncle Russ nodded. "I realize that, but this one's brand-new. You could put the old one in the box for safekeeping," he suggested.

Ryan could see Sam's struggle and the fast way she blinked to try to prevent tears from falling down her cheeks. He felt torn inside between his uncle with his good intentions and Sam with her devotion to her memory.

Zoe came up beside him and rested her hand lightly on his shoulder, letting him silently know she understood. He wasn't surprised she read him so well, any more than he was shocked by the jolt her bare hand gave to his system. He wondered if she'd have this effect on him when he was eighty. He damn well hoped so.

"Of course you could always put the new necklace on a key chain if it makes you more comfortable, but wouldn't you like to see how it looks?" Ignoring the silence and Sam's discomfort, Uncle Russ stepped forward with the obvious intention of helping her remove the old necklace.

Sam stepped back out of reach and promptly fell into the swimming pool.

ZOE DIDN'T KNOW HOW they all survived the long day, but somehow they made it through their time at the Baldwin home. During the ride back into Boston, Sam fell asleep in the back seat, and Zoe and Ryan withdrew into their own private thoughts.

Despite the events of the day, Zoe was so wiped out, she couldn't focus on anything other than her longing for bed. Ryan parked in the garage opposite the building and the three of them practically staggered up the ramp and across the street. The lights from the entryway beckoned.

"I don't think I've ever been so glad to be home," Ryan said.

Zoe nodded. "Hear, hear. I didn't know one day could be so overwhelming and exhausting at the same time."

Ryan pulled the door open, holding it for Zoe and Sam. "Ladies first."

"Hang on. I need to throw some tissues out," Sam said and before either Zoe or Ryan could argue, she darted for the large trash can on the corner, a few feet from the building's entrance.

"Hurry up," Zoe called, rolling her eyes. "Would it kill her to hang on to the garbage until we reached the apartment?" she asked, irritably.

Ryan met her gaze and laughed at the same time he heard Sam shout, "Let go!"

Ryan released the door and bolted for the corner, Zoe

right behind him. She grabbed Sam while Ryan ran after the man who'd seemingly appeared out of nowhere.

"He touched me," Sam said, practically hyperventilating from her fear. "This time he actually touched me."

Zoe hugged her tight. "We were with you the whole time," she said in an attempt to reassure Sam. But in her heart she realized she and Ryan had looked away for a split second. The same split second in which many parents lost their children in shopping malls and parking lots. She'd read about it so many times, yet despite the real danger surrounding Sam, they'd taken their eyes off her for a second too long.

"Was it the same guy?" Zoe asked Sam.

"I think so. It just happened so fast. He grabbed my arm like he wanted to turn me around to face him, but when I screamed, he ran. All I saw was the back of his head and a dark baseball cap."

Zoe swallowed hard. "Maybe we'll get lucky and Ryan will catch up with him." She hoped to calm Sam when in truth she felt anything but calm herself.

RYAN RAN HARD. The guy had youth on his side, but Ryan managed to grab the back of his T-shirt and drag him to a stop on the dark street he'd turned down.

Ryan's mouth was dry and his heart slammed hard in his chest. "What the hell do you want from my niece?" he asked, shaking him as hard as he could.

"I don't know what the hell you're talking about. You have the wrong guy." The guy was winded, but arrogant.

"Oh no?" Ryan raised an eyebrow. "Then why'd you run like a scared shitless kid?"

Ryan stared into the hooded eyes of a punk who matched Sam's description of the guy who'd broken into her room. Dark hair, big teeth, medium height and build. There was no coincidence. This was the same guy.

"I'm no idiot, man. If someone comes after me, I'm not hanging around to find out why."

"At the moment, that's exactly what you're going to do. Hang around and fill me in on why you're stalking a four-teen-year-old girl." Ryan pulled the kid's collar tighter, chok-ing him with the tight material. "Unless you want the cops to ask these same questions?"

He shook his head, the dark long hair falling into his face. "Go ahead. I didn't do nothing they can hold me for. At least nothing you can prove. It's some troubled kid's word versus mine. But if you want some advice, I suggest you get the *key* to this mystery soon. Now are you going to let me go or do I have to start yelling. This is harass-ment, man."

Ryan scowled. The guy thought he'd back down. He didn't know Ryan at all. No way would he leave this guy walking the streets.

He shoved the guy in front of him. "Walk," he insisted.

"To where?"

"Inside the building where I can call the cops and let *them* decide who to believe."

AFTER HOURS in the police station where they pressed charges against Sam's stalker, it took forever for Zoe to relax and calm down. Not even a warm bath helped soothe her nerves.

Sam, on the other hand, crashed and slept like the dead.

There was definitely something to be said for youth, Zoe thought wryly.

Now she lay in peace in her bed in the guest room at Ryan's and talked softly on the phone to her twin. She didn't want Ryan to overhear her conversation.

"The whole time I was at the house, I felt like Ryan's uncle had an agenda that involved Sam. I can just feel it. And after Ryan told the police what the stalker said about finding *the key* to this mystery, I'm more certain than ever that I'm right and it involves that key around Sam's neck," Zoe insisted.

On the other end, Ari sighed. "Is it possible he was just trying to make Sam feel welcome by buying her a necklace that the other women in the family have?"

"No, it was more than that. More than coincidence that the guy Ryan caught used the word *key*. I noticed Uncle Russ staring at Sam's keys. He definitely wanted to see them firsthand."

"You said he offered to let her keep the new necklace on a key chain. I think he's really just making an effort. After all, he's Ryan's only close relative, right? And Ryan trusts him?"

"Well, yes," Zoe admitted. And there had been other, more positive aspects to the day and Russ's behavior toward Sam.

Russ had been nothing but good and kind in direct contrast to everyone else in that mausoleum. He'd walked them to the car while Vivian had still been inside attending to Grandma Edna.

Though Sam had remained sullen and silent, when they'd reached the car, Russ had bent close to the teenager. "I'm really sorry. We all loved your mother, you know."

Sam had grunted something that sounded like, "No, I don't know."

At the time, Zoe couldn't say he'd been focused more on the keys than on Sam. She'd just had an uneasy feeling she couldn't prove or even justify—at least not until tonight when the guy had told Ryan to find the *key*. It was too much of a coincidence.

"So what did Quinn find out so far about the break-in?" she asked Ari, changing the subject since her sister would probably just continue to play devil's advocate and insist Zoe was imagining Uncle Russ's focus on Sam's beloved possession.

"He discovered that the woman who says she had something stolen has a history of filing fraudulent insurance claims in an effort to recoup money, so we're keeping an eye on her and her boyfriend, who happens to have dark hair, which matches the description Sam gave. Of course that was before Sam saw the same guy in Boston. You said the police are holding him for questioning?"

"Yes, but without further evidence or proof, they'll have to let him go," she said, her frustration mounting. Zoe bent her knees and pushed higher against the pillows, leaning back in sheer exhaustion.

"And the boyfriend I mentioned has an alibi for both the day of the break-in and the morning Sam says she saw someone lurking outside. Plus Quinn's having him watched, which means he's still in Jersey now, not Boston." Ari expelled a loud breath. "Everything just feels like a dead end."

Her frustrated tone matched Zoe's feelings exactly. "They still could have hired someone."

"And Quinn's looking into the possibility. Now, how's Sam?" her sister asked.

Despite everything they'd been through today alone, Zoe had to laugh. "Sam's Sam." She relayed some of the funnier stories and escapades about their trip so far.

"Sounds like she's charming her new relatives," Ari said, laughing.

Zoe grinned. Her sister didn't know the half of it.

"So what about the one subject you're avoiding?" Ari asked.

Zoe raised an eyebrow. "And what would that be?"

"How *you* are. How you and your social worker are doing together."

During the silence that followed, Ari remained quiet. Zoe knew the inevitable outcome. Her twin had more patience than Zoe, and she always could wait Zoe out. "Okay, okay. I'll talk about it. I'm confused," she admitted to her twin.

"About your feelings for Ryan?"

"No, those are clear. Everything just seems brighter when he's around," she grumbled.

"I see," Ari said.

"And everything tingles when I just think about him," she complained.

Her twin chuckled. "You say all this like it's a bad thing. Now granted I wouldn't have chosen Sam's uncle as the man for you, and he's pretty much persona non grata around here right now, at least as far as Mom and Dad are concerned—"

"Jeez, help make this easier, why don't you?" Zoe punched the pillow on the far side of the bed.

"But none of those things matter if you love him," her psychologist twin said.

"Whoa. Nobody said anything about love." Except Ryan last night.

He hadn't said he loved her, but he'd mentioned possibilities. She'd pushed those words aside because they scared her.

Love?

No.

Everything inside Zoe resisted the notion. No matter how mesmerizing Ryan's brown eyes were, no matter how good he was with his hands, and no matter how excellent he felt buried deep inside her body, they weren't talking about love. *Not even if he was kind and decent and protective in the best possible way,* she thought.

"I don't trust in the idea, at least not for me. If Mom and Dad—two people who couldn't be better matched—argue, can you imagine the fights that would be in store for two people as different as Ryan and me?"

"I can imagine the sparks," Ari said.

"Well sparks aren't enough. I certainly don't believe two such different people can make a relationship work."

Ari snickered into the phone, leaving Zoe with the uneasy feeling her twin wasn't about to come down on her side.

"And why not?" Ari asked.

Zoe had a sneaking suspicion her sister was leading her down a tricky path, but she answered, anyway. "Well first, have you ever met anyone more unsettled than me?"

"Give me a break, Zoe. Up until recently, you had a steady job and a place to live. What's unsettled about that?"

Before last night, Zoe had never expressed her feelings about the life she'd chosen, but now she was discussing it for the second time within twenty-four hours. "Even I can face facts. I'm thirty and I still live at home with my parents. I quit my old job and I'm just starting up a new career. Chances are I'll be living off my savings for a while, especially after I move out."

"You're moving out of Mom and Dad's?" Ari asked, obviously shocked by the news Zoe hadn't yet shared.

Perhaps because she hadn't even made a real effort to find an apartment of her own. "Eventually. When I find a place. Or even have time to look." She spouted the excuses she'd been feeding herself for the last month, even before Ryan had complicated her life.

"The point is my life is at a crossroads and I told Ryan as much."

"Hmmm. And what else did you tell Ryan?" her sister asked.

Zoe thought back to their conversation. "Just that I need to settle down and find myself before I can ever think about a serious relationship. Or something like that."

"And you had this conversation with Ryan. A man with whom you claim there is no future." Ari yawned, an obviously fake, forced sound, meant to let Zoe know she found her reasoning completely bogus. "If that's what you want to tell yourself, go ahead. And maybe you'll be lucky enough that Ryan will wait around until you decide you're ready."

"And maybe Ima will fly," Zoe said.

"Don't cause unnecessary trouble between yourself and Ryan. Let nature take its course," Ari warned. "And while you're at it, don't go spouting accusations about Ryan's uncle. Not without proof."

Zoe knew Ari wasn't finished with the subject of her and

Ryan. No more than Zoe was finished with the topic of Uncle Russ. But she would be careful around the man.

Funny how well she and Ari knew one another's unspoken intentions. "Oh, that psychic twin connection," Zoe said.

Like the time Zoe was seven and jumped out of a tree, breaking her leg. Ari had come running out of the house because she'd sensed Zoe was hurt.

"I do have a plan that doesn't involve me going off half-cocked. I'm going to start by talking to Ryan and broaching the subject of Sam's keys and his uncle's possible motives for wanting to see them. If he doesn't take it well, I'll back off and leave Ryan in peace, but I will look into those keys myself."

Without warning, she had a flash of the day Uncle Russ had visited her home. "Ari, I just remembered something. Uncle Russ mentioned that the time when Faith ran away was a very chaotic period for the business. Something about truck hijackings," she said, recalling the conversation. "Also Faith stole money from Uncle Russ. Can you ask Quinn to look into exactly what went down? The official version?"

"You got it. In the meantime, you be careful." Ari's voice sobered. "Keep us posted down here and call if you want Connor or Quinn to take a trip to Boston. They're already in touch with the police there."

"I will."

"Love you," Ari said.

"Back at you," Zoe replied.

"You know you can test those three little words on your twin before trying them on Ryan."

"Very funny." Zoe hung up the phone and leaned back.

Her conversation with Ari had convinced her she was on to something when it came to Uncle Russ. She didn't have motive for him, but she had a gut feeling and Zoe trusted her instincts. Enough to make investigating Sam's keys a priority.

At least that puzzle she had some control over, while her emotions and future provided more of a mystery.

 *Chapter Eleven*

FOR SOMEONE WHO HADN'T slept well, Zoe awoke early, and she headed straight to the kitchen to brew some strong coffee. As she puttered around and set up the coffeemaker, she tried to be quiet so as not to wake Ryan and Sam.

Morning sunlight set Ryan's apartment aglow, highlighting the new-looking chrome appliances and dark wood cabinetry. Zoe loved his apartment, which had all the warmth of the man himself and the same amount of mystery. Like just what did he keep in the cabinet above the toaster oven, anyway? Glasses? Plates? Canned goods? And why did she care?

Because wondering about his kitchen helped take her mind off her real problem. How did she tell Ryan about her hunch that his only ally in his entire family might have an agenda where Sam was concerned? Better yet, how did she make him believe her with no proof to back up her claim? Even her twin had doubts.

Zoe wrapped her hand around her coffee cup and took a sip of the hot brew.

"Someone's up early," Ryan said as he strode into the kitchen and headed straight for the coffee. His hair was still messed from sleep and he wore only a pair of jeans slung low on his hips, zipped, but not buttoned.

"I couldn't sleep."

And was it any wonder? Between her worries about Sam, her distrust of Uncle Russ and her need for Ryan, her head spun with too many thoughts and concerns. She couldn't turn to Ryan for comfort because, despite their night together, they both agreed it wasn't smart to share a bed again with Sam so close by. So for now it was hands off, but she couldn't tear her gaze away from him and the body she'd already learned so well.

He joined her at the table, straddling the chair from behind. "What's wrong besides all the obvious things?" he asked.

Somehow she managed to laugh. "Would you believe me if I said everything's fine?"

One side of his mouth lifted in a half grin. "No."

"I miss you," she said, her voice low and husky, her meaning obvious.

He reached out and toyed with the lapel of her robe, his fingers dipping below the thin fabric to tease her skin with soft circular caresses. "I miss you, too."

She leaned forward. He followed until their foreheads touched and their lips were mere inches apart. She sensed his warmth and heat and smelled his musky, morning scent.

They remained connected that way for a long silent moment, so innocent and yet so very sensual. Her heart sped up in her chest and her pulse pounded in her throat.

Suddenly his lips brushed hers and lingered, until she tasted sweetness, longing and temptation.

"Talk to me," he urged and sat back, before Sam could walk in and catch them.

She sighed, but knew he was right. Just as she knew she had no choice but to talk about what was on her mind. Drawing a deep breath, she dove right in. "Did you notice anything strange about your uncle's interest in Sam's necklace?"

His back and shoulders stiffened. His completely casual stance, and the sense of happiness she'd briefly sensed, fled. "He tried to make her feel welcome by buying her a gift."

"A necklace."

Ryan raised an eyebrow. "So?"

"He seemed very curious about the one she already wears," Zoe said. So much for gently leading him to the subject. Well nobody had ever praised her for her tact or delicate way of phrasing things, she thought.

Ryan moved his head from side to side, stretching his suddenly tense muscles. In seconds flat, he'd gone from surprisingly relaxed considering the episode last night, to wound tight.

He just couldn't believe Zoe could accuse Uncle Russ of anything underhanded. "Those old keys are odd looking. Anyone in their right mind would ask about them," he said, hating he had to defend his uncle to the woman he loved.

Loved?

He paused in shock. Long enough to think and let emotion wash over him. Long enough to realize he did love her. The feelings had been growing for a while, he now knew, building the more he got to know and admire her.

But he couldn't deal with that primal emotion right now, not when she was questioning the one stable thing in his family life.

Damn, why couldn't one thing in his life be easy right now?

"Sure, anyone might ask about the keys—once," Zoe said, interrupting his thoughts. "He asked about them once and

Sam answered. Then he bought her a necklace that she refused to take, but he didn't leave well enough alone. He pushed. He offered to put those keys away for safekeeping. It was like he wanted to get his hands on them." Zoe pulled her robe tighter.

"Uncle Russ was being his usual solicitous, kind self." Ryan rose and picked up his cold coffee and poured it into the sink. "You're reaching. I don't know what you have against Uncle Russ, but he has nothing but my best interest at heart. Which means he has Sam's best interest at heart too. God, he's the only one I can turn to."

"I know." Zoe came up behind him, wrapping her arms around his waist. "That's what makes this so hard." She exhaled and he felt her breath warm against his back. "But Ryan, how do you explain what the guy said to you last night? That you should find the key to the mystery?"

"For God's sake, it's an expression!"

"It's too much of a coincidence," she insisted.

He blinked, everything inside him rejecting the notion because it would rip apart the foundation of the only security he'd had. Uncle Russ, who'd come to all his graduation ceremonies, who'd never missed a birthday, who called him the son he never had.

"The last thing I want to do is upset you." She hugged him tight. "But if I agree to put Uncle Russ and any agenda I might imagine aside, would you do something for me?"

"What?" he asked.

She urged him around until he faced her. "Just look into the keys. We'll talk to Sam, we'll get a good look at them and we'll see for ourselves if we can figure out what they lead to. How could that hurt anything?"

Ryan didn't buy her wide green-eyed stare for a minute. She wanted to find out if his uncle somehow had a vested interest in those keys. Still he had to admit, Zoe had gotten him curious and if his uncle was as innocent as he believed, why not see if they could figure out what Faith had used the keys for? Why she'd kept them and passed them on to her daughter.

"I think it could be a way for Sam to learn more about her mother," he said, thinking Zoe's idea through.

Zoe nodded. "It's a long shot that we'll ever know the truth about her necklace, but at least we'll have looked into the last link to your sister."

"I can live with that," he told her.

She smiled, obviously happy with his agreement. At least one of them was. Now that she'd raised the specter of his uncle's odd behavior, her notion lingered in his mind. He only hoped Sam's keys held answers that put her suspicions about his uncle to rest.

JUST AS ZOE HAD THOUGHT, once they explained to Sam that the keys might provide more insight into her mother, she willingly handed them over to Zoe. All it took was a cursory examination for Zoe to discover the words *Wayham Bus Depot*, which it turned out was located in a small town about twenty minutes from Ryan's family home.

The big question was what to do with Sam, since neither Ryan nor Zoe wanted to take the teenager along and subject her to potential disappointment or upset if the keys turned out to be a dead end or something disturbing like a drug stash. There was also the fact that someone did want something from Sam and she couldn't be left alone for even a second.

Fate intervened in the form of Ryan's mother. To their surprise, she called to ask if she could spend time alone with Faith's daughter. Zoe's gut instinct was to rebel against the notion, but in her heart she understood that this woman was Sam's grandmother and any form of bonding was best for all involved, especially Sam. The teenager knew little about her mother's life growing up. After Ryan gave his mother a stern lecture, the older woman agreed to choose her words carefully when she spoke to Sam about her mother.

With luck, Vivian could help Sam feel a part of this family and make her feel more grounded when it came to her past. *With luck,* Zoe thought, still not completely trusting any members of the Baldwin family other than Ryan.

It took some convincing to get Sam to go back to the Baldwins' without Zoe and Ryan tagging along, but Ryan promised her she could pick her favorite food for dinner and then during the week go shopping at Baldwin's.

Zoe suspected it was the shopping bribe that did the trick, and they dropped Sam off with her grandmother along with strict orders: if asked, she was to say that Ryan and Zoe were off spending time together. Nothing more, not to anyone.

Ryan remained silent during the ride until Zoe couldn't take being frozen out anymore. "I'm sorry," she said at last.

One hand on the wheel, he briefly turned toward her. "For?"

That was a good question, Zoe thought. For causing distrust and upheaval in his life? For not just handing Sam over like she was a possession?

"For accusing your uncle," she said, addressing only one of the many issues between them.

He shrugged. "Just because he's been good to me doesn't mean he's the easiest person to know or like. I hope this little trip will convince you that his interest in Sam is genuine."

But from his tight jaw and steely expression, she didn't believe him. She wondered if his internal turmoil had anything to do with the fear that perhaps she was on to something with his uncle, then tossed that notion aside. In his mind, blood ties ran deep, loyalty ran even deeper and his uncle had been his only friend in a conflicted upbringing.

"How much longer till we get there?" she asked, glancing at the dashboard clock.

"About ten minutes. We have time. So tell me something."

She was happy to have conversation. "What do you want to know?"

"More about you. I know all about your family life, but I don't know that much about you."

"I'm an open book."

He raised an eyebrow at that. "Ha."

"What's that supposed to mean?"

"Just that you talk this nice game about openness and being yourself, yet I don't know much about you. Who are your friends outside of your family?"

She opened her mouth in surprise. "Are you insinuating I don't have friends?"

"I didn't meet any besides family while I stayed with you."

"My work kept me very busy and away from home. I have agency friends I left behind and some I see for drinks every once in a while," she said, feeling extremely defensive. "What about you? I haven't noticed a whole lot of messages from guys asking you to go to a Red Sox game or out for a beer. Or is it that you're too good for a cold brew?"

He burst out laughing. "Now that's the Zoe I love. Get defensive, throw it back in my face. I admit to not having much of a social life. Lawyers work long hours and we socialize with other attorneys. A quick drink with one of my partners before heading home or a date with someone if the mood strikes."

A date. "Anybody important in your life?" She couldn't help but ask, though she was shocked that as close as they'd been, neither had opened up much before now.

For someone who prided herself on her independence, she was appalled at how her palms grew damp and her stomach knotted as she waited for his reply.

He pulled off at the exit and stopped at a red light. Turning, he faced her. "No, Zoe. Nobody else important."

She met his gaze. Heat and something much more intense passed between them until a car honked, breaking the moment. They glanced up to see the light had turned green and Ryan stepped on the gas.

She exhaled a long, slow breath.

"How about you? Anybody serious in *your* life?" he asked. "I assume by your family's reaction to your turning thirty and still being single that the answer is no, but a mystery woman like you could be hiding a secret or two." His lips twitched in amusement.

She shook her head. "Nobody serious. In fact, my last re-lationship was brief and more a distraction from boredom than anything else."

She and Marco, the guy who'd been assigned to guard her at the safe house had generated serious physical sparks and had helped pass some long, lonely hours by the end of her stay there. But nothing emotional had ever come of it. Noth-ing emotional ever did.

Until now, she thought, staring at Ryan's satisfied expres-sion and handsome profile. He caused butterflies to ripple around her insides, emotions she ought to peg as adolescent and silly, yet everything about her feelings for Ryan were completely adult in nature.

And way too serious.

He drummed his fingers on the wheel and her gaze fell to his strong hands and what she knew to be a deft touch capable of arousing inexplicable pleasure.

"So not much time to socialize, not many close friends, and no serious relationships at the moment. We have more in common than you'd think, wouldn't you say?"

She murmured a noncommittal reply, hoping his question was a rhetorical one.

Before they could discuss anything else, the bus station loomed before them. He pulled into a parking space in a large lot and suddenly all the things they had in common took a back seat to those that pulled them apart.

RYAN STRODE INTO THE TERMINAL, Sam's keys in his pocket. Though it wasn't easy, he tried to push aside all that they'd discussed during their trip here. His questions during the car ride were so obviously meant to get her to think more about *them* that they were laughably transparent. Yet she still fought the notion. Considering all that was going on at the moment, he welcomed the time to bring her around.

He refused to contemplate the possibility that she wouldn't recognize their compatibility or the depth of her feelings for him. Nobody, not even this stubborn woman, would opt to be alone forever.

At least he hoped not or he was doomed to the same fate.

He approached the customer-service counter and the grumpy-looking man seated behind it. "Hi, there."

The man took his time lifting his gaze from the crossword puzzle on his desk. "Yeah."

Ryan placed Sam's key on the counter. "Does this look familiar to you?"

Yawning, he reached for the key. "Looks old, but yeah it's one of ours."

"Can you tell me who this locker number is registered to today?" Ryan asked.

The man shook his head. "No. None of your business."

Zoe slipped up beside him and leaned forward on her elbows. "We'd just like to know if Faith Baldwin's name is still on locker 811."

"Did you say 811?" His voice perked up suddenly.

"Yes. It's on the key if you'd bothered to— Ooomph," Ryan grunted as Zoe nudged him in the ribs.

"Does that number sound familiar to you?" she asked sweetly.

"Another man was here asking about that locker number around lunchtime."

Ryan took the man's words like a punch in the stomach.

"Can you describe him?" Zoe asked before Ryan had had a chance to catch his breath.

"Tall, gray hair, wearing a suit." He rolled his eyes. "He looked like any businessman with money who comes through here every day. What do you people want from me, anyway?"

Zoe patted his hand reassuringly. "You're doing just fine. Now can you tell us if you keep old paperwork on file from people who've rented lockers in the past?"

"I'll tell you what I told the other guy. He said it could have been rented as long as seventeen years ago, and that's too long a time for us to keep anything we might have found in that locker."

The description along with the time frame cemented the fact that Uncle Russ had been here asking questions about Sam's keys. He was involved in something and had an agenda, just as Zoe had thought. Disappointment churned in Ryan's gut, but he reminded himself that he didn't know *why* his uncle had interest in the keys. Maybe there was a plausible explanation.

"What did the gentleman say to that?"

"Stormed off, angry."

Now that sounded like his uncle when he didn't get his way, Ryan thought.

Zoe shook her long hair so it fell onto the counter, an obvious attempt to keep the clerk's attention. "Well I'm a little more patient and I'd like to know if you have any old records we might be able to peek at."

The other man looked into her green eyes, which she fluttered ever so nicely, and reached down to his keyboard.

"We're computerized now. Didn't used to be. So things aren't always accurate. Let's see. Nope. We only go back five years, then we wipe the files clean. Of course there's a storage room with old records. It's a dusty old place that nobody likes to go into."

"Yes!" Zoe said.

Ryan felt the excitement ripple through her.

"And if I were to make it worth your while, would you please let us into that old storage room?" she asked. "You see, our sister took that locker after she ran away all those years ago, and if there's any way of tracing her whereabouts, even from that long ago, we'd be so grateful."

The man looked from Ryan to Zoe, then down to the counter, where Ryan realized Zoe was slipping a twenty-dollar bill his way.

The guy snatched the cash and gestured with a nod of his head. "This way."

He led them down a long hall to a back room. Unlocking the door, he let them inside. "You won't be disturbed. Nobody wants to go back to the archives because of the dust," he said laughing.

"And you didn't tell the other man about this room?" Zoe asked.

The guy shook his head. "He didn't ask about it."

Ryan stifled a laugh because his uncle's temper and impulsive nature had worked against him, whereas Zoe's patience and smarts, not to mention feminine wiles, had gotten them one step farther.

Zoe turned back to the other man. "By the way, what happens to the old contents of a locker?"

"We try to contact the owner and if nobody shows up for it, it goes into lost and found for a while. Then we give the stuff away to shelters or dump it if it's garbage. If you're lucky, somebody will have written information down on the card that was filled out when the locker was paid for. Good luck," he said and shut the door behind him.

Ryan took in the old cardboard filing boxes piled one on top of the other all around and groaned. "Well, might as well get started," he muttered and started walking toward the back of the room.

"Ryan, wait."

He turned to see Zoe lingering near the door. "What is it?"

She shrugged. "I don't know. I'm sorry, maybe? I know I said it before, but I am. I'm sorry that my hunch was right. I'm sorry that your uncle was here looking for something that involved your sister and didn't tell you about it."

"Maybe he had his reasons." He could only hope.

She nodded, obviously not wanting to pick a fight on this subject. "What month and year did Faith run away?" she asked instead.

"March 1988."

"At least that's a start. Now we just have to pray these boxes are in some sort of chronological order." She started looking at one end, then walked to another section, then another.

He wanted to help her. But now he had something to say first. "Zoe?"

She peeked her head up above one of the boxes. "Yeah?"

He met her gaze. "Thanks for not saying I told you so."

She grinned and got back to work.

It felt like ages before they'd narrowed things down

enough to start digging through a select group of filing cartons. Even so, it took hours to sort through the individual boxes and papers.

The man hadn't been kidding about the mess. Zoe's eyes were tearing and her nose was running from all the rising dust that flew around each time they touched something that hadn't been disturbed in years.

"Oh my God! I found something," Ryan suddenly said, clearly stunned.

Zoe left her box and scrambled over to where he sat holding an old, yellowed paper. "What is it?"

"The card Faith filled out when she rented the box. It's dated March 15, 1988."

"Let me see." His hands shook and she eased the paper out of his grasp. She scanned the faded page and faint handwriting. There were the basic questions, but the answers didn't mean anything to Zoe. "This isn't your parents' current address."

"You're right. It belongs to a good friend of Faith's. Patty Wheaton was one of Faith's best friends. She was a couple of years older than Faith. Of course my parents disapproved of their friendship because Patty was a little fast, wore too much makeup and liked to have fun more than she liked to study."

"Hmm." Zoe narrowed her gaze. "I'm sure you followed up with Patty when you were looking for Faith."

"She was one of the few people my parents checked with right after Faith went missing. Patty said she hadn't heard from her. The P.I. I hired talked with her again, but she insisted Faith hadn't been in contact with her since she'd run away."

Zoe sighed, hearing the defeat in his voice.

He glanced at the card again. "This isn't my parents' phone number either."

"It's probably Patty's. Is it possible she still lives in the same place?" Zoe asked.

Ryan shook his head. "Doubtful. But her mother would know where she is and her parents are still local."

"It's worth a shot. We can talk to her again. See if anything from the locker ended up with her."

"Who'd keep old stuff from a friend who died years ago?" The edge in his tone spoke of his frustration.

Zoe slapped her hand on his knee. "I won't let you sound defeated before we know anything for sure." She rose and stood over him, then sat straddling him with her thighs. She felt his body heat penetrating between her legs and liquid desire pulsing through her. But her own feelings weren't what counted now.

Ryan's emotions were in turmoil, his past and present coming together in a painful way, and she wanted to be there for him as he worked his way through it. For a woman who'd always been independent, floating through life in a vacuum that only included her family, this sudden, deep need to care for another person took her off guard. Yet it was her feelings for Ryan that guided her every move right now.

She leaned forward and briefly touched her lips to his, lingering long enough to taste him and let the sensation of caring for him overwhelm her. Only then did she sit back on her heels. "We'll follow this trail as far as we can, okay?"

A smile tugged at his mouth. "We?"

"Have I abandoned you yet?" She immediately realized

the depth of her question and didn't want him to press her any further. So she held out her hand and pulled him to his feet. "At the very least, we're one step ahead of your uncle, so we can get on this first thing in the morning."

He nodded. "I'd just like some answers." His gaze never left hers—as if he were telling her he knew something deep existed between them and he wanted her to acknowledge it too.

She feared she couldn't put off facing that issue much longer.

 *Chapter Twelve*

DIRTY AND TIRED, Zoe wanted nothing more than to pick up Sam and head back to Ryan's. She intended to get a good night's sleep before she had to tackle the next part of their search. She certainly didn't need to arrive at the Baldwins' house to find Sam had gotten herself into trouble while they'd been gone. But she had.

"Accidents happen," Vivian said to Ryan and Zoe. "But when the plumber comes for a service call and finds a scrunchie clogging the toilet, then we're talking about a deliberate stuffing." Vivian shook her head, her exasperation obvious. "By the way, what *is* a scrunchie, anyway?"

Zoe bit the inside of her cheek to keep from laughing. "It's a ponytail holder. Only bigger."

"Well the water overflowed and created quite a mess." Vivian's posture and tone showed the weariness she must be feeling after a few hours with her granddaughter.

"Where's Sam now?" Ryan asked.

"Upstairs in your old room thinking about what she did and why she did it," Vivian said.

Zoe shot Ryan a glance.

"You punished her?" he asked, surprised.

"What else should I have done? She showed no thought

to basic etiquette when visiting someone else's home." His mother stiffened her shoulders defensively.

"Did you explain that to her?" Zoe asked.

"Of course."

Ryan stepped forward. "And did you yell, scream and threaten to throw her out and never let her come back as you did to Faith?"

Zoe sucked in a harsh breath, taken aback by his sharp tone and biting sarcasm. "Ryan..."

"No, that's all right." Vivian ran her hand down her bob, straightening her already perfect hair. "Believe it or not, I thought long and hard before asking you if I could take Samantha for the afternoon. I revisited many of my past mistakes."

"Say that again?" Ryan looked into his mother's eyes.

"I'm admitting I made mistakes, Ryan. It's not the time to get into this now, but I am trying harder with Faith's daughter. She's going to have to realize there are consequences to her actions, though." Vivian gestured to the circular stairs. "Shall we go talk to her?"

"In a minute," Zoe said, stepping forward, knowing she was intruding on Ryan's family, and not caring. Not when she needed answers to questions that would directly affect Sam.

"Yes?" Vivian turned her head to face her.

"Why?" Zoe asked.

The other woman wrinkled her nose in confusion. "Why what?"

"Why punish her? Why teach her that there are consequences? What point are you trying to make?" Zoe pushed the other woman to explain herself, knowing full well she had no right to do so.

Vivian paused in thought. If she was annoyed or put out by Zoe's question, she didn't show it. "Well I suppose I want to teach her the proper way to behave for one thing."

Zoe tried not to cringe or pass judgment; instead she waited.

"And I realize now that Faith never knew we loved her."

"If that bothers you, then why didn't you search harder when she ran away?" Ryan asked.

Real tears suddenly filled the older woman's brown eyes, which Zoe now realized resembled Ryan's. "We had a pattern in our home. All our fights would focus on how Faith's wild rebellion reflected on the family. We'd yell and scream as you pointed out. She'd storm off to her room and the same type of thing would happen again the next day. It became a cycle we couldn't seem to break." She dabbed at the inside corner of her eye, attempting to stem her tears.

"Did you punish Faith?" Zoe asked softly.

"We tried, but no matter what we did, she never listened. Mostly because the screaming was such a large part of our lives, nothing had any impact. So when she ran away, after we checked all the obvious places, we thought, *let her get it out of her system and then she'll come home.*"

Ryan stiffened his shoulders. "But she never did."

Vivian shook her head. "At the time we thought she made her choice, but I see now how wrong we were. We were the parents and she was the child. We should have kept trying."

Zoe swallowed hard, suddenly feeling the woman's pain.

"And all this brings us back to Samantha," Vivian continued. "When Ryan brought up the idea of bringing Faith's child here, I was completely against it since I feared the past would repeat itself. I knew when I looked at Samantha, I'd see my failures as a mother. And I did. I still do."

"Mom—" Ryan stepped forward, but his mother waved him away.

Though Zoe hurt for him, she sensed this moment was a turning point for them both. As the instigator of the conversation, but outsider to their family, Zoe could do no more than watch it play out, and in doing so she realized she was watching her family's role in Sam's life coming to an end. The thought brought a piercing ache to her own heart.

Vivian stared, focusing her thoughts. "I need to say this and I need to do it without your sympathy and without my falling apart."

Ryan nodded in obvious understanding.

"Dinner the other night was a complete replay of our lives with you children except that Samantha had you and Zoe to protect her. And the child has more spunk than anyone I've ever met," she said, with what sounded like affection in her tone.

"Spunk is a good word to describe Sam's behavior," Ryan agreed, his eyes filled with warmth when he gazed at his mother.

Even Zoe had to admit she was touched by the woman's willingness to try and change. Relief filled her, as well, since Sam would benefit from her softening and changing.

"I didn't sleep that night. And I realized then that I could continue to play the socialite who cared more for rules than her family and thereby lose Faith's daughter, too, or I could take the initiative and try to change my attitude. For the sake of my family, I decided that an old dog *should* learn new tricks." Vivian forced a laugh, but her body trembled with the emotion of the afternoon.

Emotion Zoe shared, since she now had no choice but to take the distance she'd tried to maintain and place it firmly between herself and Ryan. He was a good man and on the verge of having his niece accepted by his family. Zoe would have no place in their lives beyond that of a long-distance friend. She couldn't when she and Ryan, for all their passion, had so little in common.

She glanced at Ryan and met his gaze, her throat heavy with grief. No matter how much her heart begged her to believe otherwise, her mind told her that their different lives, different ways of doing things, and completely opposite families would never mesh long-term. On a selfish note, his family's way of life had the potential to stifle the strong woman she prided herself on being and the independent person she intended to become.

Giving him an encouraging nod, Zoe then watched as he changed his focus toward his mother and, knowing it was time, Zoe stepped back and away.

Ryan reluctantly turned from Zoe to stare at his mother and his head spun. He was in awe, completely blindsided by her admissions, her guilt and her desire to do better. Shock, gratitude, and even love for this woman who'd always remained distant swirled inside him.

Ignoring her attempt to remain stoic and alone, Ryan placed his arm around her shoulder. If *he* needed the physical connection to his parent, he decided that she must need it, too. To his never-ending surprise, she wrapped her arm around his waist, acknowledging his gesture.

But he couldn't take his eyes off Zoe. She stood off to one side, her expression soft as she smiled. She was clearly touched by the mother-son moment. But as the silence continued, she grew more uncomfortable. She shifted from heel to heel and appeared unusually alone for a woman normally filled with confidence.

He wanted to pull her into the moment, but she obviously wasn't ready for such a move.

"I want you to understand that I was questioning you for Sam's sake, not for my own," Zoe said into the silence.

His mother eyed Zoe warily. She obviously still didn't know what to make of Zoe's place in this situation and Ryan wasn't ready to fill her in. Not when he knew even Zoe wasn't ready to hear the truth.

Before he could ease the tension, Zoe started to talk. "You see, my family has been where you are. Sam has tested us, too, and we discovered that she responds well to punishment based on caring, but she rebels against rules for their own sake. All Sam wants is to be loved, accepted and to know she fits in." She finished quickly, out of breath.

"That's…"

"I'm rambling." Zoe interrupted his mother. She waved a hand through the air. "This is all between you and your son." She took a step backward, and then another.

Ryan knew she was searching for distance. He couldn't allow her to find it. Zoe was used to love and acceptance from her family, yet she'd closed herself off to the possibility of finding love with him.

Ryan had every intention of changing that.

NEAR MIDNIGHT, Ryan, unable to sleep, opened his door to find a light shining from the living room. He figured it was Zoe, but instead found Sam wandering around the room, looking at his framed pictures. Most were of family and he could understand her curiosity. He still had a lot of questions about Sam herself. They hadn't spent much time alone since they'd met and he figured now was as good a time as any to try and forge a deeper bond with her.

He strode into the room and cleared his throat.

Sam jumped back, a squeal escaping her throat. "You scared me." She hugged a framed photo tight against her chest.

"I didn't mean to. What are you doing up so late?"

She shrugged. "I couldn't sleep."

"Me neither. So what are you looking at?" he asked.

She placed the picture face down on the table and stepped back almost guiltily.

He joined her and turned over the frame. It was the one he had of her mother. He stared at the familiar blond hair and bone structure and shook his head. "It's amazing how much you look like her," he said, turning the photo so she could see it again.

"My memories were getting blurry." Sam pulled the picture from his hand. Glancing at the photo, she blinked and a tear fell.

In her oversize pajama pants and tank top, she was an odd mixture of child and young adult. He wanted to hug her, but knew she wouldn't accept comfort from him yet. "You can keep the picture," he said instead.

"You mean it?"

"I wouldn't have offered otherwise."

She looked at him with gratitude in her wide eyes. "Do you have one for yourself?"

He shook his head.

"Then—"

Realizing she was about to decline his gesture, he came up with a more acceptable idea that would help them both. "How about we take this to a photo machine and make you a copy? You can even pick out your own frame."

She smiled. "I'd like that a lot." She paused, biting on her lower lip. "Can I ask you something?"

"Sure." He leaned against the wall and studied her.

"Why are you being so nice to me?"

He hadn't known what to expect, but she'd stumped him with that one. "Any reason I shouldn't be nice to you?"

She glanced down at her bare feet. "I don't deserve it."

He swallowed hard, surprised at how her sudden insecurity and vulnerability affected him. "I'll admit you can be a pain in the ass sometimes, but it's part of your charm." He laughed. "Besides, you're family."

"So?" She curled her toes into the hardwood, her body a bundle of raw nerves.

He wondered if she was serious. Glancing up, meeting her gaze, he realized she was. As Zoe had tried to tell him time and again, Sam didn't understand being loved and accepted. It would take a long time to convince her there was nothing she could do to change the way he felt about her.

"*So*, you're my niece and that binds us. You can stuff all the toilets you want and it won't get you tossed out of here. You can run away and, mark my words, I'd find you."

"You mean it?"

His throat filled as he looked at the young girl. "I mean it. I guess what I'm saying is, you're my family and I love you." He held his breath, wondering if he'd gone too far too fast.

But when Sam unexpectedly stepped forward and gave him a quick hug, he realized his honesty had been a good thing for them both. "You should get some sleep," he told her.

"Yeah. I have a big day ahead of me. I promised Grandma Vivian I'd help her fix up the garden."

"You did, huh?"

Sam raised her shoulders. "Ima messed it up. It's right I help fix it. Besides Grandma said if I did, she'd build a special pen for Ima to stay when we come visit."

Ryan blinked. "You're kidding."

"Well she wouldn't build it herself, but she did say she'd have one built for Ima. It works for me." Sam yawned, then flipped her hair out of her eyes with her hands. "I guess I'm beat." She started for the hallway, then turned. "Night, Uncle Ryan."

She padded down the hall, leaving him with a warm, fuzzy feeling of family that he'd never had before. A feeling he wanted to share with Zoe, so rather than head for his room, he paused outside her closed door.

On the other side was another female with whom he had unresolved issues and feelings. He didn't believe any talk with Zoe would be nearly as productive or end as well as the one he'd just had with Sam. But he was too wound up to sleep and decided it was time she hear what he had to say.

Although it was late, he knocked once and walked inside. Zoe lay in bed under the covers, but she didn't seem shocked to find him standing by her side. She moved over to make room for him to sit, while she propped herself up against her pillow.

"What's going on?" she asked, her voice rough from sleep.

Ryan tried like hell not to focus on her skimpy tank top or think about the matching pair of equally skimpy panties she likely wore beneath the covers. Instead he reached for her hand and chose his words.

"I had a bonding moment with Sam."

A smile touched her lips. "That's great. You and your family are beginning to make headway with her." Her voice held a somber tone.

"You don't sound thrilled."

"It's a mixed blessing," she said. "As much as I'm happy for you, your progress with Sam means that my family's role in her life is coming to an end."

"We'll work things out. You *will* see her again."

Through the darkness, Zoe merely stared. "We have to be up early," she said at last.

In other words, she was asking him to leave. Not yet, he thought. "You don't believe me, do you?"

"About what?"

"That you'll see Sam again."

She sighed. "Actually I do believe you. We agreed early on that you're a man of your word and I've seen that for myself many times since we met."

He appreciated her belief in him—because faith was a solid basis for a long-standing relationship.

"Then what's going on in that beautiful head of yours?" he asked, and to make certain she couldn't avoid the issue or him, he turned on the lamp on the nightstand.

With her long black hair tangled around her face, she'd never looked more endearing or desirable.

"I was thinking that since you have things under control with Sam—"

"Relatively under control," he joked and got a laugh in return.

"I thought that as soon as we solve this key mystery, I'd take her home. I know we haven't figured out who's after her, but at this point she's as safe here as she is at home… I mean in New Jersey. I hope you'll give my parents the courtesy of a few weeks more with Sam to say goodbye before you move her up here for good."

He narrowed his gaze, wanting to hear more before he jumped to any conclusion about where this conversation was heading. "Go on."

"Well since Sam will have to start school in the fall, you'll need to register her, and she'll need time to get settled in at your parents', of course. But it's still early and I'm sure my parents would appreciate some quality time with Sam, that's all." She toyed with the blanket, her nerves clearly showing.

He swallowed hard. Just as he suspected, Zoe was making plans to pull out of Boston and his life as soon as possible without consulting him or asking him what he wanted.

"Let me ask you something. Just whose plan is this? Because I don't recall mentioning registering Sam in school or her living with my parents, of all people."

She blinked. "I just assumed—I mean I didn't think your schedule would be that flexible when you returned to work. So you'll be able to be home with her in the mornings and after school? Because she really needs a watchful eye, what with her tendency to get in trouble when she's left alone."

He rolled his shoulders, but the tension remained. "I haven't had time to think it through yet, but you apparently have it worked out. And that plan seems to include running away from your own feelings," he accused.

Maybe he was dense, but he thought after all their closeness, she'd at least treat him fairly. But then if she was truly running, she wasn't being fair to herself, either.

"Quit raising your voice or you'll have Sam running in here to see what's going on," Zoe said in a harsh whisper.

In an effort to calm down, he inhaled and counted to ten, then exhaled before speaking again. "I see."

"You see what?" she asked, her brow wrinkled in confusion.

"You just changed the subject. We were talking about *your* feelings."

Zoe pushed her hair out of her eyes. "This isn't about me. It's about Sam and what's best for *her.* Now you tell me you don't have a plan." She maneuvered up in bed and perched her hands on her hips, which had the unfortunate effect of pushing out her breasts and erect nipples, distracting him.

She frustrated him as much as she turned him on and he swallowed hard, determined to force her to acknowledge the truth about *them,* her fears and her hang-ups be damned. He wasn't about to lose her now.

"What about what's best for you? And for me? Doesn't that have to be decided. too?" he asked, fingers clenched into fists at his side.

Zoe tried hard to hold onto her anger because it was the only way to keep Ryan at a distance and she needed that kind of barrier between them right now. From the moment his mother had turned her attitude around, Zoe had accepted the end. She'd tried to explain as much to Ryan the night before, but apparently he hadn't understood.

Or didn't want to, said a small voice in her head, one that mimicked her parents when they accused her of being afraid to commit to anyone, anything or any man. She wasn't giving him an easy time, but he'd thank her in the end. With time and miles between them, he'd see she was right and they couldn't have a future.

"We come in second to Sam," she explained slowly. "That's what happens when there are kids involved. So I'll go home and get my business on track. I know Quinn and Connor need me back soon. And—"

"And you'll go back to living at home?"

"Until I find my own place to live, yes."

"You are so full of crap," he said, taking her by complete surprise.

"Excuse me?" She sat up even straighter in bed.

He groaned. "We've had this discussion before. You say you'll find a place to move, but I've come to realize that you won't. You'll continue to live at home because you love your family, but also because it's the easy way out. You won't have to face moving out, growing up, or having an adult relationship, which might lead to, God forbid, having to compromise with another human being who is also independent and knows his own mind."

She blinked, shocked he'd analyzed her so deeply, thoroughly and possibly correctly.

"I'll prove it," he said.

She stiffened, readying herself for another verbal attack. "Go ahead."

"I love you."

She reared back.

And smacked her head against the wall in the process. "Ouch." She rubbed the sore spot with her hand and glared at Ryan. Her heart galloped in her chest, fear of everything Ryan represented rising faster than any other emotion brewing inside her.

He lived in Boston. She lived in Ocean Isle and she couldn't bear being separated from her family. He wore conservative suits and she preferred outrageous miniskirts. No way his fancy partners and their wives would embrace her style. Her family liked a good con and a slimy pig. His preferred the other side of the law and the only person they'd accept on their own terms was Sam because she was blood. Zoe had already been frozen out by everyone in that house except Ryan. At thirty years old, she was too old and wise to change everything about herself for a man.

And in the end, that's what Ryan would not only expect, but what he would need. It's what he deserved, someone who could fit into the lifestyle he had in Boston.

That someone wasn't her.

She realized he'd covered her hand with his.

He squeezed hard. "Did you hear me, Zoe? I said I love you."

A tremor shook her body. "You don't mean that."

"I most certainly do. Because unlike you, I know my own mind and I don't run from something that's threatening." Equal measures of what seemed like satisfaction and disappointment flashed across his face.

"Run? Me? That's a good one. I was a Secret Service agent. I protect people for a living. I thrive on a challenge and on new experiences, so don't tell me *I* run away."

His lips quirked in a grin that seemed to mock her claim. "Well, how I see it is you're running from me and from what I make you feel."

"That's ridiculous." She rolled her eyes.

"You admitted that I threaten you and your lifestyle." He spoke too smugly for her pride to handle.

"That's true. It's also true and completely like a man to say *I love you* and when the woman doesn't say it back, claim *she's* afraid, as opposed to—" Realizing her next words, she clenched her jaw shut tight.

"Go on. Say it. I dare you," he said, getting into her personal space. He'd taunted her, but even in the face of his dare, she couldn't bring herself to hurt him with what she knew to be a lie.

"You can't say it, can you?" he asked, his voice softening. "You can't say, as opposed to admitting the woman doesn't feel the same way about him." He touched her face and lifted her chin to meet his gaze. "It's okay."

To her dismay, her eyes filled with tears and she couldn't speak, not without falling apart.

"You don't have to say 'I love you' back." He wiped the moisture from her face with his thumb. "I can wait and do you want to know why?"

She swallowed hard and nodded.

"Because you're worth waiting for."

Chapter Thirteen

EARLY THE NEXT MORNING, Ryan, with Zoe beside him, pulled up to a beautiful house in a residential neighborhood. Each property on the street was perfectly kempt and manicured with swing sets in the yard.

"Patty did well for herself," Ryan said, glancing around at the nice neighborhood. "If Faith had gotten her life together..." He stopped and shook his head. "No sense going there. I can't change the past."

Zoe placed her hand on his shoulder and he appreciated her silent support. Last night's harsh words and frank discussion still hung between them, yet she reached out to him when he needed her most. That fact proved to him that their connection went further than any place she could possible run to.

He stopped the car in front of the address he'd gotten from Patty's mother, and together he and Zoe made their way up the flower-lined walk.

"So last time you spoke to Patty, she said she hadn't heard from Faith at all?" Zoe asked.

"Actually the P.I. I hired spoke to Patty. I left it to the professional to follow all leads. I was so emotionally vested, I figured he'd have more success."

Zoe nodded. "Okay, so with a little luck, it's your emotions that'll get Patty to open up now."

"I hope you're right." He rang the doorbell, which set off an interesting combination of chimes. Then they waited.

Soon the door opened and a familiar face appeared before him. His sister's friend looked older, but she was still an attractive brunette, who'd obviously outgrown the punk stage.

"Patty?"

She blinked, staring at him until he saw the recognition dawn in her eyes. "Ryan Baldwin?"

"It's me."

"Wow. It's good to see you!" She sounded genuine, but he also caught the wariness in her expression.

"Patty, this is a friend of mine, Zoe Costas." He gestured to Zoe. "Could we come in and talk to you? It's about Faith."

The other woman shook her head. "I don't know. It's been so long and I probably can't be of any help to you."

"Faith had a child," Zoe blurted out. "Can we please talk? It's important."

Patty's eyes grew wide. Obviously whatever she might know about Faith, she had had no idea about Sam.

"We won't keep you long," Ryan promised.

Patty stepped back and eased the door open wide. "Of course. Come in."

They followed her into a modern kitchen, with white cabinets and dark Formica countertops, and joined her at the table.

"You have to understand how hard this is. Faith was my best friend. My loyalty ran pretty deep." Patty intertwined her fingers as she tried to explain.

"Nobody would be upset if you knew something and didn't tell my parents," Ryan assured her. "At the time, who knows what, if anything, would have brought Faith home and who knows if my parents could have made it work a second time. I appreciate your loyalty to my sister. She didn't have much of that, so I'm not angry if you didn't tell my P.I. something, either."

Patty nodded, obviously grateful. "How did you find out Faith had a child?" she asked, sounding stunned.

"Eventually we got a lucky break that led to her ex-boyfriend who's serving a life sentence. Once I found out that Faith died, we were able to track her last whereabouts and it led to the fact that she had a child."

Patty shook her head. "I had no idea. I wasn't lying when I said I didn't hear from Faith after she ran away. Where is her daughter now?"

"Sam's been living with my family in New Jersey," Zoe explained.

"So what made you look me up now?" Patty asked.

While Zoe reached for the keys in her purse, Ryan pulled the old paperwork out of his pocket. "All this," he said. "We're hoping that somehow you were called before they dumped the contents of Faith's locker."

As Patty looked at the paper, her hands shook. "I was. And I picked up a stack of papers from the bus terminal years ago."

Hope flared in Ryan's chest. "What did you do with them?"

"Well I kept them, because I thought maybe Faith would come back one day." She blinked and he noticed her glassy eyes. "She didn't, of course."

"I'm guessing the papers are long gone by now?" Zoe asked.

"Actually..."

Patty stood and started walking, so Ryan rose and followed, Zoe behind him.

"I'm a pack rat," Patty explained as she headed into the hallway and paused at a closed door. "We've moved since I received the papers, but I kept all my old things in boxes. I never could bring myself to part with anything and since those items were my only link to Faith, I held on to them. I can't promise you that the papers are there, but if you don't mind dust, there's a good chance you'll find it if you dig around in the basement." She opened the door and flicked on an overhead light.

Ryan glanced at Zoe in her pink skirt and white halter top and asked, "Are you up for another dusty recovery mission?"

"I'm game if you are." In her eyes, he saw the same glimmer of hope and excitement that had flared to life inside him.

They shared this goal. He hoped in time they'd share many more. He didn't know what he'd find here, but he was glad she'd be with him no matter the outcome.

"Go right ahead," Patty told them.

He clasped her hand. "I can't tell you how much I appreciate this."

She waved away his words. "I wish I could have done more. I wish I had done more. Then maybe—"

"Don't go there," Ryan warned her. "I've learned it does no good. You were Faith's friend. The best kind of friend. Nobody could have asked any more of you."

Patty nodded. "Thanks, Ryan. You two stay as long as you need to."

"We appreciate that," Zoe said.

He led the way, helping Zoe down the long stairs in her

heels and together they began to search through the large, unfinished basement. Hours later, they were only halfway through the unmarked, unlabeled boxes.

"Patty's not only a pack rat, she's an unorganized one," Zoe said, wiping her dirty hands against her light-colored skirt. "The bus depot was a breeze compared to this."

As he took in the dirt marks on her clothing and the smudges on her cheeks, she sneezed with gusto. "You're being a great sport."

She shrugged. "It's no big deal. I want to help you find whatever your sister left behind. Besides, the alternative is hanging out at the house with Grandma Vivian." Zoe gave an exaggerated shudder. "And I don't think she likes me very much."

Ryan shook his head. He needed to dispel that notion immediately. Although he hadn't thought his mother would take to Zoe, her turnaround where Faith and Sam were concerned gave him hope that she'd soften her ideas about what kind of woman made suitable marriage material for a Baldwin.

Personally, he didn't care what his mother thought, since his life was his own and he'd long since stopped doing what his parents desired. Yes, this woman could potentially cause a rift in the family, but then, so what? They weren't all that loving on the best of days.

Until very recently he'd feared the family shutting him out the way they had Faith, but he'd grown in the short time since meeting Zoe. He feared losing *her* much, much more.

"My mother doesn't know what to make of you. There's a difference between confusion and hate. If she can come to understand Sam, you'll be a piece of cake." He winked and, watching the blush suffuse her cheeks, he chuckled.

Zoe rolled her eyes. "Are you saying to know me is to love me?" she asked teasingly.

"You said it, I didn't."

Realizing her word choice, she glanced down and began rifling through her next box. Obviously *love* wasn't a term she wanted to discuss at the moment. He refused to take those concerns of hers too seriously right now. He'd already decided to keep things between them light and normal in the hopes she'd see how easy they were as a couple. So he began digging through his own treasure chest looking for something, anything, familiar.

Hours passed. His lower back hurt from bending, his shoulders ached from remaining hunched over and his neck was strained from tension and frustration. He was about ready to give up for good.

Zoe had already finished her share of boxes and now sat on the dirty floor leaning back against the cement wall, eyes closed. She appeared so fragile, a complete contrast to the strong woman he knew her to be. But seeing her this way made the ache inside him grow, made him want to take care of her.

He shook the fantasy out of his head and forced his gaze to the bottom of his last box. Unexpectedly, a sheath of papers caught his eye. At first glance they were just numbers on computer paper. Old computer paper, that looked as if it had come from a dot matrix printer, with the perforated edges still attached.

He pulled the papers out and, though the text and ink had faded, the words *Baldwin's Department Stores* headed the page.

His heart began to race. "Bingo!" he said, excitement rushing through him.

Zoe jumped to her feet and huddled beside him. "What'd you find?"

He sifted through the pages. Although Baldwin's was far more technologically up to date today, these were obviously old insurance claims.

"Old business statements from Baldwin's and…a letter or actually a diary of sorts. It's Faith's handwriting," he said, the familiar scrawl from the past making him feel as if his sister were here with him now. He shivered involuntarily.

"Are you okay?" Zoe asked.

"Yeah."

"Are you going to read it?"

A part of Ryan wanted to get the hell out of the dark, dank basement and read his sister's words in warm, familiar surroundings, and another part of him wanted right now to see what she'd left behind.

Curiosity won out. "Yeah I'm going to read it now. Want to see?" He wiped a hand over his forehead and lifted the old pages closer so he could see.

Zoe inched nearer and read along with him. His first glimpse was shocking and what he saw only became more horrifying as the meaning and intent in the letter grew clearer.

Nausea rose in his throat as Zoe stepped back and met his gaze. "It seems you were right," he said dully.

"Ryan, I'm so sorry."

"For forcing me to see the truth about my uncle? Someone had to shed some light for me." His laughter sounded harsh and gritty to his own ears.

"Could she have made things up?" Zoe asked of Faith.

"Don't try to protect my feelings now," he said wryly.

"It's possible, isn't it? Faith might have blamed your uncle for being thrown out of the house and left these notes, hoping your parents would find them when they found her."

He shook his head. "These sound more truthful than anything I've heard in quite a while."

He was beyond angry that his uncle would betray his sister. He was even more furious that the man would feign such ignorance over the years. Faith had left a thorough diary of her experiences and Uncle Russ's role in her running away. In fact, if his sister's words were to be believed, and Ryan did believe her, his uncle had every reason to want to get his hands on the keys. He'd want to see what Faith had left behind, if for no other reason than to cover his own ass.

"What's next?" Zoe asked.

"It's time I pay a visit to Uncle Russ."

She nodded. "Feel free to drop me off sat your parents' while you go."

Considering how much she disliked his family and their home, her offer meant a lot. "Actually since this revelation is a result of your persistence, you deserve a front-row seat at the confrontation."

"I never *wanted* to find anything incriminating on your uncle. For your sake, I hoped I was wrong," she said, her eyes huge, her voice imploring.

"But you aren't surprised."

She shook her head.

He rose and extended a hand, pulling her to her feet. They started for the stairs when suddenly he turned and she bumped into him. He grabbed her around the waist to steady her, then lowered his head and kissed her hard. Though he'd taken her by surprise, she responded. Her tongue tangled with his and as he pulled her closer, a soft moan escaped the back of her throat.

He'd needed this, needed her and the reassurance of something good and trustworthy in his life and she seemed to understand. He deepened the kiss, slanting his mouth first one way, then another, their mutual desire building with each passing second.

Slowly he pulled back with immense regret. He hadn't had his fill, not by a long shot, but he had gotten the fortification he needed for what lay ahead.

"What was that for?" she asked, her tongue dragging over her lower lip, taking in the moisture he'd created.

"It's been too long and I needed sustenance."

She laughed. "That's a unique excuse."

Despite it all, he grinned. "I didn't know I needed one."

"Well, I can't have you thinking I'm yours for the taking, now can I?" She patted his cheek and strode past him up the stairs.

He appreciated her sass and the way she didn't treat him with kid gloves or pity. Another reason this woman was a keeper, whether she knew it or not.

BALDWIN'S DEPARTMENT STORE was located in downtown Boston. With traffic and construction hampering them, the trip took over an hour. A silent hour that left Ryan alone with his thoughts and Zoe with hers.

Faith's words had been a bombshell, Zoe knew, one big enough that Ryan wanted her by his side when he confronted his uncle, a man he'd always trusted and loved like the kind of parent he should have had. *The kind of parent he'd deserved,* she thought.

Finding out his idol and mentor had feet of clay had obviously hurt him badly. Zoe saw the pain in his eyes, the disappointment in his expression. She'd even felt the desperation in his kiss. She couldn't deny him what he needed and she would be there to see him through this difficult time. *Then* she would put her plan in motion and begin the painful process of separation—Zoe and her family from Sam—and Zoe from Ryan.

She let Ryan walk ahead of her and, acting on a hunch, placed a quick call to Quinn. He'd been looking into the Baldwin family during the years right before and after Faith had run away and she wanted to know what he'd found out. Sure enough, the guy in custody in Boston who'd been following Sam was connected to the mob. The son of a man who'd been involved in the hijacking of the Baldwin's trucks years before. Zoe was certain Uncle Russ had hired the man to stalk Sam. Anger, fury and pain for Ryan all surged through her.

Uncle Russ had a lot of explaining to do and Zoe knew it would take all of her restraint to allow Ryan to deal with his uncle without her going after him on her own.

They entered Baldwin's from an underground parking structure and took the elevator to the main floor. Since they hadn't yet taken Sam on her promised shopping trip, this was Zoe's first excursion into one of their stores and she was impressed with the upscale establishment.

They made their way to a bank of private elevators that

led to the office level, and once there, Ryan asked to see his uncle. He was granted immediate access and Zoe followed him down a long hall to a corner office. He knocked once and walked inside.

Since Russ's secretary had called ahead, the other man was standing when they entered. "Well this is a nice surprise." His gaze shifted from his nephew to Zoe. "To what do I owe the pleasure of this visit?"

Zoe merely waited.

Ryan shut the door behind him. "It's time we talk."

She heard the strain in his voice and her heart went out to him, but all she could do was stand there and listen.

"I always have time for you, but we talk all the time. Why the visit to my office?" Russ glanced from the closed door to his nephew's severe expression and grew suddenly wary, shuffling papers on the desk for no apparent reason.

When Ryan didn't answer right away, Uncle Russ gestured to the chairs circling his desk. "Shall we sit?"

"I'd rather stand." Ryan rolled his shoulders and Zoe could only imagine the tension sitting upon them. "You know, when Zoe told me she thought you had an unusual interest in the keys around Sam's neck, I told her she was crazy."

Maybe it was Zoe's imagination, but she thought the older man lost some of his ruddy complexion, paling at Ryan's words as he eyed Zoe with barely concealed anger before shifting his gaze back to his nephew.

"Even when I agreed to look into the keys, I was humoring her. I figured best-case scenario, Sam finds out a little more about her mother, and worst case, I waste an afternoon. Not once did I believe you'd been involved in Faith's disappearance. Not you, the man who'd undertaken his own investigation to find her." His voice rose with all the hurt, anger and betrayal he must be feeling.

Zoe sensed the power behind Ryan's words. Her stomach jumped with equal doses of anticipation about what his uncle would admit to, and empathy for Ryan's obvious pain.

"And what exactly did you find?" Russ asked, suddenly more relaxed.

Zoe felt certain the man figured Ryan's fishing expedition had been as fruitless as his own. Ryan's initial indignation no longer threatened the older man, but he would soon find out he was deluded, she thought.

"The first thing I discovered was that Zoe's hunch about you was correct. You'd visited the bus station a few hours before we did. So I wondered, what in the world could you be looking for?"

"Ryan, surely you know I've always had your best interests at heart."

"I thought so. Up until our search led us to the contents of Faith's locker."

"That's impossible!" His uncle propelled himself forward, righteous certainty in his voice. "They told me there was nothing to be found."

"Unless you know the right questions to ask," Zoe said, unable to contain her pride in Ryan.

"It doesn't matter how we found Faith's things," Ryan said, stepping between them. "What matters is that she left behind a note documenting everything that led up to her running away."

Uncle Russ walked to his side of the desk and lowered himself into his large, leather chair. "You can't possibly believe the ravings of a seventeen-year-old drug addict." That he was no longer eye to eye with Ryan, but gripping the armrests hard, gave away the measure of his fear.

"You wouldn't look so worried right now unless you knew for sure Faith's words were more than ravings."

"That's nonsense," his uncle said in return.

A muscle ticked in Ryan's jaw. "Still in denial?"

Tension radiated between the men and she sensed Ryan's disappointment in the uncle he'd idolized throughout his life. Even cornered, he wasn't man enough to own up to his actions.

She had to clench her fists in order to prevent herself from calming Ryan down. He needed to do this and she needed to let him.

"So tell me just what it is you think you know," Russ said dismissively, speaking to Ryan as if he was nothing more important than an annoying little boy.

A pathetic old man's last bid to dominate the nephew he claimed to love, Zoe thought. But she knew Russ's attempt to cause Ryan to back down was doomed to failure.

"What do I know?" Ryan mimicked, then stormed across the room and braced both arms on the desk. In mood and in action, he took charge. "Dad already mentioned the mob-related truck hijackings that took place during the years Faith was most troubled. Thanks to her letters, I know *you* were involved with organized crime. That you gave them Baldwin's trucking schedules." His voice was filled with disdain. "And I know that select vehicles with hundreds of thousands of dollars worth of electronics were hijacked."

"Coincidence."

"Bullshit," Ryan countered. "Because I also know you'd increased the insurance appraisal and made yourself a hefty sum of money without revealing *that* to my father. And I'm certain the mob sold the goods they stole and made a bundle. It was the perfect scam until Faith found out and confronted you, so you needed to get her out of the way."

"It sounds like a work of fiction." But Russ's eyes darted from side to side, his panic obvious.

And Zoe clung to every word. Though she'd thought Russ had an unusual interest in the keys, in her wildest dreams, she'd never imagined Russ was involved in something like this.

"By the way, I also know that it wasn't Faith's choice to run away. You gave her money and told her to take a hike because everyone at home would be better off with her gone and nobody would miss her once she disappeared."

Zoe winced as Ryan revealed the most painful betrayal of all.

Ryan's throat hurt from hurling the truth at his uncle without letting his anger overwhelm him completely. His heart ached with the knowledge that the one man he'd trusted had let him down in this way. The only thing keeping him together right now was Zoe, who stepped up and silently clasped her hand inside his.

"You must be taking Faith's words out of context," Russ said, his voice shaking, his fear real.

But not as real as his sister's must have been, Ryan thought. "How could you?" he asked barely concealing his disdain.

Russ's eyes suddenly blazed with emotion. "How could

I? I'll tell you how. I was Faith's only ally in that house, just like I've been yours. I was the one who comforted her when her parents yelled and passed judgment. I bailed her out of trouble more times than your family knows about. Especially that last time."

Ryan's legs shook and he lowered himself into the nearest chair. Zoe remained behind him, her hand on his shoulder and he appreciated her steady support. "What are you talking about?" Because for all his sister had revealed in her letter, he'd sensed there was much she hadn't said.

And unfortunately, Uncle Russ was the only one who could fill in the blanks. It was up to Ryan to decide whether or not to believe him.

His uncle rose and paced the small area behind his desk. Sun shone in from the plate-glass window behind him, but Ryan felt as if the sky were full of black clouds.

"Your sister had been doing drugs for years," Uncle Russ began. "I didn't know where she got them and I didn't ask. I tried to get her into treatment and I paid for shrinks your parents didn't know about, but the bottom line was, Faith was messed up and she still had to go home to that dysfunctional house every night. Therapy wasn't working. So when she came to me that last time, I had no choice."

"But to throw her out?" Ryan asked, unable to contain his sarcasm.

Zoe's hand squeezed his shoulder tighter.

"To bail her out and send her away." Russ shook his head, the bachelor looking older than his years for the first time in Ryan's memory.

But Ryan wasn't ready to believe that easily. He swallowed hard. "What do you mean?"

"Your sister ran out of money to support her habit. Your parents weren't giving her cash and I sure wasn't helping her kill herself. We all thought she'd give in and let herself be helped. But she began to borrow money from a *friend* at school. The *friend* turned out to be connected and when Faith couldn't pay him back, he threatened her. And she came to me."

Ryan rubbed his hand over his burning eyes. He refused to be conned, but so far the story made sense. "Go on."

"I met with this *friend* who brought his boss. They were only too willing to let me take on her debt. In fact they'd had it planned all along, using your sister's addiction to further their bottom line. Threatening Faith was never about the couple of hundred dollars she owed. They wanted a cut of Baldwin's profits. And they wouldn't leave her be until they got it."

His voice cracked and his eyes glazed over as he remembered. "They promised the truck hijacking would be a one-time thing. If I turned over the trucking schedule, they'd pick the shipment. They'd let me know with plenty of time to up the insurance so I could make some money off it too." He looked down, shame briefly clouding his expression. "But that was peanuts in comparison to their take when they sold the goods on the street."

Ryan's head began to pound, but he forced himself to focus on what was most important. "Why did you pay Faith to leave?"

Uncle Russ slammed his hand on the desk, making Ryan flinch.

"You're a smart man, Ryan. Use your brain. Faith had a drug habit. She wasn't getting better. Hell, she just didn't care. Living at home, she was destined to repeat the cycle and I was afraid Baldwin's would be in bed with the mob forever, to use a cliché. But I hoped that if she got away from the situation that caused her to turn to drugs in the first place, maybe she'd get better."

"That's the most naive thing I've ever heard," Ryan muttered.

"And stupid. But this was seventeen years ago. What did I know about addiction? As the only person who was thinking clearly about the business and the family, I had to consider the possibility that Faith was on such a destructive path, eventually she'd cause someone in the family to get hurt. We were already involved with the mob. What was next?" He glanced at Ryan, his eyes imploring. "You have to believe me. At the time I thought I had no choice."

Considering what a shock all this was, and knowing his uncle had made a profit off the scheme, at the moment Ryan wasn't sure what to believe. "Yet you lied and told us all that Faith stole money from you to run away."

"That wasn't far from the truth. She stole the key to my briefcase along with false insurance papers documenting a shipment worth more than the actual goods."

Ryan narrowed his gaze, confused. "You'd been helping her. Why would she turn on you before leaving?"

Russ spread his hands wide. "She was a drug addict, Ryan. Who knows why she did what she did?"

"Why did *you* continue the scam over the years?" Ryan asked.

Russ frowned. "Who says I did?"

"You did. Through your actions." Though Ryan laughed, he recognized the hollowness in the sound. "If you'd done it once to help Faith, you wouldn't have been in a panic when you saw Sam's key. Your actions were screwed-up, but sort of justifiable and eventually forgivable."

"I don't see you believing in me at the moment," his uncle said, his voice laced with bitterness.

"That's because Faith's letter indicated you made money off the scheme more than that one time. It seems she kept those papers in the locker for a year or so, adding to them on occasion."

His uncle opened his mouth, closed it again, then finally said, "How the hell would she have known?"

"Because like you said, she was a drug addict. She needed drugs after she ran away and turned to her 'friend' to supply her before she finally took off for New York. He must have filled her in."

"Good Lord." Uncle Russ turned toward the window.

"Yeah," Ryan muttered. "So what the hell was going on?"

Russ faced them again. "It was supposed to be one time. Then a year later, they called on me again. Between their veiled threats to reveal my insurance scam and the fact that the extra money in my pocket helped my lifestyle—"

"You're hardly hurting for cash from the business," Ryan pointed out.

"And neither is your father or brother and they don't work nearly as hard as I do. After a while, it seemed like I wasn't getting what I deserved from Baldwin's," he admitted. "Who was it hurting?"

"How about the small-business owner who sees insurance

rates skyrocket year after year?" Zoe said, making her presence known.

Not that Ryan had forgotten.

Uncle Russ scowled, but the slight incline of his head acknowledged her point. "I heard from your sister from time to time."

"What?" Ryan asked in shock.

"She'd call collect or drop me a note. She'd remind me of what she knew and I lived in abject fear of her revealing all. But then after a while the threats stopped. It seemed as if she was cleaning up her act and I was able to justify sending her away. But then it was silent for too long. I was petrified of her going back on drugs, or exposing me. That's when I began my investigation into her whereabouts."

Ryan's head pounded and he braced himself for his uncle's next admission.

"I found out she'd died in a drug dispute," he said, his voice cracking.

"You kept that from my parents? From *me? You* let me investigate and search and *hope*?"

Russ nodded. "Please hear me out. When I first found out, the guilt nearly killed me. I blamed myself and I stopped my part in bilking the insurance company. It helped that the feds were cracking down and the guys I dealt with wanted to lay low and focus on other things."

"And with Faith gone, so was the threat of discovery," Ryan said.

Russ nodded. "I stayed clean and focused on you, but the guilt never went away. Guilt over sending her away, over her death, over keeping the news from you, but I couldn't see what good it would do to tell you. I couldn't hurt you that way."

"Or deal with my reaction to your role in it."

Russ hung his head. "That, too."

"But then I started investigating on my own. With only partial information to go on, since you withheld the important things, like my sister's death," Ryan said with contempt.

"Guilty as charged," Uncle Russ admitted dully.

Ryan leaned back in the chair, his body heavy with the weight of everything he'd just heard.

"How did you feel when Ryan found out something you hadn't? When he found Sam?" Zoe's voice startled Ryan and he glanced her way. She was face-to-face with his uncle.

Uncle Russ merely shook his head and Zoe continued. "I can answer that. You got nervous that maybe *she* knew something or had something that could implicate you, isn't that right?"

Ryan's gaze shot back to his uncle. "Is she right?"

Uncle Russ nodded and nausea churned in Ryan's gut. He'd had enough revelations today to last a lifetime, but Zoe obviously wasn't finished.

"You were so nervous this child of Faith's might know something or have something of her mother's that you hired someone to break into my family's home and tear the place apart, starting with Sam's room," she said, accusing him of something that had never even crossed Ryan's mind. While he'd been consumed with the past, Zoe had been focused on the present.

"She's right about this, too, isn't she?" Ryan said, knowing the answer before he'd asked the question.

Defeated, Russ merely nodded. "But how did you know?"

"The guy's in jail in Boston and we found out he has a mob connection to the same people involved in the truck robberies. I also had my brother-in-law run a check on you during Faith's troubled years." She shot Ryan a regretful glance, but he wasn't about to be angry at her.

"Do you know how badly I wanted to be wrong?" she asked Russ. "Ryan loves you. He believed in you. I didn't want to think that you were capable of something so low," Zoe said, her anger and fury evident in the clench of her fists and the barely controlled tone of her voice. "Do you realize you scared a fourteen-year-old girl half to death and you violated my parents' home, all to save your sorry—" She stepped forward.

Ryan rose and grabbed her by the waist to prevent her from going after his uncle. Her Mediterranean blood was fired up and though he'd like nothing better than to let her take care of the man, he was compelled to protect her from her own anger.

When her breathing slowed and he knew she'd calmed down, he released her, holding her hand to be sure.

"You also pretended to extend an overture to Sam just so you could get your hands on her keys," Zoe said in disbelief. "She's a child and you violated her trust in the worst way. But then you'd already done the same thing to her mother, so why should Sam get in your way?"

With each word, with each revelation, Ryan's stomach rolled in sick disbelief. "I don't know who you are," he said, glancing at his uncle.

"Sometimes I don't know the answer to that, either," Russ said.

Zoe's hand still in his, Ryan pulled her toward the door.

"Ryan," his uncle called to him.

Ryan paused.

"I've always loved you—you and Faith," Russ told him. "And I pray that someday when you've had time to think this over, you'll see through my weakness and stupidity and realize that."

Unable to see anything at the moment, Ryan strode through the door with Zoe without looking back.

Chapter Fourteen

ZOE FOLDED HER LAST TANK TOP and placed it into her suit-case. A few more items and she'd be good to go. She glanced around the small guest room she'd called home for a short time and realized she'd always felt comfortable here. Not just here in this room, but here in Ryan's apartment and in his life. Surely that was because he hadn't been in his normal routine any more than she'd been in hers.

As she'd told him already, they needed to return to their jobs, their friends, their *lives* and then their differences wouldn't just be apparent, but dramatically so. Of that she was sure—no matter how much her heart hurt at the thought of leaving him.

Sam knocked, interrupting Zoe's thoughts. She bounced into the room and plopped herself cross-legged on the bed. "So we're going home?" she asked, her gaze on the bag.

Zoe nodded. "It's about time, don't you think?"

"I guess."

Catching the uncertainty in Sam's voice, Zoe knew the young girl had started to care for her new family and would find it difficult to leave them behind—even if it wasn't for good. The next chapter in all their lives promised to be a challenge.

"You had fun here, didn't you?" Zoe asked.

Sam twirled a long strand of her hair around one finger. "This last day or so, yeah I guess I did. Even the old lady isn't so bad as long as I keep Ima away from her." Sam snickered.

"Be nice, you," Zoe chided, but she was laughing, too.

Suddenly Sam sobered. "Am I gonna have to come live here?" she asked, her eyes deadly serious and too wise for her fourteen years.

Zoe turned and sat down beside her, joining her on the bed. "I wish I could say no, but there's a good chance you will."

Sam nodded slowly. "I figured."

Zoe narrowed her gaze, wanting to be sure she was reading Sam's mood correctly. That her lack of tantrums and yelling meant she'd begun to accept the inevitable and even look forward to her future a little bit.

"You're okay with this?" she asked the teen.

"I don't have much of a choice, right? The Baldwins are my real family. I love you guys, but even I know the law and kids always end up with their relatives even if it's not what's good for them."

That damnable lump rose in Zoe's throat. "Is that how you feel? That Ryan's family isn't good for you?"

"No," Sam whispered. She hung her head, shaking it from side to side at the same time. "They're not bad people. Grandma Vivian said she's learned from her mistakes. A person who says that can't be too awful."

Zoe smiled. "Good point."

"But I feel guilty."

Sam looked up with watery eyes and Zoe felt her pain like a punch in the stomach. "Why? All we want is for you to be happy."

"You guys took me in and wanted to adopt me." Her bottom lip quivered as she tried to find the words to explain. "I love you all so much and I feel bad liking these uptight people at all."

Zoe shook her head, rejecting Sam's guilt. "Liking them doesn't mean you love us any less." She reached for Sam's smaller hand. "You have a big heart, honey. Big enough for everyone in your life."

"As big as my mouth?" Sam grinned and at that moment, Zoe knew the teenager would be okay.

"When's Ryan driving us back?" Sam asked.

"Actually I thought we'd fly. I didn't want to put Ryan out and—"

"Isn't that for Ryan to decide?" The man himself stood in the doorway, eyeing the open suitcase with an unreadable expression.

Zoe's stomach cramped at the thought of the conversation to come. "Sam?" she asked pointedly.

"I know, I know, you want privacy," the young girl said with an exaggerated tone and a roll of her eyes that said she thought the adults in her life were complete dorks.

But Ryan didn't appear anything like a dork. Wearing a light blue short-sleeve polo shirt and khaki shorts, he looked completely masculine and self-assured. He was so sexy he literally took her breath away, reminding her exactly why it was time for her to leave.

Ryan cleared his throat.

Sam jumped off the bed. "I'm going, I'm going," she said, ducking underneath his arm.

He stepped into the room.

Sam shut the door behind her and yelled, "I'm gone." Her footsteps sounded behind her as she walked down the hall.

"Gotta love her," Zoe said, forcing a smile.

He strode toward her. "Please don't change the subject or make light of leaving. This is serious."

She inclined her head, feeling the guilt Sam had spoken of earlier. She didn't want to cause Ryan to feel bad. "You're right."

His gaze bore into hers. "And I'm serious about you."

She swallowed hard. "Ryan."

"Zoe," he mimicked, but he wasn't laughing. "I'm not going to say what you want to hear. I can't make it that easy on you."

She wondered if he could hear her heart pounding in her chest, wanting to leap out and—she didn't know what her heart wanted. Nor did she know what he desired from her.

"What is it you want from me? From us?" she asked him.

He held up his hand and she laced her fingers through his. His touch was warm, their connection solid, yet she couldn't discount what separated them—physical distance and social differences, she thought.

"I'll take an open mind to start," Ryan said.

She narrowed her gaze. "Meaning?"

"Meaning I agree that we have our own individual lives and we need to go live them."

She blinked, unsure she'd heard him correctly. He was letting her go? "Say that again?"

"I agree with what you've been saying, that we need to get back to our daily routine and the things that define our lives."

She nodded slowly. "Okay, then." She could zip her suitcase and hop on a plane. He wasn't stopping her. Just the opposite, in fact. He was giving her what she wanted, so why did she feel so bad?

Like her heart had been sliced open and would never heal?

"I'd just like to know that while we're apart, you'll keep an open mind. Remember the good times we shared. Can you do that?" he asked.

His voice soothed her emotions like warm honey and she savored the liquid heat and delicious feelings he inspired. He was giving her time and space. He respected her feelings and, as a result, she respected him even more.

"Of course I can think about the good times." It was probably all she would think about. "Besides, we'll keep in touch through Sam." She forced a smile, refusing to think about how difficult a mere friendship with him would be.

"Definitely," he said easily.

Too easily.

"Speaking of Sam," he continued. "I thought through everything you suggested, and you were right about that, too. You should take her home for the summer. Not only will your parents get time with Sam, but I'll have a chance to organize things around here."

Zoe waved her arm through the air. "Her school, her room, things like that?"

He shrugged. "Things," he said vaguely.

Well, he was entitled to his privacy no matter how much she disliked being shut out. "So what did you mean when you said you weren't going to make it easy on me or tell me what I want to hear?"

He curled his fingers around hers. "I'm not letting you go without reminding you that I love you. And remember, nothing is forever." He kissed her forehead, his lips lingering. "Not even goodbye."

On that enigmatic note, he released her without even a kiss on the lips.

ONE WEEK HAD PASSED since Ryan had driven Zoe and Sam to the airport, and he still felt as if he'd put his heart on the plane with them. Letting Zoe go, allowing her to think he wanted the break, was the most difficult thing he'd ever done.

He hoped it was the smartest.

He hadn't been able to think of another way to force her into realizing that she missed him when they were apart and that they could easily make a life together—if only she came to terms with her fears.

She had to believe he loved her for who she was and that he had no intention of destroying her independence or strong personality, the very qualities he'd fallen in love with. She needed to believe that despite their different backgrounds, he accepted her unique traits. But, most important, she had to believe in herself, and trust that she wouldn't allow anyone to change her. Knowing all she had to come to terms with, Ryan planned to give her time before coming after her.

He refused to contemplate what he'd do if she turned him away for good. In the meantime, he'd used his own time wisely, doing as Zoe had suggested.

He'd returned to the business of living. His days consisted of getting back into the routine of work, dealing with clients, attending meetings, returning phone calls and scheduling business lunches.

Somehow the days passed, yet every time he returned to his condo, he was reminded of all he'd briefly had and lost. He missed hearing the sounds of female voices. When he woke up, he expected to find either Sam or Zoe making themselves at home in his kitchen. And on the nights when he managed to get some sleep, he'd roll over hoping to find Zoe had joined him in his bed.

Amazing how fast a man got used to things that were once foreign to him. Only now those things were nothing more than spectacular memories. He spoke to Sam every couple of days, but not once had Zoe answered the telephone when he'd called. When asked, Sam always said Zoe wasn't home. He doubted the kid would lie since she seemed to want Ryan and Zoe together as much as Ryan himself.

In his free time he'd done a lot of soul searching about his sister, her life and his uncle's role in both her running away and the way she'd died. Though Ryan had come closer to accepting and comprehending, he hadn't yet reached the point of complete forgiveness, so he hadn't returned Russ's calls. Since Ryan had always had his uncle as a sounding board, a mentor and a friend, now he had no one. And he felt the loss.

He hadn't been in touch with his family since Sam had left, but he was ready to deal with them, which was a good thing since his secretary informed him he was "expected" at the house for dinner this evening. Well, it wasn't like he had anything better to do, Ryan thought.

It had been so easy to admit to Zoe that neither one of them had many friends or much of a social life. It was more difficult to acknowledge to himself how empty that now made him feel. He shook his head and laughed at how pathetic his life was and had been for a long time. Something he could see clearly now, faced with her absence.

She'd given him purpose and laughter, and he longed for warmth and intimacy to fill the void she'd left behind. A void he hadn't before known existed.

The question was, could he ever get her back?

RYAN ARRIVED at his parents' home at 6:00 p.m. sharp. Instead of the help greeting him at the door, his mother welcomed him. "Hello, Ryan." She kissed him on the cheek.

"Mother." He glanced over her shoulder to see his father pouring drinks in the study. "This informality is interesting. What's going on?" he asked.

His father, who until now had avoided Ryan and any discussion of Sam's entry in their lives, stepped forward, bar glass in hand. "I can answer that. Your mother has spent the last couple of nights explaining our mistakes and convincing me we can do better with Sam than we did with your sister."

Ryan raised an eyebrow. "And you agreed so easily?"

His father glanced down, and when Ryan returned his gaze, he took in the graying hair and stooped shoulders he hadn't noticed before. "I lost a daughter, Ryan. Just because I never show the pain doesn't mean I don't—and didn't—feel it."

Ryan's heartbeat tripled as he heard the words nobody in this house had ever expressed while he was growing up. He couldn't believe how emotional they made him feel now.

His palms sweated and his relief nearly overwhelmed him. "I'm so glad to hear you say that." He forced the words from his tight throat.

His father's gaze never broke from Ryan's. "It's a start, son. It's a start."

They were a long way from normal, but thanks to a young girl named Sam, they were taking small steps.

"So this do-it-yourself attitude is a part of that?" Ryan swept his arm around the room, encompassing the lack of servants and more casual atmosphere. His father, Ryan realized, wasn't wearing a suit, but a collared shirt with the top two buttons opened.

The other man nodded. "Apparently, we need to lose our snobbery. Your mother's words." A slight smile touched Mark Baldwin's lips.

Ryan stopped short of calling it a grin. "And you listened to her? Will wonders never cease." As much as Ryan appreciated the changes in his family home, he couldn't hide his sarcasm.

"Give us a chance," his father said. "You might be surprised." He extended the drink he'd poured and Ryan accepted the peace offering.

"To…change," Ryan said in return, coming up with the most apropos word he could find under the circumstances.

"To change," his father echoed.

"Is Uncle Russ coming for dinner?" Ryan asked.

His mother shook her head. "He had to work late. He said to send his regrets."

Ryan nodded, relieved he wouldn't have to face him just yet. He wanted time with his father to figure out what Mark

Baldwin knew and fill him in on what he didn't. He hoped that together they'd come up with a way to handle the past—and minimize any future damage to the company or to the family. Soon though he'd have to pay his uncle a visit and begin to tie up those loose ends.

"I was sorry to hear Samantha and Zoe went home," his mother said, interrupting his thoughts.

Her words took him by surprise. "Does that apply to both Zoe and Sam? Or is the truth that you were glad to see Zoe go?"

His mother blinked, obviously surprised. "Of course I mean them both."

Ryan studied her, trying to assess her sincerity.

"That Zoe has character." Grandma Edna walked slowly into the room using her cane. "Reminds me of myself in my youth."

"Then why did you make her feel like a pariah?" Ryan asked.

His grandmother laughed. "Because the only way to be accepted is to earn your place."

More old-fashioned wisdom from the Baldwin family, Ryan thought. The more things changed, the more some things stayed the same.

Grandma Edna smacked her cane against the floor for emphasis. "We couldn't make it too easy on the girl, now could we?"

"You didn't make it easy on my sister and she's gone for good. Were you trying to repeat history?"

The older woman, whom Ryan had never known well, snorted in reply. "Zoe's made of stronger stuff. I knew it the moment she stood up to me over those napkins at dinner. I, for one, respect her."

"Well it would have been nice if you'd told her so."

"She didn't ask."

Ryan rolled his eyes. "You could have shown her, then."

She tapped the cane again. "Zoe was too busy assuming we didn't like her and protecting Samantha from us, for no good reason. What about you? Why didn't *you* tell her so? Maybe then she wouldn't have taken Samantha and gone home."

"Mother's got a point," Vivian said.

Ryan opened his mouth, then shut it again. Were they really advocating *for* Zoe?

Grandma Edna sniffed. "I'm hungry," she said before he could formulate a reply.

Ryan knew that in her mind, her proclamation ended the subject, which was just fine with him. He turned and started for the swinging doors leading to the dining room.

"Dinner is in the kitchen tonight."

His mother's voice stopped him and Ryan paused mid-stride. "We've *never* eaten in the kitchen."

"Then it's about time we start, isn't it?" his father asked.

"Uhh...Why?" Ryan leaned against the nearest wall, exhausted from trying to keep up with the new pace here.

His mother walked over and locked her arm with his. "Because if Samantha's going to live in Boston and be happy, she can't be subjected to all the formality and structure her mother couldn't handle."

A swell of gratitude rose in Ryan's chest as he realized how much his parents were willing to change for the sake of their granddaughter. He knew how hard it must be for them to acknowledge both their mistakes and their role in Faith's death.

He'd never been prouder of his family.

And he'd never been more certain of what he had to do next. Because despite the one-hundred-eighty-degree turn in his parents, he still couldn't envision Sam growing up anywhere near here, the place that destroyed her mother.

In the same instant he accepted his family, he also acknowledged that he needed to do what was best for Sam and that meant allowing Sam to be raised by two people who loved her. Who understood what a teenage girl needed. People who wouldn't stifle her spirit, yet would provide the proper discipline. People who'd be there when she left for school in the morning and when she came home in the afternoon. Most important, people who Ryan trusted not to deny her access to her blood relatives who also loved her.

Sam belonged with Elena and Nicholas Costas.

He spent the next hour explaining his decision to his parents, who, to his surprise, understood. He even sensed their relief at not having to deal with a teenager again this late in life.

After they ate dinner, his mother and grandmother retired early for the evening. "An after-dinner drink?" Mark asked Ryan as he poured himself a cognac.

Ryan shook his head. "How about an after-dinner discussion instead?"

"That would be a novelty," Mark said.

He had a point, since Ryan and his father hadn't been close. Ever. Perhaps it was time they began some sort of relationship based on truth and understanding. "When you had your heart attack you cut back on running the business, right?" he asked his father.

"I cut back on traveling from store to store, yes." He narrowed his gaze. "Why do you ask?"

"In the years before you cut back, were you focused on the nitty-gritty? Like financials and insurance?"

His father waved a hand. "That always was your uncle Russ's forte, not mine. In time it'll go to J.T. I preferred the hands-on dealings and once I slowed down there, I focused more on golf." He smiled at his words and swallowed a gulp of his drink. He regarded his son and his expression sobered. "What's going on, Ryan?"

As succinctly as possible, Ryan began to explain everything he'd discovered about Uncle Russ.

"Impossible," Mark said.

"Unfortunately, it's true," Uncle Russ said as he entered the room and joined them. "I wanted to be here when you heard everything, and I assumed Ryan would tell you tonight."

"I can't believe you sent my daughter away. That you made money off of our family's tragedy and our business." Mark raised his voice to his brother in a way Ryan hadn't heard in years.

"It was a long time ago," Ryan said to his father, expressing some of the things he'd come to terms with over the last week. "And I do believe Uncle Russ thought he was bailing Faith out."

"You're defending him?" Mark yelled.

Uncle Russ placed a hand on his brother's shoulder. "Don't. You'll wake the women." He turned to Ryan. "But that's a good question. Why *are* you defending me?"

Ryan drew a deep breath. "You've always been there for me. I can't forget that. Plus I know you, and I have a hard time believing your intentions were all bad. I'm not saying I'm over it or that it won't take time to rebuild trust, but…" He shrugged. "Life's too short to waste time hating or holding grudges. Faith taught me that."

His uncle extended his hand and Ryan took it, going so far as to pull him closer and pat him on the back.

"I'll leave it to the two of you to deal with the business and the past," Ryan said to his father and his uncle and started for the door. He hadn't been involved in the family business before and he wasn't about to start now.

"Ryan?" his uncle called to him.

He glanced over his shoulder. "Yes?"

"I suggest you attend to your future."

Ryan didn't need to ask his uncle what he meant.

Chapter Fifteen

ZOE LET HERSELF into her parents' house around 3:00 a.m. and quietly placed her keys on the console by the front door. She slipped off her shoes so she wouldn't wake anyone and silently headed toward the stairs.

"Did you ever hear the expression, *too busy to think?*"

At the sound of an unexpected voice, Zoe jerked around and shrieked aloud. "Mom! Jeez, I didn't expect anyone to be up at this hour. You scared me to death." She placed her hand over her rapidly beating heart.

"What were you doing out so late?" Elena asked, rising from the couch. She stepped forward, nearly tripping on her kimono before catching herself and hiking up the sides of the flowing garment with her hands.

Zoe shook her head, but knew better than to comment on Elena's clothing. "Why don't you sit, Mom?"

Elena complied.

"I was working covering security at a show tonight." Zoe's company, now officially named All-Hours Security Specialists, was up and running and doing extremely well for a fledgling business. "Since when do you keep tabs on me?" Zoe joined her mother on the couch and settled in beside her.

"I just worry about you."

Zoe leaned her head on her mom's shoulders as if she were a little girl again. "And I love that you care." She curled her legs beneath her, allowing exhaustion to take over. "But you know I work long hours and you know not to worry. So why wait up for me now?"

She stroked Zoe's hair with gentle hands. "Because your heart is hurting. That's what I'm so concerned about."

Zoe shook her head, her denial automatic. But she knew she was lying. She'd been home from Boston for two weeks and she hadn't been able to forget anything about Ryan and their time together. She remembered what his lips felt like kissing hers and how his very presence reached her on a deep, intimate level.

"Baah. You miss him." Her mother had always been able to read her well.

She could no longer lie to herself, nor did she want to. "Of course I do, but that doesn't make us right for each other." She bit down on the inside of her cheek, but her words were even more painful.

"What does this *right for each other* mean?" her mother asked, all the while running her hand over her daughter's hair with soothing strokes. "Do you love him?"

Zoe forced a nod. "But that doesn't change that we live miles apart or that our backgrounds are completely opposite."

"So? Does he eat with his hands or does he use a fork?"

Zoe laughed. "Too many forks, actually. Mom—"

"Does he respect your feelings and who you are as an individual?"

Zoe nodded, knowing her mother would feel her reply even if she couldn't put it to words.

"Has he tried to change you?" Elena pushed on.

"No," she whispered, her words making a mockery and a lie of everything she feared.

"I see," her mother said. "You are right to distrust him and think things won't work. Ryan Baldwin is an awful, awful man."

"Mom!" Zoe said, laughing once more. Her mother knew just how to twist a point in order to make her own, and she'd just cornered Zoe with her own words.

And Elena wasn't finished yet. "On top of everything, you're willing to trust him with our Samantha." She paused on purpose. "And yet you refuse to trust him with your own heart. Why not, my beautiful daughter?"

Zoe sighed and closed her eyes. How could she explain her deepest fears? "Ryan may act one way now, he may promise all the right things and say he loves all my 'unique' qualities. He may even believe all these things, but eventually we'd clash on issues. Important issues."

Her mother waved her hand dismissively. "All married couples argue. After all, common wisdom says opposites attract, no?"

"Opposites divorce, too," Zoe reminded her.

"Baah. You're grasping at reasons to run away from him because you're scared."

"Of?" Zoe asked, affronted her mother would think such a thing.

"Of love." Her mother's voice dropped, her sadness and disappointment obvious. "Didn't your father and I set a good example?" she asked.

Zoe swallowed hard, reaching for Elena's hand and holding on tight. "Of course you and Dad set the best example, but you're both so...so...intense."

There was that word again, Zoe thought. *Intense. Extreme.* She on one end of the spectrum, Ryan on the other, only their passion uniting them.

"You inherited the same qualities. Much more so than Ari," Elena mused.

Far from being reassuring, her mother's words cemented the fear in Zoe's heart. But there was no time like the present to confront it.

"It's that intensity that frightens me," she admitted. "When I was younger, I thought if I put all those feelings into my career, I could handle it. I realize now the Secret Service and all my training with the Bureau was a way for me to try and control the intense part of myself."

"The Greek part of you? We're hot-blooded people. We fight strongly and we love strongly. It's not something to fear but to embrace." Her mother smoothed Zoe's hair with her hand again.

Zoe nodded, understanding her mother's words in a soul-deep way she couldn't have before. Not when she was young and searching for adventure, and not when she'd first met Ryan. Only after. "I feel that kind of intense emotion with Ryan in a way I never did for another man," she admitted to her mother.

"I understand. It was the same for me and your papa."

Zoe sat up. She glanced over at the wedding photograph of her parents on the mantel and smiled. "You married young. I'm already thirty."

"Way past time to settle down."

"Way past time to get set in my ways," Zoe countered. "What do I know about sharing my life?"

Another wave of her mother's kimono-sheathed arm followed. "You'll learn together. Zoe, Zoe, even when we joked about you being afraid to commit to anyone or anything, I never thought I raised you to be a coward."

"Well then surprise, surprise." Because Zoe was a coward.

She was damn scared of discovering she couldn't have it all, that she couldn't be herself and keep Ryan happy, too. She was afraid of having to answer to him and failing, afraid of disappointing him.

Elena pinned Zoe with her contemplative gaze. "So you're afraid even to try. You're unwilling to compromise so that you and Ryan can be together."

Ryan had accused her of something very similar, Zoe recalled.

Her mother made a tsk-tsking sound that Zoe knew signaled her disappointment in her. "And is Ryan a coward, too? He must be since he let you leave without fighting for you. Another one unwilling to change or compromise."

Zoe rose from the couch, her anger flowing on Ryan's behalf. "I'm willing to admit my flaws, but don't paint Ryan with the same brush."

"What is this brush?" Elena asked, confused by the English expression.

"I mean don't just assume that Ryan is like me. He's come a long way since the first time he set foot in our backyard."

Her mother leaned forward, her chin in her hands. "Really? How so?" she asked as if she doubted Zoe's claim.

Zoe tossed her hands in the air. "After all Sam and I told you about our trip to Boston, I can't believe you need to ask. He understands Sam. He will raise her to be independent without crushing her spirit. He's mellowed and he looks for reasons before just applying ridiculous rules or codes of behavior."

"So what makes you think he's incapable of doing the same for you?" Elena asked, her mother's words doing the near impossible, silencing Zoe, and also forcing her to think.

Ryan *had* changed since they'd met. He'd found a balance between his Boston upbringing and Sam's cherished independence.

He'd told Zoe he loved her and was willing to wait for her.

And he'd gotten nothing back in return, she realized. Not a single, solitary thing. Not words of love, not promises of tomorrow or even a future. Nothing.

"Zoe?" Her mother's voice interrupted her thoughts. "You're quiet."

"I'm thinking."

"About?"

"What an idiot I've been."

"How so?" her mother asked.

Zoe sighed. "Ryan's a good man. A decent man." A sexy man who *loved* her and accepted her, stubborn flaws and all.

And she'd walked away.

Her pulse raced. Nausea threatened as reality struck, hard and unyielding. She'd been so stubborn, so unwilling to believe in love, or in Ryan. Or even in herself. She placed a trembling hand over her churning stomach. Why hadn't his word been enough?

Hadn't he proven himself since he met her? He'd loosened up and learned to accept things new and different. Like the Costases and their pet pig, she thought wryly. And he'd promised her that he'd never make her change. Yet she'd still felt the need to run.

Why?

Fear had motivated her, just like Ryan had said.

And now? What had changed in her mind? She bit down on her lower lip. She was still scared of the emotions and the intensity they shared. Only now she saw things clearly and she was much more afraid of losing him than she was of giving them a try.

Ryan had already found his balance in life. It was time she showed him she had done the same. And she knew exactly what she had to do in order to prove herself to him. She only hoped it wasn't too late or else she was doomed to spend the future alone. Because an intensity and love like she shared with Ryan only came around once in a lifetime.

RYAN SAT IN HIS OFFICE, legal pad in front of him, case files surrounding him, but his concentration wasn't on work. Instead all he could focus on was Zoe. Ryan had every intention of telling her family about his decision to let them raise Sam, and he planned to tell them in person. He didn't want to delay the revelation because he understood how much pain and misery was involved in preparing to say goodbye.

But his plans to leave immediately had been cut short when one of his partners had been rushed to the hospital with appendicitis. Ryan had stepped in to take over the workload. As a result, the soonest he could leave for New Jersey would be this coming weekend.

Not that it mattered. Whether he left for Jersey late Friday night or early Saturday morning, beach traffic would prolong his commute. And no matter when he made the trip, he'd still have hours alone in the car to think about all the things he could and should say to Zoe. Not that any of them would make a damn bit of difference. Apparently in his world, *I love you* was destined to be a one-way street.

He glanced down at the empty pad when the buzzer on his intercom rang. Ryan ignored it, hoping Nadine would take the hint and assume he was busy. Unfortunately she was persistent and suddenly the buzzer turned into knocking on his office door.

"Come on in," he called, annoyed with the interruption.

Steeling himself to deal with the intruder when he wanted nothing more than to be alone, he glanced up. Zoe was the last person he expected to see standing in the doorway. But there she was. Wearing her trademark miniskirt and not much of a top that fell seductively off one shoulder, she looked tanned and as fresh as the summer morning.

He couldn't deny the absolute pleasure he took on seeing her here in his office, on his turf. Coming to him.

"Hi," she said, lifting one hand in a hesitant wave. Her expression was just as wary, and since uncertainty wasn't something he normally associated with Zoe, Ryan was immediately on guard.

Still, she'd made the trip here and his heart leaped in his chest. He rose, not bothering to hide his surprise at seeing her. "What are you doing here?"

She shut the door behind her. "I needed to talk to you."

He raised an eyebrow. "I've called every couple of days to

speak with Sam. You've avoided every possible opportunity to talk."

Though he didn't know why she was here, he wasn't about to make this visit easy or let her off the hook without an explanation. Surely he deserved that much from the only woman to whom he'd ever professed his love.

"I've been working long hours."

"So have I," he said, pointing to the stacks around his desk. "But that didn't stop me from calling the people I care about."

She briefly bowed her head. "You're going to make me work for this, aren't you?"

"Work for what?" he asked her. "I have no idea why you're here or what you want."

And Zoe wondered if he even cared anymore. She swallowed hard and resisted the urge to wipe her sweaty palms against her skirt. Nobody promised her an easy meeting and certainly nobody had guaranteed her the happy ending she wanted. For all she knew, there would be no second chances for herself and Ryan.

She stepped forward, coming up close to his desk. "When I met you, I thought I knew who I was and what I wanted out of life. Or at least I told myself I knew."

He waited, his steely gaze never leaving hers.

"I thought I was a hot-shot ex-fed who was about to start her own business and have it all." She shook her head at her naïveté. "I told myself I hadn't fallen in love and it just wasn't in the cards for me. Then you came along in your suit and tie and your uptight ideas about rules and propriety, and I was so damn sure I could handle the attraction."

She shook her head and laughed at herself and the fool she'd been. "I mean, after all, I'd had affairs, I'd had sex, and what else would it be with a guy like you, who was so different, so opposite of me and everything I believed in?" She glanced at him through lowered lashes. "Are you with me so far? Because if you don't say something soon, I'm going to lose my nerve and bolt," she warned him.

"I'm listening," he said in a deep, compelling voice. "In fact, I'm hanging on every word."

But he remained on his side of the desk, thick mahogany wood and deep emotional distance separating them. Distance only she could bridge and, drawing a deep breath, she somehow found the courage to go on.

"Then I got to know you." Closing her eyes, she remembered their first awkward meeting, then immediately recalled how she'd found him shirtless, digging a place for Ima to root. She couldn't forget how he'd shown up with pig-raising books for Sam and realized she'd probably fallen in love with him then. "And I saw there was so much more than someone from a completely different world than me."

"And that scared you," he said, finally contributing to the conversation and helping her out.

"Yeah. Along with the intense heat and chemistry we generated, *you* scared me."

"Why?"

She rolled her eyes because in her mind, the answer was obvious. However, it wasn't apparent to Ryan and she owed him every word of explanation. "You scared me to death, Ryan. Because I'd grown up watching my parents' marriage.

It was always hot and passionate and always ended in one of them compromising their beliefs for the other."

"So? Isn't that what love is all about? Nobody has to change, but sometimes one or the other person has to give a little." Confusion laced his tone.

She almost smiled because he'd just provided her with his view on relationships. And love.

Nodding slowly, she continued, "Yes, that's what love is all about. And at thirty years old—"

"Hell, you make it sound like thirty is ancient." He ran a hand through his hair, his frustration clear. "It's a goddamn excuse, Zoe, and it's about time you admit it, if not to me then to yourself."

He'd raised his voice at her and a swell of emotion rose in her throat, tears forming in her eyes. And she wasn't even halfway through with what she had to tell him.

"Yes it was an excuse," she yelled back at him, her harsh tone and criticism aimed at herself. "You think I don't know that? But if I don't explain why I needed the excuse, then we have no hope of getting past it. So if you don't mind, I'd like to continue." She forced a deep breath into her lungs and only when she was sure she wouldn't cry, she started to speak again.

He grinned.

Damn the man.

"By all means. Go on." His voice had softened as had his expression, giving her courage and hope.

"At the time, when I couldn't face how I felt about you, I started focusing on our differences. And I told myself that after doing exactly what I wanted when I wanted, I wasn't capable of having an intense, committed relationship while maintaining my independence."

"And you didn't trust me not to demand you change," he said, his disappointment strong.

"Because I didn't trust *me*. I didn't trust myself not to give in to you, to do anything to keep you happy, even if I lost myself in the process."

He shook his head. "I wouldn't let that happen."

She nodded. "I know that now. Just like I know I wouldn't lose myself to any man." She couldn't help but smile. "Not even to you, despite how charming, sexy, and charismatic you may be."

He stood up straighter. Then the man in the Italian-cut designer suit and silk tie, the man she'd first met with the twinkle in his eye and the ability to make her laugh, strode around the desk and came up beside her. "Say that again."

"What?" she asked, fluttering her eyelashes and feigning innocence.

"Tell me again how charming, sexy and charismatic I am." He sat on the desk and leaned closer.

She laughed. "I think you're missing the point."

He shook his head. "With any luck, I think I'm just catching on."

Not only were they joking and laughing, but he'd closed the physical and emotional distance between them. When she inhaled, she took in his musky cologne and heady scent, and arousal hit her hard. Only this time, her desire didn't frighten her. It just made her more determined to explain and win him back.

"So just how did you come to these momentous conclusions?" he asked.

She sensed the seriousness in his question and settled herself beside him on the big desk. "That's probably the easiest answer I can give. I realized I was faced with losing you forever and *that* scared me a hell of a lot more than overcoming my fears."

"What are you saying?"

Although they sat side by side and though they were more relaxed with each other than before, something very important was missing and Zoe knew that move was also up to her.

Reaching out, she placed her hand over his, making that connection for the first time today. "I love you, Ryan."

"Zoe—"

She placed a finger over his lips to silence him and felt the electric zing straight down to her toes. "I'm not finished yet." And she wasn't, since words of love weren't nearly enough to make up for not returning those words after he'd uttered them, and for leaving him in the first place.

She licked her lips, dry from nervousness. "I love you, but that's not all. And after all you've said and done, it's certainly not enough, I know."

His gaze met and held hers.

"I want to be with you and I'm willing to move to Boston to make that happen, assuming you want the same thing, that is. You see? I've learned my lessons well and I'm willing to compromise." She laughed nervously, and was perilously close to passing out on the spot.

"You are, huh?"

She swallowed hard and waited, but he remained silent for too long. "It won't work, will it?" she finally asked.

He shook his head. "I can't see that it will."

Again silence surrounded them.

The pit in her stomach grew wider, her disappointment profound. "I guess I can understand, considering how I jerked you around. You said you loved me and I didn't say anything back, and whether it's an ego thing or you just can't trust in what I say or feel, I get why it won't work anymore."

Zoe knew she was rambling, but she didn't think she could stand the pain that would fill her once she allowed herself to think.

"I really don't think you understand." He spoke in a gentle, compassionate voice and she hated that he was trying to let her down easy.

She stepped backward. "I need to be going." Pivoting, she started toward the door, unable to leave her hurt and mortification behind fast enough.

"Wait."

She turned in time to see him jump off the desk and dart around her, blocking her exit.

"If you're leaving, you really don't understand and I need to explain," he said with what sounded like panic in his tone.

Confusion along with anticipation took hold inside her. "You're damn right I don't understand."

"But you will." His expression softened before her eyes. "I'm trying to say that it won't work because you can't be in Boston if I'm going to move to Ocean Isle."

She blinked and shook her head, certain she'd heard him wrong. "You're going to what?" she asked.

He grasped her hand and pulled her toward a chair. She willingly let him lead her. Once she was seated, he knelt beside her. "I'm going to move to Ocean Isle."

Her head spun and she was glad she wasn't standing. "Ryan," she said, completely overwhelmed.

"You need to know a few things. First, I was planning to drive down and see your parents this weekend."

She tipped her head to one side. "Why?"

His bigger hand covered hers. "Because I needed them to know I'm not going to take Sam away and I wanted to tell them in person."

She opened her mouth then closed it again. "I'm...I'm floored. Confused. What's going on?"

He didn't respond immediately and she sensed him searching for a way to explain.

"Even though my parents have come a long way and are willing to work hard at being a different kind of family, in my heart I believe Sam's best interest and ultimate happiness lie with your family. Not mine."

His heartfelt words along with the magnitude of the gesture reached out to Zoe. The man already owned her heart, but now he had the key to it, as well.

Still, knowing how Ryan felt about his sister, about Sam, and about blood ties, she couldn't let him make such a huge sacrifice and she shook her head hard. "No. You should—"

"Be her uncle. My parents should be her grandparents. We'll all be a part of her life, but she deserves a real family that understands her." His smile grew wider as he said, "Your parents provide everything she needs much better than we ever could."

"I don't know what to say except thank you." A tear rolled down Zoe's face and she wiped the moisture away with the back of her hand. "You're an incredible man, Ryan Baldwin."

Amazingly, he flushed.

She realized that *they* were still unresolved and she pushed on with a question. "So you were going to move to Jersey to be closer to Sam?"

"No. I was going to talk to your parents and work out a schedule for weekends and holiday visits." He inhaled deeply. "And then you showed up here first, saying everything I dreamed about, but never thought I'd hear." His voice was gruff and deep.

Zoe glanced down, ashamed of the pain she'd caused him while she'd searched her own heart and soul. "I wish I could have come around sooner."

"Then you wouldn't be *you*." He nudged her chin up with his hand and looked into her eyes. "And I love you, too," he said.

Warmth filled her heart replacing most of the fear that had lodged in her chest. "Are you sure I didn't wait too long?" she asked him, still uncertain.

Ryan shook his head. He'd probably have waited forever for her, but thank God it hadn't come to that. "All I wanted to hear was that you loved me. Offering to uproot your life for me was an added bonus."

She'd provided him with the proof he hadn't realized he needed. Proof that Zoe had come to terms with her fear of losing herself in their intense relationship—which he intended to turn into an intense marriage as soon as humanly possible.

"You deserve someone who's willing to compromise as much as you already have. I can do that for you now. I can do that for *us*." She smiled the sexy smile he adored.

"Compromise is nice, but you don't have to. Since Sam's already going to live in New Jersey, don't you think it makes more sense for us to live there?"

"What about your law firm?"

He shrugged. Although he couldn't say he'd thoroughly thought this move through, he was able to improvise based on certain helpful facts. "I can already practice in New York since I'm licensed there. And if it makes sense, I can always take the New Jersey bar exam."

"You'd do that for me?" she asked, green eyes wide with wonder and gratitude.

Despite that the thought of Continuing Legal Education classes and bar exams made him shudder, he assured her, anyway, "I'd do that for us."

She responded with a quick kiss.

"Don't you realize that I've never been as happy as I am when I'm with you? You and your wacky family," he said, laughing. "I just have one prerequisite."

"And what would that be?"

"Do you think you can move out of your parents' house now? I'm not sure I could live with my in-laws and stay sane."

"In-laws?" Her voice cracked as she said the word.

He nodded. "That is what I want them to be."

"Are you asking me to—"

"Marry me, Zoe." He hoped it helped that he was already on bended knee.

"Yes!" She laughed and threw her arms around his neck,

knocking him to the floor. Her body snuggled into his, the fit perfect and right.

Since driving her to the airport over two weeks ago, he'd been holding his breath. Now he was breathing easy and damn it felt good. *She* felt good.

She straddled him with her knees, her flirty skirt hiked high, only a thin scrap of lace covering her underneath. She kissed him senseless, her tongue tangling with his, her hands in his hair, tugging on his scalp, without ever coming up for air.

"Mr. Baldwin—" Nadine said, stepping into his office. "Oh my gosh! I knocked, but… Oh my gosh!" she said again and started to back out of the room.

"Hold my calls," he said as she quickly slammed the door shut behind her.

He glanced at Zoe.

Her cheeks were a deep red, but she laughed aloud. "The look on Nadine's face was priceless," Zoe said.

"She won't forget to knock loudly anytime soon, that's for sure." Ryan grinned, happier than he ever remembered being and he had the woman lying on top of him to thank. "Know what I want to do now?" he asked her.

"What would that be?"

His hips jerked upward, making his plan perfectly clear. And in case Zoe wasn't sure what he meant, Ryan leaned up and whispered his intentions in her ear.

 *Epilogue*

"When you said you wanted to make little Baldwin babies, I didn't think you meant right that minute!" Zoe whispered as she covered her still-flat stomach with her hand.

Once she'd left Ryan in Boston, she'd gone off the pill because of a series of headaches she'd attributed to the birth control. In reality, it had been nerves, stress, and stupidity for leaving Ryan that had caused the pain. Regardless, she'd completely forgotten about birth control after he'd proposed. It was that intense, passionate, Mediterranean blood of hers, she thought, with pleasure this time.

"I didn't hear you complaining," Ryan replied. "In fact I distinctly remember you screaming with pleasure. If I hadn't covered your mouth with mine, Nadine would have come running back in and then where would we be?"

Zoe chuckled.

"Shh!" Ari glanced over her shoulder and reprimanded them in her most professorial tone. "We're in church and the wedding's supposed to start any minute."

They were all at Connor's wedding to his fiancée, Maria, two people who'd worked hard to come to this point in their lives. Zoe still recalled how they'd fought their feelings at first. And look how well things had worked out for them, too.

Zoe grinned, but, duly chastised by her twin, she settled

down. Her hand remained on her stomach while Ryan placed his warm palm over hers.

Seconds later, Maria and Connor's wedding processional began. Sam, dressed in a gorgeous burgundy dress, walked down the aisle looking older than her fourteen years.

Ryan sucked in a breath and Zoe knew he was seeing shades of his sister in his beautiful niece. But he could rest easy knowing Sam would have a happier life than Faith had had.

Next came Joe, Maria's son, followed by Connor, the groom. A glowing Maria walked down the aisle with Quinn by her side.

The lump in Zoe's throat grew larger as she remembered her own wedding a few weeks ago. As intimate a family affair as she could manage by Costas standards, the day had been filled with magic moments.

Including the spectacle caught on video camera, when Spank the monkey had attempted to dance with Ryan's mother. After both Vivian and Grandma Edna turned her down, Spank mooned them both. Zoe still cringed at the memory. It had taken Zoe a long time to calm the monkey down while Ryan had seen to his grandmother with the smelling salts she kept on her at all times.

Zoe held in laughter, then cried happy tears as Maria and Connor said *I do*. Later that afternoon, after the reception at Paradeisos, the couple left on their honeymoon.

Ryan glanced at Zoe and she couldn't mistake the love in his eyes. "Want to tell Ari and Quinn?" he asked, like the proud, expectant father he was.

They'd kept the news of her pregnancy quiet up until now, not wanting to spoil the wedding. But after today's trip to the doctor, no way could she remain silent any longer. "I didn't want to upstage the bride and groom, but now that they're gone—"

"I thought Maria and Connor would never leave," Ari said, coming up to Zoe, dragging Quinn along with her.

"Hey," Quinn said to Ryan who shook the other man's hand.

Zoe couldn't help but notice that the hard-edged ex-cop had developed a grudging respect for Ryan, especially since he'd let the Costases' adoption of Sam go through.

"We have news," Ari said, excitedly.

"So do we." Zoe laughed. "You first."

"No you," Ari said.

Zoe shook her head. "No you."

Quinn rolled his eyes. "Women," he muttered.

"We're having twins," both Quinn and Ryan said at the exact same time and loudly enough to be heard over the music, chatter and the sisters' bickering.

All the talking in the room seemed to come to a halt.

"Our babies are having babies!" Elena said, her voice cracking.

She strode forward with Nicholas, their gazes encompassing both daughters. Elena kissed first Zoe's cheek, then Ari's, then repeated the gesture kissing Ari first and next Zoe again.

"Aah, that Costas sperm is potent!" Nicholas slapped each man on the back.

"Don't you think someone ought to explain the facts of life to him?" Ryan asked.

Zoe laughed. "And ruin the moment where he takes all the credit?"

Quinn shook his head. "Unbelievable," he said, but his joy and pride were evident.

As Zoe glanced around the diner where she'd practically grown up, she took in the faces of the people she loved most and decided at that moment, she was the luckiest woman on the face of the earth.